Steve Mosby was born in Leeds in 1976. He studied Philosophy at Leeds University, worked in the Sociology department there, and now writes full time. He is the author of ten psychological thrillers which have been widely translated. In 2012, he won the CWA Dagger in the Library for his body of work, and his novel *Black Flowers* was shortlisted for the Theakston Old Peculier Crime Novel of the Year. He lives in Leeds with his wife and son.

www.theleftroom.co.uk
🐦 @stevemosby
📘 /theleftroom

Also by Steve Mosby

I Know Who Did It
The Nightmare Place
Dark Room
Black Flowers
Still Bleeding
Cry for Help
The 50/50 Killer
The Cutting Crew
The Third Person

YOU CAN RUN

STEVE MOSBY

ORION

First published in Great Britain in 2017 by Orion
This paperback edition published in 2019 by Orion Fiction
an imprint of The Orion Publishing Group Ltd
Carmelite House, 50 Victoria Embankment
London EC4Y 0DZ

An Hachette UK company

1 3 5 7 9 10 8 6 4 2

A CIP catalogue record for this book
is available from the British Library.

ISBN 978 1 4091 8890 2

Typeset at The Spartan Press Ltd,
Lymington, Hants

Printed and bound in Great Britain by Clays Ltd,
Elcograf S.p.A.

www.orionbooks.co.uk

To Carolyn

Acknowledgements

Many thanks to all the people at Orion who helped with this book and all the others, especially Laura Gerrard, Genevieve Pegg, Bethan Jones and Jane Selley. I also deeply appreciate the support I've received from friends and fellow writers in the crime fiction community, with an extra special nod to the Blankets. You know who you are. As always, massive thanks are due to Lynn and Zack, for putting up with me while writing this book, and for everything else too.

You Can Run is my tenth novel. My agent, Carolyn Whitaker, was with me from the very first, and this book is dedicated to her, with affection and gratitude.

Prologue

Once upon a time there were two boys.

But we can be more specific. It was twenty-five years ago and one of those boys was me. The other was my best friend Rob. It was a warm August day and we were out on an adventure. We were ten years old and we had our bikes, our small rucksacks and our internal maps of the village we lived in.

My mother had an old, weathered road atlas that I liked to look through on long car journeys. Grown-up maps, as I thought of them back then, show grown-up things: churches and pubs and petrol stations. I'd had to learn the various Ordnance Survey symbols for them at school. But a child navigates by an entirely different set of waypoints, and so at that age I thought not of street names and landmarks but of the Quarry, the Field, Killer Hill, the Chalkie, the Old Oak. Places that were unknown and unnamed by adults. They might as well have been legends that children told each other, important only because we met and played in them. Grown-up places were where adults needed to go. Kid places became places simply *because* we went to them.

As we rode along the quiet streets of the village that day, Rob was always slightly ahead of me. I remember the way his T-shirt billowed slightly at the bottom, and the angle of his arms as he gripped the handlebars. His clothes and bike were much more expensive than mine, but we were best friends and had been since we started school together six years ago, all but inseparable from the first day. Although we did get along with other children, there was perhaps something different about the two of us. We were both quieter than the other boys: a little more sensitive; not quite so rough. Our parents were very different – Rob's were well off, whereas my mother certainly wasn't – but we were similar children. *Best friends forever*, my mum had beamed at us one day. *That's what I think I'm looking at here.* I remember that. It didn't feel embarrassing when she said it. And on that day in August, it still held true.

Rob looked back over his shoulder.

'The Bridge?'

'Yep,' I said. 'The Bridge.'

The Bridge didn't really go anywhere. At one side was the corner of our village; at the other, a dirt path and a load of farmers' fields. The field we played in the most was behind Rob's house, and it had a climbing frame and a slide. These other fields were unknown territory that looked like they stretched away for miles, and were too large to be considered a place. The Bridge itself was more contained, though, and interesting in its own right. There was a thick wall on either side, and the ground between them was uneven: neglected and overgrown. On both sides there was a vast drop to the train tracks below.

Rob and I cycled up and leaned our bikes against the wall. The world whirred into silence.

We walked a little way along, stones crunching beneath our feet. There was no real purpose to being there apart from to be there, so we stopped about halfway across. The walls at the sides were as high as the top of our chests, but if we reached over and grabbed the far edge, we could hoist ourselves up on to the rough stone surface and peer down.

'Do you think the fall would kill you?' Rob said.

I stared down. We were very high up, sixty feet or more, and all that space between us and the ground seemed full of echo and potential. The twin tracks below stretched away ahead, surrounded on either side by an infinity of tiny dirty pebbles, and then the steep sides of the embankment, thick with ferns and trees and jutting rocks.

'Too right it would,' I said.

'I don't know. I wouldn't be so sure. You might survive.'

'Maybe,' I said. 'Not in one piece, though.

'No. No way. And not for long.'

Still clinging on, I spotted that there was a snail between us on the top of the wall. The pattern on its shell was striking, and I loosed one hand to reach out and trace the whorls there with a fingertip. Round and round they went, circling down to a black dot, but I thought that if you could see much better, and your finger was small enough, you could trace those circles forever...

'What are you doing?' Rob said.

'I don't know. It's just cool.'

'You're not going to flick it off, are you?'

'No,' I said. 'Of course not.'

I moved my hand away immediately. The thought would never have occurred to me, although I imagined it then, of course: the snail tumbling almost weightlessly through the air, its tough shell clattering on the pebbles far below. Actually, I thought, the snail would probably survive the fall just fine, but I would never have done something like that.

Rob looked genuinely concerned, though. It was how he'd been all year. Over the last twelve months, he had become preoccupied with death. The summer before, his little sister Mary had died, and he'd not been the same since. We were still best friends, but there was a sense that Rob had aged a little quicker than I had, in a way I would never be able to catch up with. He seemed to see the world differently now: as a place full of bad things and threat and danger. He worried about everything. In turn, because he was my best friend, I worried about him. I wanted him to feel safe.

'Of course not,' I said again.

And then I looked up and saw that a train was approaching in the distance. I took hold of the wall with both hands again to steady myself. From this far away, the train appeared slow and lumbering as it curled towards us, its carriages locking into place one after the other. It was only as it reached the Bridge and thundered underneath that the speed and power of it became obvious.

Sixty feet above, I felt the air folding and pushing up at us, and the whole world rattled and shook. I could even feel it in the stone beneath my arms and my chest. Carriage after carriage – the train seemed to go on forever, impossibly long. And then suddenly it was gone again, a furious sound receding into the distance behind us.

I turned my head towards Rob, feeling exhilarated, and was about to say something when I saw that he looked terrified. He was still clinging on to the edge of the Bridge, but he was staring straight past me now, and his face was pale, his body trembling.

'What's the matter?' I said.

'There was someone there.'

He was still staring to my right, his gaze fixed somewhere beyond me, and he spoke with such conviction that, when I looked that way a moment later, I was almost surprised to find that the Bridge was empty and we were totally alone.

'Someone where?' I said.

'Just there,' Rob said. 'Right next to you.'

I looked again. 'Don't be daft.'

'I'm not. I saw him. A man with long hair. He was sitting on the wall there, looking right at me. And his face, Will...'

'What about it?'

'He looked so *sad.*'

'Really?'

I tried to sound low-key about it, but the truth was that he was scaring me a little. I could always tell when he was joking about something, and this wasn't remotely like that. He meant it; whatever he'd seen had really shaken him. It had been a sunny day before, but I realised that a cloud had drifted over the sun and the world had become darker.

'Maybe you saw a ghost,' I said.

'I don't know.' He shook his head and lowered himself back down on to the Bridge. 'Or maybe I'm just going nuts.'

'What do you mean, "going"?' I said.

'You're really funny, Turner. You should take that act on tour.'

'Maybe I will.'

'You could take Anna with you.'

'No way. Why would I do that?'

'Because you're in *love* with her, of course.'

He made kissing noises, and I rolled my eyes. Anna Hilton was a girl in our class who Rob liked teasing me about. While I always denied it, he was right, of course. I was totally in love with her.

'No way,' I said again.

'Race you to the Chalkie?'

'Yeah, you're on.'

But as Rob walked back to where we'd left our bikes, I found myself hesitating. He was a little bigger than me, but right then he looked very small, and I felt that protective instinct again. I wanted him to be okay. I wanted him to feel safe. A moment later, I reached out and picked the snail from the stone, then placed it safely in the undergrowth at the base of the wall. It was a pointless gesture, and Rob didn't even see it, but it still felt meaningful in a small, quiet way.

We never spoke about that day again, or the man with the sad face Rob thought he'd seen. I did think about it from time to time, though, especially when I saw Rob staring off into the distance, lost in thought and preoccupied by something that remained invisible and out of reach to me. I suppose I always thought it must just have been a hallucination of some kind. A daydream. Or an instance of pareidolia: that strange sensation when shapes in the world around us come together and momentarily form a pattern, an image, a face.

It was only many years later, after the Red River Killer came into my life, that I began to wonder if it had been something else.

Part One

One

She has nothing left to do now but make up stories.

As a child, Amanda would do that all the time. That's what children do, of course. Confronted with the confusion of the world around them, they create fantasies to shape and make sense of it. They turn what happens to them into narrative. They tap their toys against each other and make a noise.

But unlike other children, Amanda would write her stories down.

Her mother would fold sheets of coloured A4 paper in half, sew them together and say: *Here is an empty book, Amanda; fill it for me.* They were poor, her family, but her mother encouraged her to believe that there could be worlds within pages, and it was a lesson she learned well. She wrote stories about other planets, and princesses, and dashing heroes and winged horses. The stories she wrote became more elaborate just as she did, but one theme remained constant: good always triumphed over evil, and the monsters in the stories could always be beaten. When you confronted them, they were never as scary as you imagined them to be.

Of course, she knows differently now.

Once again – in the silence, in the dark – Amanda eases her wrists forward. Once again, there is absolutely no give in the makeshift pillory. The man has clearly constructed it himself – or at least adapted it, perhaps carving three holes in some sturdy old dinner table, then sawing it in half and adding metal hinges. The two holes to either side are smaller; they hold her wrists in place. The central one is for her neck, and angled so as to force her head back. She is kneeling on the rough stone of the garage floor, with only her hands and head visible above, like some kind of macabre dinner tableau on the stained, pitted surface.

She is not sure how long she has been here now.

Nothing left to do but... Well. Write stories in her head.

She imagines the canal path, still dappled with spring sunlight even in the early evening. In the stories she tells herself, she cycles along it slightly earlier or later – or even avoids it completely. The man makes a mistake, and there is someone there to save her. Or else the man isn't waiting in the undergrowth at all.

What if...?

She might have stopped writing stories down over the years, but she knows she never stopped telling them, because that's what adults do too. The childish toys might be replaced by news articles and promotions and relationships, but they're still all knocked together to create stories that make sense of the world. As a grown-up, she has told fictions about herself and the things that have happened to her. She has sought meaningful constellations in the random sky of her life.

But, like most people, the stories she has told herself have always been subplots or chapters. Until now, she has never really thought about the final conclusion: The End. But now it's hard not to. The man has shown her photographs of some of the others: the women who came before her. She knows exactly what The End will involve.

Hopefully it will be soon.

The tape is wrapped so tight and high around the lower half of her face that she has to concentrate every single second on breathing through her nose. How long has it been now? Not since the canal – that time is endless and infinite and can't possibly be counted in human terms – but since she's seen *him*? Well over a day. Probably longer, actually. Her body is rigid; her mouth is parched. Perhaps she is finally going to die. And in her delirious state, it is hard to separate reality from the vivid stories she keeps replaying in her head.

What stories, though!

On the first day of her captivity in this place, Peter found her somehow. That was a sweet story. She imagined Peter taking one of the things the man has hurt her with and swinging it into his head, then holding her and telling her it's all okay now, that she'll be okay and that nobody will ever hurt her again.

Peter at home with Charlotte, their daughter. At the breakfast table for some reason. *Is Mummy home yet? Where is Mummy?* Peter looking sad, hardly able to answer. *Not yet, sweetie. Soon, hopefully.* And then a knock at the door, and it's the police, and she has been found alive.

In the darkness and silence now, she tells herself one last story.

The world is a river of cause and effect, and one single change, however small, can divert the later course of it an enormous distance. So Amanda imagines herself as that little girl again, staring at her bookshelves – *we can always find money for books, Amanda* – and sitting cross-legged on the floor in the local library, and then writing her own stories. But this time she changes a single word – a letter, even – in one of them, and in the present she lurches from this hideous dungeon into the body of a subtly different woman. A woman who has lived a gradually divergent life and reached a much better end than this.

If only.

And yet. Lives are stories, and sometimes stories have twists and surprises in them. The world keeps secrets from us until it's ready to reveal them at exactly the right time.

Here is a secret.

As Amanda squats there in the darkness, lost in the past and imagining a different present, the constraints of the pillory force her to stare in the direction of the front of the garage. She has been kept in here now for nearly a month, and has actually been alone for well over forty-eight hours without food or water. Right now, she thinks she knows exactly how her story is going to end.

But she doesn't.

Because right now is when the front of the garage explodes loudly and violently in a sudden, shattering burst of brightness and noise.

TWO

There are people who think you can tell.

My mother was one. She believed in ghosts. When I was a child, she told me that when something terrible happened in a place, the events imprinted themselves on it, and that a person who was sensitive to such things could pick up on that. That was what a ghost was, she said – a vivid memory, held not by a person but by a place. It was as though the houses and alleys and isolated pathways where bad things occurred ended up dreaming of them over and over again, unable to wake, just as a person might relive some awful event in a nightmare.

I believed it as a boy. As an adult? Not so much.

As a police officer, I've turned up at plenty of places where bad things have happened, and the truth is that you often can't tell. Houses are stone and cement and fixtures and fittings. They don't know or care. It's people who know, and it's people who care – or who don't.

Places can often be granted power and meaning, but only in hindsight. It's why the concentration camps feel like hallowed ground, and on a much smaller scale, why people leave flowers tethered to lamp posts after an accident. Some places of horror and sadness are maintained forever: tended like gardens. But then you have the houses where atrocities have been committed that are razed to the ground in the years that follow, leaving their streets like mouths with a missing tooth. It's the tension we feel between the desire to erase and forget and the need to always remember, and that only happens after you know, never before.

But there have been a handful of times when I've questioned that. Occasions when I've pulled up outside a house and felt like I knew that something was very wrong inside, and been proved right. Confirmation bias, people might say, except I don't always believe that. In each case, the feeling has been different from simple unease. It's more a sense of dread throbbing in the back of my skull, like an unpleasant memory of something that hasn't happened yet. A part of me still believes the things my mother told me, and I've always paid attention to that feeling, confirmation bias or not.

And I had it that day, as Emma and I arrived at the house of a man named John Blythe.

There were already three police vans parked by the house when we arrived, but aside from that, there was little to distinguish the property from its neighbours – or indeed from any of the other houses in this drab area of the city. Fifty years ago, this was all waste ground. When I'd transferred here, over ten years earlier now, it had been transformed into a square mile of superficially aspirational suburb, but even back then you could tell the dreams were going nowhere. All the streets here were the same – endless rows of all-but-identical conjoined semis, with nobody caring enough to paper over the cracks that appeared and spread over the years. Some places are just like that. You can build or plant whatever you want in them, but it's as though there's something in the ground that stops things growing.

I parked up behind the nearest police van, then folded my arms and leaned on the steering wheel. The house was two up, two down. Because the day was gloomy, it was possible to tell there were lights on in the two upstairs rooms, the bare bulbs visible behind the red curtains. The front door was open. An officer was waiting there, his hands behind his back.

And there it was. The sick feeling at the back of my head.

Something is wrong here.

Easy to dismiss it as confirmation bias, of course, because in this case we already knew a little about what was wrong. My gaze drifted to the half-demolished garage on the side of the house, where the remains of the crashed car were still quite spectacularly embedded. The collision had taken out a good quarter of the external structure, and the roof had collapsed towards the front, so that the garage looked a little like it was frowning at what had been done to it.

'What are you thinking, Will?' Emma said.

'I'm not thinking anything yet.'

She sighed quietly to herself. Emma and I had been partners for years now, and she was used to me. My introspection, my moods. They were well known enough for them to be considered a character trait of sorts throughout the department. I was not particularly well liked. Apparently.

'You're not going to get weird on me, are you?' Emma said.

I stared at the house.

'It looks like a face,' I said.

'What?' Emma leaned over and peered out. 'The house? I suppose so. But all houses look a bit like faces, don't they?'

'Pareidolia.'

'Exactly.'

Which was true, but that effect was especially striking here, and for a moment it was all I could see. The pale grey outside walls transformed into dead skin; the open door became a thin mouth; the pinpoint lights in the upstairs windows were pupils that seemed to be staring at me from the centre of bright red eyes. The house looked like a head half buried in the ground, crying out in pain or anger.

And then the effect was gone again.

'I'm not going to get weird on you,' I said.

'I don't believe you. But let's go and see what we've got.'

Outside the car, Emma led the way. She usually did, though we were equal rank. The fact that we were both in our mid thirties was one of the very few commonalities we shared, the others being that we were both tall and slim. But Emma was appealing and confident. People warmed to her easily, and she had the kind of relaxed charisma that pointed towards promotion and a career much higher up the chain than partnering the likes of me. It's safe to say I was neither charismatic nor appealing. Where Emma strode, I tended to slump as I walked, subconsciously minimising my presence; I didn't like to be noticed. Emma said once that even when it was sunny I looked like I was pulling my coat around me against the rain. *You look like everything's weighing you down on some philosophical level*, she'd said. I'd told her she might be right. *And like it's always making you miserable.* And again.

Approaching the house, I noticed there were already reporters assembled on the opposite side of the street.

'Can you tell us about the woman, Detective?'

A TV crew was setting up a little way down, but the ones closest to us were mostly just hacks for the local papers. Well, I vaguely recognised the guy who had just spoken, and he certainly was. Almost instinctively, I moved to the far side of Emma, pulling that metaphorical coat around myself.

'No,' Emma said cheerfully. 'We've literally been on the scene for ten seconds, Joe. With your keen journalistic eye, I'd have thought you'd have seen us arrive.'

Her response got us a sneer from Joe. There's always a bit of a dance between police and reporters – a push and pull of information – but it's generally good-humoured. You all understand the music, and God knows you've practised the moves often enough, and so with some of them you can joke around and banter a bit. Not with Joe, by the looks of things.

'Apparently it's Amanda,' he said.

'If you say so.'

'Word is that she's in hospital.'

'That's more than one word, Joe,' Emma called over her shoulder. 'You'll probably need to watch that when filing copy.'

'Word is she's not going to make it.'

Despite myself, I stopped at that and turned around slowly.

Joe looked pleased to have got a reaction, and looking at him, I didn't think it was just from scoring a hit on me. He actually seemed pleased that the story might have an unhappy ending. I wasn't sure exactly what I was going to say or do, but I found myself taking a step back towards him.

Emma placed a firm hand on my arm.

'Let's keep moving, Will.'

I stared at Joe for a moment longer, then turned around again and followed her towards the officer guarding the cordon.

'What exactly were you going to do just then?' she said.

'I have absolutely no idea. Maybe try to make him understand he was talking about someone's life.'

'Joe doesn't care, trust me.'

'There's always a first time.' I frowned. 'Anyway, how come he knows who this woman is and we haven't been told?'

'Finger on the pulse, our Joe. Plus, you can't expect anyone to tell us anything, can you? We're only in charge here, after all.'

'True.'

Something about what Joe had said bothered me, though. It was almost subconscious, the same way it might register when someone said your name on the other side of a loud, crowded room but when you looked across you couldn't tell who. And the bad feeling remained. After we'd showed our IDs at the cordon, I stared up at the house again and couldn't shake the sensation that it was watching me.

'I want to see the garage first,' I said.

'Naturally.'

We walked along the front of the house until we reached the garage at the side. Rubble and glass were scattered over the short driveway in front. Most of the debris, of course, would be inside. From the back, the car itself looked surprisingly fine, although enough of the passenger side was visible to see the damage there, along with a portion of the crumpled bonnet.

The car was – or had been – a black Honda that had been reported stolen yesterday. Just after eleven o'clock this morning, a patrol car had spotted it, and when they put their siren on, the driver had decided to attempt to get away instead of pulling over. He'd been lucky not to kill anyone during a five-minute high-speed pursuit through the streets, but when he'd approached the corner here, he'd finally lost control, careered off the road, and ploughed straight into the edge of this garage, taking a chunk of the structure down with him.

The driver himself was in a stable condition. He had been placed under arrest and then taken to hospital.

Along with the woman.

I moved to the side of the crashed car now and knelt down beside it, just as the first officer at the scene had done. In the immediate aftermath of the collision, nobody had emerged from the house to inspect the damage. The officer had wanted to make sure that there was no one inside the garage. But there had been.

I peered in. A bare bulb was hanging from a cord, lopsided due to the tilt of the roof. The two walls that stood intact were lined with metal shelves, and my gaze passed over piles of tools, irons and heaters, cans of petrol and paint, unidentifiable clusters of metal pieces. It looked like the garage of a mechanic, the idea supported by the concrete pit in the centre. That was where the attending officer, upon turning on his torch and shining it through the exposed corner, had seen the naked woman, gagged and strapped into a home-made wooden pillory, staring back at him in shock.

Word is that she's in hospital.

Word is she's not going to make it.

We were less well informed than the dregs of the local media, as I had no idea right now how the woman was doing. All I knew from the initial report was that she had been severely dehydrated when found, and that she'd suffered obvious and serious injuries.

My gaze moved from the now empty pit back to the racks on the walls. The tools there. The irons. Breathing in, I could smell an awful congealed stink of bodily fluids.

'SOCO?' I said quietly.

'On their way.'

It was time to go inside the house, but I continued to stare into the garage for a moment longer. Nothing was moving in there, but the stillness felt strange and heavy. Portentous.

Something terrible has happened here.

Of course, I knew enough by then for that feeling to be entirely justified. Except that I didn't. Not really.

I had no idea how much worse it was about to get.

Three

As we carefully explored the ground floor of the house, we got word through about the owner. His name was John Edward Blythe. He was forty-two years old and he actually *did* work as a mechanic, at a large chain garage a few miles from the house. Officers were en route there now to arrest him.

'Nice place,' Emma said.

'You think it's nice?'

'No, of course not. You need to work on your sarcasm detection.'

Excluding the kitchen, there were two large rooms downstairs. Both of them were filthy and cluttered with so much bric-a-brac that it was actually difficult to move about. There was an unnerving lack of organisation to it all. While a normal house might have had a lounge and a dining room, it wasn't remotely clear here which was intended to be which, or if either of them was. In one room, a settee had been placed at an angle, facing a bare wall. In the other, battered armchairs were clustered backwards around a pillar of weathered boxes that stretched almost to the ceiling. There were old wooden chairs balanced upside down, like a bar after closing time, and piles of magazines arranged in haphazard patterns. Everything smelled musty and damp. Faded canvas prints of nature scenes had been tacked to the walls, but the angles were all skewed, as though the house had leaned to one side, or the person placing them hadn't really understood what pictures were for.

It only exacerbated the feeling I'd experienced when we'd arrived here. While the house seemed well maintained enough from the exterior, that was purely a matter of appearance – a careful act of fitting in with the neighbourhood as much as possible. Behind the front door, everything was not just a mess, but almost *alien*. If the outside had reminded me momentarily of a head half submerged in the ground, then the interior offered a disturbing insight into the thoughts that went on in that head. Disordered, distracted, uncaring. A confused attempt at normality that had gone deeply wrong.

As we walked into the kitchen, Emma seemed to read my mind.

'It looks like madness, doesn't it?' she said.

'Looks like it. Smells like it.' *Feels like it too*, I wanted to say, but didn't. Although by this point, I thought that Emma wouldn't have disagreed with me.

Flies buzzed around the unwashed plates and dishes piled on the kitchen counter and lining the floor around the edges of the cabinets. The sink was full to the brim with filthy grey water. Like the rest of the downstairs, the room didn't seem like it had ever been cleaned, or the window opened. There was an unpleasant meaty smell in the air.

Emma gestured around the room.

'What kind of person *lives* like this?'

'John Blythe, apparently.' I checked my phone for updates. There was nothing so far. I put the phone away. 'Hopefully we'll get to find out in person shortly.'

'Cellar door?' Emma said. 'Or a pantry?'

I looked across at where she was pointing. There was a door in the far wall, directly opposite the one that led into the attached garage. Most of the white paint had flecked off it, leaving swathes of bare black wood; it looked like something that had charred in a bonfire. The unease inside me deepened.

'Let's find out.'

I snapped on a pair of gloves and approached the door. Just before I grasped the cold handle, I imagined a slight tingle of electricity in my hand. When I opened the door, a waft of old air escaped from the stairwell beyond, and I grimaced.

'Cellar,' I said.

The stench came next. It was the same meaty, unwashed aroma that permeated the kitchen, but much more intense than that. And on some primal level, I understood. Whatever was down there was the source of it. The rotting heart of the place.

Something is terribly wrong here.

Emma said, 'Oh God. Can you ... ?'

'Smell it? Yes.'

There was a light switch on the nearest wall beyond the door. I flicked it on, and a bulb came to life at the top of the stairs, the cord wrapped in strings of dust. Lights had come on below me as well. I could hear a faint, ominous buzzing sound emanating from the cellar.

'Will, we should wait for SOCO.'

I nodded. We should. But I couldn't stop now. I stepped through the doorway and stood at the top of the dusty stone staircase. The house felt more alive than ever, and I couldn't shake the ridiculous feeling that it recognised me somehow. As though, below the surface of the world, two cogs had come together and were now turning in unison.

With every step down, the smell grew stronger. I knew what it was. Old meat and decay, but with an added element that wasn't a smell so much as recognition on a deeper level. I knew full well what I was descending towards, if not what form it might take.

It still wasn't immediately apparent when I reached the bottom of the stairs and stepped into the cellar. It was a small, square space, and in comparison to the first floor of the house it was relatively clean and tidy. There was a mattress beside the bottom of the steps. As hard as it was to believe, perhaps John Blythe slept down here sometimes. Otherwise, the room was empty. But as I looked over to the far side, I saw another door in the wall there.

Emma joined me at the bottom of the steps, her arm across her face.

'Oh God, the stench.'

I didn't reply. Instead, I walked over to the closed door. An old black key had been left in the lock. I turned it, then pulled the door open slowly. There was a smaller, secondary part to the cellar beyond, and as I stepped inside, I saw what had been stored in there.

Barrels.

There were four of them. They were made of opaque white plastic, their black lids clipped around the top with enormous metal clasps. All the same size – probably about ten gallons each. And I could see enough through the plastic to tell that at least three of them were full of something.

I crouched down in front of them.

'Will...'

'I'm not going to touch them.'

I tilted my head slightly, peering at the obscured shapes within and trying to make sense of them. There was no light in this second room, and I was casting too much of a shadow over them. After a moment, I pulled out a pen torch and played the light across the plastic.

I forced myself not to recoil. This close, the things inside looked like a crowd of people pressed up behind a blurred-glass door, contorted around each other. As the light moved here and there, I made out a web of hair swirled against the inside, a splayed hand pushed against the plastic, the fingers dissolved at the edges...

It felt like the heart of the house was beating too quickly now.

Apparently it's Amanda.

I'd been so intent on forgetting the reporter outside and getting to the scene that I hadn't chased the thought – the name. Now, though, it clicked into place. I remembered where I had heard it before, and I understood what I was seeing in front of me right now.

I stood up suddenly as the consequences unfolded in my head. John Edward Blythe was not here. Our best chance was to arrest him at work, but we didn't know for sure he was even there.

'We need to get to the press outside.' I moved quickly past Emma, back through the cellar, almost running up the staircase. 'We need a press blackout on this whole scene.'

Too late, of course.

Way too late by then.

Four

It doesn't matter who gets him.

That was part of what I was telling myself two hours later, when Emma and I were sitting in the office of DCI Graham Reeves, our direct superior.

It doesn't have to be you.

Which was a good thing, because right now I didn't think it was going to be me. Reeves was a thin, wiry man in his late fifties, with tight muscles and salt-and-pepper hair that he kept shaved neatly to grade one. He was not beloved throughout the department. His mood could most correctly be judged by betting on the exact inverse of how he appeared, in that the angrier he was, the calmer he seemed – and right now, he seemed very calm indeed. That calmness was very obviously directed at Emma and me. The room was threateningly silent.

We had been joined by DI James Ferguson. He was a large man in his late forties, and he naturally slumped when sitting, like something partially solid that had been poured on to the chair. A good officer, I suppose, but very much an arch-careerist. He had led the investigation into Amanda Cassidy's disappearance, and I very much doubted he would want to relinquish it now that it had exploded into the kind of case you could pin a promotion on.

Without speaking, Reeves turned the monitor on his desk around to face the three of us, but specifically Emma and me. An open internet window showed rolling coverage from a news website. There were plenty to choose from right now, I was sure. This one was being streamed live from a press helicopter, and showed footage of officers moving in and out of John Blythe's property. A red banner at the bottom of the screen proclaimed: AMANDA CASSIDY FOUND ALIVE. HAS THE RED RIVER KILLER BEEN IDENTIFIED? The volume was muted, but I didn't need an audio commentary to understand the message. Reeves was staring at us with blank, almost dead eyes. I wasn't sure he was actually even breathing.

'Well?' he said finally.

I left it to Emma to reply. I would have done so at the best of times anyway, but right now I was distracted by a hundred different thoughts and trying hard to suppress them all – or to keep them from showing on my face, at least. I couldn't afford to let anybody know what was going on in my head. If I did, there was a good chance I'd be removed from the investigation before it even began. And even though it didn't matter who got him – *it doesn't have to be you* – I didn't want that.

'The situation was out of our hands before we even arrived at the scene, sir,' Emma said.

'Was it now?'

'The name had leaked to the press, sir. They had it already.'

'And how did that happen?'

'I don't know, sir. We arrived on the scene blind.'

Reeves let the silence pan out for a moment and then turned to me.

'What about you, Boy Wonder? Anything to say?'

'Not really, sir.'

'"Not really, sir"?'

Emma leaned forward.

'It was Detective Turner who made the connection, sir. By the time we got outside, it was too late.'

'I've seen photos from that second room in the cellar, Detective. I imagine it wasn't a particularly *difficult* connection to make.'

This was the worst part of the job – the jostling and the

politics – and I knew there would be more to come. This was only the beginning. Assuming the reports on the screen were correct, we were facing an investigation on a huge scale, taking in numerous forces across the country, and I already knew only too well what would happen. The victims would become less and less important, and the man behind their abductions and murders would be reduced to the status of a trophy. Hundreds of officers at every level would be squabbling for authority over the case: fighting to lead; straining for credit; ruthlessly apportioning blame for any mistake made along the way. The capture of John Blythe was a huge piece of pie, and everyone involved was going to want the biggest slice they could get.

Normally, none of that would have mattered to me. Under different circumstances I'd never have been bothered enough to fight for my piece. I'd have been happy enough just knowing that the man responsible had been caught. And perhaps that remained true here in a sense, in that it wasn't the idea of taking credit that made it so important to me. Not exactly, anyway.

I slid a photograph across the desk.

'John Edward Blythe,' I said.

Reeves stared at me. I resisted the urge to stare back – to make this into some kind of competition. If he wanted to remove Emma and me from the investigation, then he would, and I wasn't going to beg. In fact, I figured the best way to win this game was to bypass it altogether and refuse to play. So I just waited as he stared at me. After a moment, he picked up the photo and stared at that instead.

It was a head shot. Blythe had shoulder-length dark hair, and a hard face. There was something bad in his eyes – or maybe something missing, as though the concept of other people being real didn't quite make sense to him. There was danger there, even in a still image. If you'd accidentally met his gaze in a pub, you'd have looked away quickly.

Reeves slid the photo back across the desk.

'He looks utterly charming.'

'Blythe is forty-two years old,' I said. 'He's five foot ten, and apparently quite heavily built. Dark brown hair, worn as you've seen. Blue eyes. Beyond his size, he doesn't appear to have any distinguishing features. He moved to his present address in late 1998.'

'He works as a mechanic?'

'Yes, sir. A garage just a couple of miles from his house. According to his boss, he's very good at his job. One of the things he said to the officers was that Blythe "enjoys taking things apart".'

'Jesus. That'll be one for the tabloids, won't it? They'll love that.'

Reeves leaned back and ran his hands over his hair. In his short-sleeved shirt, the biceps on his thin arms stood out. He seemed a little less angry now, or at least, angry at something other than me. Probably thinking about the press coverage. With a case like this, the surrounding media scrum would equal the jostling amongst the police, if not surpass it. The articles would pile up, the focus and emphasis twisting back and forth, and the press would turn on us quickly if we failed to deliver an arrest. That was always how the story unfolded.

And the truth was that, right now, none of us knew how far away an arrest might be. When officers had arrived at the garage Blythe worked at, the owner had informed them that he was on annual leave. He hadn't been in work since the week before. Had the Red River Killer been identified, as the press were saying? Most likely yes, he had.

The problem was that we had no idea where he was.

'We're already running checks,' Emma said. 'Blythe's credit cards and so on. Last withdrawal was for two hundred pounds, taken from a local cashpoint on Sunday. There's no record of any booked travel abroad. His name's not listed on any flights. I think the next step—'

'Getting a bit ahead of yourself, aren't you, Detective Beck?'

'Sir?'

'It's not your case.'

Emma said nothing, but I could feel her bristling. She was considerably more ambitious than I was, and she knew what this case represented. It was as important to her as it was to me, albeit for different reasons.

Finally Ferguson came to life beside me. He had spent most of the meeting with his big arms folded across his belly. The abduction of Amanda Cassidy had been his investigation, but Emma and I had found the bodies, which made this unknown territory in terms of who would have primacy on the expanded case. I figured he'd be more than ready to plant a flag. And for once, I decided I would be ready to try tearing it down.

Reeves didn't give either of us an immediate chance.

'Tell me, Detectives Turner and Beck, do you think John Blythe is enjoying his holiday?'

'I literally have no idea, sir,' Emma said.

Reeves nodded to himself. 'I imagine perhaps he is. After all, a man's got to unwind, hasn't he? But I suspect that enjoyment will shortly cease, assuming it hasn't already. And while I'd dearly love for that to be because he's unexpectedly taken into custody, I think it's *far* more likely right now that it will be the result of him seeing his house on the news.'

'Yes, sir.'

'And we have to ask ourselves, don't we, what will happen then? Will he run? If so, where? We don't know where, of course, because you have no idea where he is. Or indeed, how fast he can run. Perhaps he'll kill himself. Some of them do.'

I shook my head.

'You don't think so, Detective Turner?'

'Blythe's not the suicidal type, sir. It would make life easier for us, but you don't do what he's got away with for nearly twenty years and then just turn the knife on yourself. Not unless you have to. Whether he'll allow himself to be taken alive is a different matter. But I think he'll ride it out for as long as he can.'

'Oh yes? And what makes you think you know him so well?'

I shrugged. There was no way of knowing for sure, but it was what I thought. Reeves appraised me for a few silent moments. I imagined my reputation for gut feelings had drifted far enough up for him to be aware of it, and he was a man who would hold such notions in contempt.

I picked up the photo of Blythe and held it up.

'For the record, whoever's case it is, I think we should get this out to the media as soon as possible. Along with his name. His house is already all over the news, so we've lost any chance of keeping him from finding out that he's been identified.'

'Unless he's camping in the wilderness somewhere.'

'No harm done if so. With a name and a photograph in the public domain, we've got a much better chance of someone coming forward. Someone must have seen him. So I suggest we go all out.'

Reeves stared at me again, considering it. At only a few hours into such a potentially controversial investigation, it was early to release the name and a photograph of a suspect, but time was pressing. Blythe wasn't going to kill himself, I was sure of that. Which meant we needed to find him quickly.

'All right,' Reeves said finally. 'Let's get that done.'

'Yes, sir.'

'And now let's talk ownership.' He smiled thinly at that. I could tell he was relishing being the one to close a two-decade-old high-profile case. 'DI Ferguson is nominal lead. But you two are on it as well. Can you all play nicely together?'

I felt a flood of relief.

'Yes, sir.'

'Yes, sir,' Ferguson said. 'But the house is where Amanda was found, and that was my case. I'd like to handle that angle. The searches and so on.'

It might have seemed an odd choice – no obvious glory there – but I understood why he wanted it. Blythe was the prize and the hunt for him was the story, but the press were focused on his house right now. If Ferguson could show himself around there as lead, he'd end up on camera, get himself quoted a little. He'd become the name. And when Blythe was found, it wouldn't matter to the media who'd done the hard work behind the scenes; there'd already be a face attached to the case in the public's mind.

That probably mattered a little to Emma. It didn't matter to me at all.

'Fine by me,' I said.

'Sort it out amongst yourselves.' Reeves leaned back. 'Keep me updated on anything and everything.'

'Yes, sir.'

And as we stood up and left his office, I finally allowed myself to think about my connection to the case. To think about *her*. Because while it shouldn't have mattered who took Blythe down, it did. It really did.

And I'm in the room, I thought.

I am in that room.

Five

The woods around John Blythe's small campsite are already growing dark.

It's nowhere near evening yet. That's just the way it is here. The trees are so overgrown that little sunlight reaches ground level. The surrounding undergrowth is thick with shadow. Whenever he camps here, whatever the time of day, it always feels like dusk, and Blythe likes that. After night falls, and it becomes pitch black instead, he likes that even better.

Breathing in deeply now, he can smell the trees and the fire and the meat cooking. It's reassuring; he always feels at home out here, surrounded by nature. There's something comforting about coming back after the things he does. He spent so much time in the wilds as a child that it feels warm and welcoming when he returns. It's like an embrace. While he doesn't believe in ghosts – he would have seen one by now, surely – he finds it easy to imagine a smaller version of himself sitting cross-legged in this exact spot, by a much older fire, sensing in turn the presence of the man he would eventually become. Stupid, yes, but the connection feels real. Maybe that's why he was always at peace here all those years ago, and why it feels so good returning as an adult. Cotton threading together, two points in time.

The woman will be dead by now, he thinks.

Probably, anyway. Blythe has never been present when the women have died, so he has no idea how long it takes. No real idea of the cause, either. He's done with them by then, so what does it matter? They die, and there's no need to think any more deeply about it than that. At the end of his trip, he will return home and flick on the light in the garage, to be met with the familiar scene, silent and still.

In one of the homes he stayed in as a child, he kept a rat as a pet. The cage was in the dark basement, and it would sometimes be a week or more before he remembered to go down there and feed it. Whenever he opened the door, he'd hear it scrabbling. Week after week – until the day he heard nothing. He remembered the emptiness in the cool air as he descended the stairs and found the thing dead, small and curled up in the corner. It is no different with the women.

He carefully pokes the fire with a stick, turning over a couple of scratchy white coals. It's burning well – small and hot and bright; warm on his face – and it makes the woods around seem even darker. From one side he can hear the hiss of the small gas burner and the water boiling, the peeled potatoes rolling and banging against the sides of the pan. The rabbit he snared earlier, skinned and gutted and tied, is on a spit above the flames. He puts the stick down and turns it now. Fat drips into the fire with a sizzle. The rabbit looks and smells ready. Blythe tests the potatoes and decides they're soft enough to eat, so he retrieves a metal plate from the rucksack beside him. With his meal assembled, he sets about separating the rabbit meat from the bones and the stringy tendons, all of it steaming in the cool air.

As he eats, he turns on his laptop. There's no real reason, but he has a Wi-Fi device with him and he likes to look at certain things. By default, the browser opens on Yahoo, so he sees the news headlines there immediately. The top three are all about him.

AMANDA CASSIDY FOUND ALIVE.

RED RIVER KILLER IDENTIFIED?

POLICE CONFIRM HUMAN REMAINS FOUND AT 'HOUSE OF HORRORS'.

The photograph at the top of the web page is of his house.

Blythe continues to eat just as before, but as he does so, he clicks on the links, reading each article blankly and dispassionately. Then he loads up a number of other news websites and reads the reports there too, attempting to put together a picture of exactly what is happening.

After he's finished the food, he puts the plate on the ground beside him. The inedible parts of the rabbit are already beginning to congeal. He dabs his mouth with a paper napkin, then wipes his fingers. Aside from the occasional crackle of the fire, the world is silent.

They have found him.

From the reports, it appears to have been down to sheer luck. That is unfair on one level, but there is also some consolation to be had there. He has always been very careful, and he would be annoyed with himself if he'd made a mistake. But he hasn't. It was an accident. So there is that, at least.

He takes a long, deep breath.

It is not to calm himself. As always, he feels no real panic. In general, he feels little at all. His situation has changed, that is what it comes down to, and this is just a new scenario to understand and react to. It requires a shifting of perspective and attitude. That's all. So he sits there quietly for a time and lets the subconscious machinery of his mind turn developments over and work out what to do next.

Actually, there *is* a little anger. Amanda Cassidy should not be alive. She should not be in hospital. She should be there in his garage, her body waiting quietly for his return. The others should be there too. They belong to him, after all, and the police are currently in the process of stealing them from him, which is not right. There is a genuine sense of loss – the sensation that he is a victim of theft – but none of these emotions are useful right now, so he pretends he is at work or in public, and the emotions go away quickly. He needs to concentrate on what is important.

What to do next.

The answer is that it depends. Blythe reads through various online reports again. What he needs to know is what *the police* know – but of course, the news will be incomplete; they will not release everything. They will assume that he will see all of this, and they'll want to keep him in the dark as much as possible. Hunt him like an animal rather than a man. Not let him know how many paces behind him they truly are.

So: assume they know more than they say.

Blythe thinks carefully. Since his arrival in the area, he's more or less avoided human contact altogether, but he paid cash at a petrol station a couple of days earlier, filling up the jeep and buying some supplies, and it is possible the attendant there will remember him.

So: assume that he will.

The police will therefore soon be aware of his general location, and while he has been alone at this campsite the whole time, it is reasonably well known locally. As he was buying camping supplies, that means it will be searched, and probably sooner rather than later. Therefore he has to move on immediately.

Where to?

The village itself is obviously out of the question. There are too many people there, several of whom might have recognised him even before his name and photograph appeared on the news. Ultimately, he needs to get out of this whole area, but they will be watching for the jeep on the roads. Their cameras can be programmed to search for it. So that's already too much of a risk. And yet he can't escape easily on foot.

All of which naturally leads to heading north for the moment: towards the deeper woods and the mountains. He spent most of his childhood living half wild in this particular area. He knows the land here well, and he can camp and hunt and live off it for a time. As long as necessary, perhaps.

It would be good if the police didn't know exactly where he is heading, of course. The local officers may well know the land as well as he does, even if they're soft and unaccustomed to it, and not as capable, so he should give them as little as possible to go on. He wants to keep *them* in the dark. Because he's good in the dark. It feels natural to him. Always has.

Slowly Blythe clambers to his feet.

He clears the site as much as he can, packing only the necessities: knife, tent, clothes, cooking equipment, some basic supplies. He needs to travel fast, which means light. Is there time to collect all his snares from the surrounding woods? No, but he can always make more. He kicks over the remains of the fire and scatters what's left of the rabbit amongst the trees.

The jeep is a problem, though. Parked to one side of the small site, it's too large to manoeuvre into the trees out of sight, and he can't risk taking it out on the roads. There is little point in removing the registration plates; the act will buy him less time than it takes to perform.

The last thing he packs is the laptop and Wi-Fi device. He will have no means of charging them now, and he's momentarily annoyed with himself for leaving them both active while he's been busy. That's a mistake. He can't afford to make mistakes.

He allows a little of the anger to surface as he logs into his email.

Very soon he will have the shadow of a huge police investigation falling over him, and he has no doubt they will throw the full weight of their formidable resources at him. So it is true that he now has some serious disadvantages to work with. He has certain assets of his own, though. His ability to live off the land is one. But far more important is something the police will be entirely unaware of.

The police don't know about the Worm.

Blythe writes the email quickly. If it comes across as a threat, that is fine, because it is. He can't escape from this area on foot, which means he needs help. And so the Worm is going to help him, whether he likes it or not.

When he is finished, he shuts both devices off and stores them in his pack. He hoists it on to his shoulder as though it weighs nothing. The anger remains present as an undercurrent, but there is still no panic. He has a plan, and for the moment he is in control of the situation. And so, less than twenty minutes after learning of his new predicament, John Blythe steps into the undergrowth and disappears into the shadows between the trees.

Six

I want to tell you a story...

With his hands gripping the steering wheel tightly, Simon Bunting imagined the man from work cowering. The exact scenario didn't matter, but he pictured this particular confrontation occurring in the man's bedroom. He'd never seen it, of course, so his mind conjured up a dirty little area: a single bed with filthy sheets; old paper peeling off the damp walls; clothes strewn everywhere. The kind of place such an individual deserved.

Andrew Reardon.

He was the manager in the warehousing department of the company Bunting worked for. Reardon had been with the company since he left school, working his way up from the floor, and he was still more blue-collar than white: shaved head; broken nose. At well over six feet tall, he towered over Bunting, and was muscular and tough – or so he thought, anyway. But in Bunting's imagination now, Reardon had an expression of utter terror on his face as the Monster approached him.

I want to tell you a story, Andrew.

A story about what happens when you bully people.

Bunting nodded to himself as he drove. It would be *Andrew*, of course. The Monster would always be superficially polite; when you were that dangerous, you could afford to be. First-name terms were all about power. Its voice would be dripping with menace, though. He liked that, actually. *Dripping with*

38

menace. He might write that one down when he got home, he thought. It sounded professional.

In reality, Bunting knew that Andrew Reardon was probably anything but afraid right now. Most likely he wasn't even thinking about their encounter at all – he was probably drinking a beer or hitting his wife. Bunting recognised his type from childhood: the boys who couldn't do anything with their heads, only their hands, and who took their frustration at the world out on the quieter, softer, more academic children like him. Boys with violence inside them who quickly learned the lesson that hitting downwards felt good. Bullies never changed. They just grew older, the exact same behaviour manifesting itself in more adult ways.

Take today. Bunting was in the IT department. Last month he'd been charged with creating a new database for Reardon's team, which he'd dutifully done, even working late last night to finish it on time. And he had, of course, produced something that, on paper at least, hit the given spec perfectly. This was no surprise. He liked databases. He enjoyed the step-by-step complexity of constructing the foundations, and then designing the front end so that less intelligent people would be able to use it. He liked the sensation that he had programmed something intricate and clever, and that he was the only one who understood the underlying code. Any problems, they'd have to come to him, the same way a dim-witted motorist with a faulty engine would need to visit a mechanic. It was a trivial but satisfying use of his talents.

Not good enough for Reardon, though. In the meeting today, he'd demanded a last-minute change – something else the database needed to do that hadn't been specified at the beginning. Bunting had considered it quickly on the spot and realised it was impossible. That was the thing about databases, he'd tried to explain to the room full of people staring at him. You needed to build them from the ground for a specific purpose. If it were a building, it would be like asking him to add a new floor halfway up. *It should have been on the plans to start with*.

Reardon had barely been able to hide his contempt. He'd sat there, sneering openly at Bunting, with his big arms folded aggressively, and told him it should be easy for a man as clever as he was. He'd made *clever* sound like an insult, for God's sake! Someone had actually laughed. Bunting had looked around the room and felt himself reddening. He could see himself through their eyes: short and soft; pudgy; an easy target for picking on. He'd remembered the way the girls at school had called him *Slimon*, and he'd felt little again.

Not so easy now, though, is it, Andrew?

I'm sorry, Reardon said in his imagination.

But the Monster moved towards him. *Sorry won't cut it with me.*

Was that another good line? Bunting wondered, just as the blare of a horn shook him out of his thoughts. In the rear-view mirror, a car was disappearing away behind him, the vehicle stopped. Shit. He realised that, lost in his fantasy, he'd just gone straight through a red light. Fortunately, the traffic was sparse. He could have been killed!

He tried to calm down and laugh it away. No harm done. 'Yeah,' he told the car in the distance behind him. 'That's right. I don't give a fuck.'

But he stopped at the next set.

Lost in his fantasy, though – that wasn't quite true, was it? Fantasy was the wrong word, because what enabled him to get through days like this was something that men like Andrew Reardon didn't know.

The Monster was *real*.

In his lonely teenage years, Bunting had gorged on comic books. He'd found a world of escape and support in the stories of superheroes and villains in the comics, which he saved up for and bought secretly from the local newsagent. The old man had taken to ordering them in specially, keeping them behind the counter ready for Bunting to pore over privately until they fell to pieces. He left the tattered pages in woodland the way other children did pornographic magazines.

What he loved most about them was not the heroes and the things they did, but their alter egos: the people they became without their costumes. They seemed like ordinary men and women. Nobody around them suspected the secret powers they had and the things they were capable of. How easy it must be to be bullied or belittled when you're Peter Parker or Clark Kent, when you know you could stop it at any moment. That was a different kind of power. It wasn't flying or crawling up walls or invisibility; it was a by-product of those things, and actually far more profound. It was the power of knowing you could hurt someone if you wanted to, and every time he'd been pushed over or spat on as a kid, and every occasion he was mocked as an adult, he'd tried to summon that spirit inside himself.

I could stop this whenever I want.

You don't know how lucky you are.

It had been a fantasy back then. But it wasn't any more. Because the Monster was real. It was like a costume he could put on if he chose to – a mask and cape he could wear. Reardon didn't know how lucky he was. Because Simon Bunting, the small and apparently defenceless man he was abusing, was really just an alter ego. Simon Bunting had a monster he could unleash if he wanted to. All it would take was an email. And that knowledge gave him the power to choose not to. Which was why he'd taken the contempt, smiled politely at Reardon, and then left work early for time in lieu, albeit clocking out without anybody seeing him.

The lights changed.

Bunting decided not to head straight home. Instead, he would drive a couple of streets along from his own house to where the Monster lived. He liked to do that from time to time, especially when he knew the Monster was entertaining a guest. There was no danger in doing so. He knew the location of the CCTV cameras in the city and avoided them by instinct. And there was little risk of the Monster noticing him. Some nights, he would park a way down the street and leave the engine idling while he peered over the steering wheel at the house, feeling the thrill of having a monster under his control.

I know who you are, even if you don't know me.

You're my secret power.

And so Simon Bunting drove past the end of his own street, and towards the house of John Edward Blythe.

He was almost there when he saw the congregation of media and police outside, and realised that his life was about to change forever.

Seven

'You've done well for yourselves,' Ferguson said.

We were heading down the corridor towards the main operations room, where the teams we'd been assigned had assembled and were waiting to be briefed. Ferguson was leading the way, conspicuously and deliberately so. Emma was making more of an effort to keep up than I was.

'What are you talking about?' she said.

'Crowbarring your way in like that.'

'Rubbish. Our scene. We found it.'

'A car thief who couldn't drive found it.'

'Oh come off it, James.' She made it sound breezy. 'Anyway, you know what this is going to be like. By the time we're done, every officer in the department is going to be involved.'

Ferguson smiled over his shoulder. 'Yeah, but we both know that it helps to be in at the foundations.' He glanced at me, slouching along behind. 'You're wrong, by the way, Turner.'

'Oh?'

'I think he's going to kill himself.' Ferguson turned back, sniffing loudly as he walked. 'We'll look for him, and look for him, and six months down the line some walker will find a bunch of bones in the woods somewhere. Bet you.'

'I don't want to bet you,' I said.

'Well then, there you go.'

'You sound quite happy at the prospect, though.'

'I'm not crying about it.' Ferguson shrugged. 'Plus, it would tie things up neatly enough for us. I don't see it matters much.'

I thought of the barrels I'd seen in Blythe's cellar. They were being removed – covered, of course, to hide them from the prying eyes of the media. I imagined Blythe's collection of dead women still packed away inside, their bodies pushed down like rubbish. The families would be watching the news right now and wondering.

'It might matter to the victims,' I said.

'Yeah, but the thing is, I don't believe in ghosts, Turner.'

'Me neither.'

'Don't you? What the hell is it you do believe in, then?'

'He believes in pareidolia,' Emma said.

'What's that?'

'It's kind of when you mistake inanimate objects for human beings,' she said. 'So it's basically the opposite of the problem you have.'

Ferguson thought about it.

'Very funny. But the point stands. The victims are beyond caring now.'

I had a strange flash in my mind at that: an odd sensation of the way time can knit together, fold on itself, forming shapes and patterns that you can only see if you look at them right. In that moment, Ferguson's question made no sense to me. I didn't believe in ghosts, but I wasn't sure I believed in that division of *then* and *now* either.

'They would have cared once,' I said. 'That's the point. But actually, I was thinking of the survivors. The relatives. They're victims too. I'm sure they'd want him to face justice. And you're forgetting something.'

'What?'

'Amanda Cassidy,' I reminded him. 'She's not dead.'

'Yeah, I guess.' He was silent for a moment then, and I realised I'd stung him a little. That had been his case, his way in to this investigation, and he'd already moved on to the other victims. 'I guess we can ask her what her ideal end scenario is if she pulls through.'

He paused as we reached the operations room, considering what he'd just said. Adjusting it.

'*When* she pulls through.'

'Yes,' I said. 'When.'

Ferguson opened the door.

Inside the room, we were met by a warm hum of activity. Over two dozen officers were arranged at the various desks or leaning against the walls, talking quietly amongst themselves. As we walked through the throng towards the front of the room, they all fell silent, leaving only the quiet whir of the standing fans.

'Good afternoon, everybody,' Ferguson said. 'I'm DI James Ferguson, and I'm in charge of this operation. This is DI Emma Beck and DI Will Turner, who will be assisting.'

Emma kept her expression neutral, but I knew that inside she'd be bristling at that. I didn't mind. I stood there with my hands clasped in front of me, head bowed slightly. You don't need to win everything. You don't need to be the main character or the hero. When you don't let it bother you, and instead quietly concentrate on what matters to you, it makes it much easier to deal with people like Ferguson.

And all I cared about right then was that I was in the room.

'Right,' Ferguson said. 'Let's talk about the Red River Killer.'

As far as we knew for sure, the man who would eventually become known as the Red River Killer abducted his first victim in May 1999.

There would have been others beforehand, I was sure. Killers as accomplished as this rarely emerge out of nowhere. It takes cunning, organisation and practice to make a person vanish from the face of the earth the way he did. It also, of course, takes the desire to do so. That all develops over a period of many years. It seemed likely to me that there would be earlier victims who had, for various reasons, never been connected to the case. But, for now, we had to work with what we knew, which began in 1999.

In the intervening seventeen years, another fourteen women had gone missing, bringing the Red River Killer's total to fifteen, including Amanda Cassidy.

Until today, no bodies had ever been found. The women he abducted seemed to vanish without a trace, roughly at the pace of one a year. They were taken from different locations around the country, possibly suggesting the killer was transient, but there was no definite geographical pattern from which to work. It had never been clear if he was travelling for his job, or whether he was deliberately visiting other cities to obscure his trail.

The women were generally abducted on their way home from work, often from footpaths, isolated side streets or canal towpaths, but there was little else to link the cases at first.

Not until the so-called 'Red River letters' were sent to the police.

One was posted for each missing victim, always sent from the town where she had lived. At first, they had not been taken seriously, but when the sender finally included evidence with his correspondence, several separate investigations were immediately brought together into one, albeit fragmented across various departments.

I hadn't followed the case at first. Like most people in the country, I was aware of it, but the crimes were distant. Until Amanda Cassidy, only one of the other abductions, years earlier, had fallen under our jurisdiction, and I hadn't been involved back then.

In addition, I had an instinctive dislike of the way the media handled such things: the way the victims' lives were pored over and dissected, their images all but fetishised in newspaper pages, the press tripping over itself to unearth the prettiest picture or the most emotional anecdote; the intrusive photographs of grieving friends and family; and – most of all – the elevation of the killer himself. Somehow the existence of the letters leaked, gifting the press with a title: the Red River Killer. It wasn't enough for him to be a man. Instead, he had to be transformed into a monstrous figure with a super-villain's name. I found it all distasteful and exploitative, and so for a long time I only vaguely followed the reports.

That changed in 2008.

'How many of you are experts on the Red River case?'

Ferguson looked around the room. Among the assembled officers, not a single hand went up. They all knew the invest-igation, of course, but they recognised the trap in that word *expert*. I resisted the urge to raise my own hand, and continued to stand there with my head slightly bowed.

'Well,' he continued, 'you will all shortly become experts. And that includes Detectives Turner, Beck and myself. Let's start with the victims.'

There was a laptop hooked up to a large plasma screen on the wall behind us. Ferguson worked at the keys. I remained facing forwards for a moment – preparing myself – and then turned around.

The screen showed head shots of fourteen of the victims.

There's always something disconcerting and sad about the photographs used in these circumstances. We always ask for recent shots: the best quality possible, showing the missing person clearly and recognisably. Sometimes that's a passport photo, but for others – and it was the case with many of these – it means ordinary and prosaic everyday shots: snaps in which the women looked unguarded and happy; captured moments of their lives when they hadn't known what awaited them.

I scanned the screen until I found her.

I knew the photograph off by heart, of course, but it was still jolting to see it projected so large. I did my best to remain implacable at the sight of her. In the picture, she was looking back over her shoulder towards the camera. She was blonde and beautiful and smiling.

And, for a moment, I found myself transported back in time,

from the pain of the ending of our relationship, through the intense, heady teenage years we'd spent as a couple, all the way back to the day I'd stood on a bridge with my best friend Rob, and he'd teased me about the girl in our class who he knew I was in love with. Even then, years before Anna and I had actually got together, I'd known he was right.

You could take Anna with you.

No way. Why would I do that?

Because you're in love with her, of course.

Typical little-boy bravado – and yet only a handful of years after Rob had said that to me, I would have given anything to do exactly what he had suggested. And I would have readily admitted how I felt, too, even if it hadn't already been obvious to everyone who saw us. She was the first girl I held hands with, the first I kissed, the first I ever told I loved. The first everything.

Ferguson let everybody take in the screen for a few moments, and while he did, I felt held in stasis: trapped, almost, in two times at once. I stared at the photograph. Anna was probably about twenty-five when it was taken. That was two years or so before she disappeared from life altogether. And about seven years after she'd already disappeared from mine. Long enough ago that my name had never come up in the initial investigation into her disappearance. Long enough that I could be in this room now, even if I knew emotionally, in terms of what the case meant to me, that perhaps I shouldn't be.

Ferguson tapped on the keyboard, and the image changed. I didn't shake my head; I didn't need to. The memories were gone: still present, but out of sight now, the way you might slip a photograph into your wallet and put it in your pocket. On the left-hand side of the screen was a list of women: their names, ages and the dates of their abductions.

1. Rebecca Brown (28), 6 May 1999
2. Mary Fisher (23), 22 November 2000
3. Kimberly Hart (32), 2 October 2001
4. Grace Holmes (41), 15 January 2003

5. Sophie King (16), 7 May 2004
6. Melanie West (29), 30 August 2005
7. Chloe Smith (19), 26 January 2007
8. Anna Parker (27), 12 June 2008
9. Amy Marsh (32), 19 January 2010
10. Ruby Clarke (30), 4 July 2011
11. Olivia Richardson (29), 7 December 2012
12. Carly Jones (31), 22 May 2013
13. Emily Bailey (36), 12 August 2014
14. Angela Walsh (32), 10 June 2015
15. Amanda Cassidy (34), 26 May 2016

On the right-hand side there was a map of the country, complete with numbered markers detailing the sites of the abductions. Even from a cursory glance, the geographical spread was obvious. The Red River Killer had hunted far and wide. My gaze turned to number 8, which was several miles away. Even though numbers 6 and 15 rested exactly on our city, number 8 still remained the closest to me.

Anna Parker.

'Amanda Cassidy,' Ferguson said.

For the last minute or so, the room had been entirely silent. Ferguson had let the photographs and names speak for themselves. Although officers might joke amongst themselves, letting off steam, everybody here knew deep down how serious this job was. They might forget that as the investigation progressed, especially with the possibility of glory in front of them, but for now, this was a stark reminder of what we were dealing with.

'As those of you who were in my earlier team know, Amanda was abducted a little over a month ago. The current word from the hospital is that she's in a serious but stable condition. It looks like she's going to make it. There was some speculation at the time about a possible connection to the Red River case, but nothing conclusive. Now, we know for sure.'

I wanted to frown at that, but kept my face impassive. Yes,

we almost certainly *did* know, but if it had been me delivering this part of the briefing, I would have been more cautious.

'As many of you will also be aware, today we found several sets of remains at the house of this man, John Edward Blythe.'

Ferguson clicked on the keyboard, and the names and the map on the screen were replaced by that now familiar photograph of Blythe. Displayed this large, he looked even more intimidating than before; he seemed to be glowering down at the room. I tried not to imagine how it must have felt for his victims, or to think that this image right here was probably the last thing at least fourteen women had ever seen.

'The remains were located in the cellar, stored in four plastic barrels. Blythe moved into the property in October 1998, and so I fully expect that the remains we have found will account for the list of victims you've just seen. In terms of workload, myself and my earlier team will search the house, evaluate the evidence and begin to make links between Blythe's life – his work, his activities, his travels – and each of these women. They were taken from different parts of the country at different times of year, and it's going to require a great deal of co-ordination between ourselves and other forces. But we'll do it. We'll make sure that Blythe, when he is caught, is held responsible for everything he did to the women you just saw on the screen up there. Yes?'

There was a murmur of assent from the room. I glanced from face to face. Every man and woman seemed focused and keen. Ferguson turned to Emma and me.

'Detectives Beck and Turner?'

As usual, Emma took the lead. She moved over to the laptop, while I tried hard to analyse the unease I'd felt over what Ferguson had said a minute earlier. We *did* know for certain that Blythe was the Red River Killer, didn't we? Unless there were two equally prolific killers out there, one flying all but impossibly below the radar, then he had to be. But something about it made me uneasy. Maybe it was just a case of dotting the i's and crossing the t's, but this investigation was too important to take anything for granted.

'As DI Ferguson suggested,' Emma said, 'the investigation will have two connected but separate areas of focus. The first will be handled by him and his team, and that is a matter of tying the victims to John Edward Blythe. The second – and most important right now – is to locate Blythe himself.'

I glanced at Ferguson to see how he'd taken the barb. He did well; his expression barely changed. If anything, in fact, I thought there might even have been the wryest of smiles there – the look of a man appreciating a skilful move made by an opponent. Both he and Emma had more of an aptitude and an appetite for the jousting than I ever would, and for a moment I felt a brief tinge of jealousy, as though they were united in some way that excluded me.

Emma ran through the basic details with the team: Blythe's age, height and build, car and registration number, last known movements.

'This information,' she said, 'along with the photograph, will be released to the media shortly. DCI Reeves will be giving the statement. We'll be appealing for Blythe to turn himself in at the earliest opportunity. Given the circumstances, we don't feel that's a likely outcome. At this point, he knows he has nothing to gain from doing so. So it's likely we'll be facing either a suicide or a fugitive situation. Until we find him either way, we're going to be involved in one of the largest manhunts this department has ever taken part in.'

From the atmosphere in the room, everybody knew it.

'We'll also be interviewing extensively. We need an idea of where he might have gone. Neighbours. Work colleagues. Friends – assuming he has any. And of course, anybody who comes forward with information. We can expect an avalanche of potential sightings over the time it takes to find him. A couple of you lucky officers will have the job of sifting through those for the tiny percentage that might prove useful. The others will simply have to envy you that task.'

Under different circumstances, there might have been a few good-humoured groans about that. We all knew how monotonous and unrewarding such work was. But today Emma's words were greeted with silence. Everybody was willing to play their part. And that was good, because it was going to be how we got him. Assuming he stayed on the run, Blythe would only have to make one mistake and we'd have him in custody.

Emma began to divide up the various assignments. Unlike me, she knew the names of all the officers. I did marvel sometimes at her ability to work a room. Really, she was wasted with me.

'Detective Turner?' she said finally. 'Anything to add?'

I stood there quietly for a moment, looking at the room as the room looked back at me. Many of the faces seemed blank; a few were curious. Most of these officers had heard more about me over the years than from me. My reputation for weirdness would certainly have spread, though, and it wouldn't have been helped today by the fact that I'd spent most of the briefing lost in thought. The screen at the back of the room no longer showed Anna's photograph, but I could somehow still *feel* her there behind me, staring out at me from my past, my memories. Demanding something of me. And with the weight of that gaze pressing against my back, I found I had to force myself to speak.

'Detective Beck has covered most of it,' I said.

I wasn't quite sure what I was going to say next. But then, just as the room seemed to be accepting that that had been the sum total of my contribution, I started speaking again.

'There's something else, though, and actually, I can't emphasise this enough. To all of you – not just the teams working under DI Beck and me. There's going to be a lot of interest in this investigation, and if anybody's getting too involved, too attached, we need to look at them. We need to look at them closely.'

Emma was watching me, unsure of what I meant or where I was going with this. And I was far from certain myself. Across the room, Ferguson had folded his arms and was looking at me with something entirely different from the vague camaraderie he'd shared with Emma earlier. I didn't care. It felt important to say it, even if I didn't understand why. We couldn't afford to miss anything here. For Anna's sake. For all of them. For me, even.

A hand went up. The officer was frowning, reading between the lines of what I'd said.

'Are we not assuming Blythe is our guy then?'

Silence again for a moment.

'It looks like he is,' I said eventually. 'But I don't want to assume anything just yet.'

Eight

'So what was *that* about at the briefing?' Emma called through from the lounge.

'Nothing.'

She and I had been living together for over two years now. It was a good arrangement for both of us. When my previous lease had expired, I'd needed somewhere cheap to stay, and Emma had had a spare room she was thinking of renting out anyway. We got on well enough beneath the superficial bickering, and we both knew there was zero chance of any kind of relationship occurring between us, so it hadn't been a difficult decision. We had one rule: any romance was to take place off the premises. To be honest, while Emma occasionally had her absences, it hadn't been a rule that had affected me much.

I was not a hoarder. My bedroom was actually the largest in the house, and my meagre belongings fitted comfortably in there, so most of the rest of the house was unequivocally hers, in the sense that it had remained pretty much unaltered by my presence. The spare room downstairs was full of books. Three of the walls were lined with heaving bookshelves, and there were several haphazard piles on the floor, too. Emma was a reader. Her favourite authors had entire shelves to themselves: hardbacks bought on the day of release pressed tightly together, along with the weathered copies she'd searched out from charity shops to complete her collections. That was one of her preferred weekend activities – browsing the aisles and turn stands in second-hand bookshops. She bought new and she bought old, and it seemed she rarely if ever threw any of them away. As little impact as I'd had on the rest of the house, my contribution to this room was precisely nil.

'Nothing?' Emma appeared in the doorway carrying two glasses of white wine. 'I don't believe you.'

I shrugged. 'Just a gut feeling.'

'Ferguson didn't like it, you know.'

'Ferguson doesn't like anything.'

'He likes me. But then who wouldn't? Here.'

'Thanks.' I took the wine, then turned back to the bookshelves. 'I'm just worried there might be something we're missing. Pinning everything on Blythe. Not looking for other possible angles.'

'Putting all our eggs in one barrel? No, wait, that's too much even for me.'

I shrugged again. 'It's probably nothing. You know what I'm like.'

'Yes. A source of constant irritation and sorrow.'

'But you'd be lost without me.'

'No, I'd be DCI without you.'

'Maybe you will be soon anyway, if we play our cards right with this one.'

'Yeah, maybe.' She looked at me curiously. 'You don't care about that at all, do you? Your reputation, I mean. How you come across.'

'No, not really.'

'Probably a good thing, considering.' It was a joke, but for a moment it seemed like she was going to expand on the topic. Instead, she came and stood next to me. 'What are you doing, anyway?'

'Admiring your library.'

'Glorious, isn't it. Anything take your fancy?'

'Not really, no.' I looked around. Most of the books were crime thrillers or horror. 'I'm genuinely not sure why you like

55

this kind of stuff. You live the reality of it all day, and then you spend your evenings reading deeply unpleasant things that people have made up about it.'

'Escapism.'

'Exploitation.'

'Ha! You're way too serious sometimes. You do know that, right?'

'Yes,' I said. 'While I don't care, I am aware of my reputation and how I come across.'

I'd meant what I'd said, though. In much the same way the newspapers amped up the gory details to sell copies, these books were filled with violence as entertainment, and it all felt the same. Dead women shifting units.

'I like the fact that at the end of them the bad guy gets caught,' Emma said. 'Doesn't always happen like that in the real world, does it?'

'No, it doesn't. Although it will with this one.'

'Yes. It will.'

'Anyway.' I turned away from the shelves. 'I'm too serious. I know that. Maybe I'll give one of them a try some day. See if it surprises me.'

'I'll be happy to guide you in the right direction.'

'And I'll be happy to be guided.'

I sipped the wine. It was ice cold, and exactly what I needed right now. Only one tonight, though; we remained on call. If Blythe was located, we needed to be on the move.

'In the meantime,' I said, 'I think I've got enough reading material for tonight.'

The first letter from the Red River Killer was received by police on 28 July 1999. In common with the correspondence that followed, it was printed on one side of a single sheet of generic white paper, double-spaced, in twelve-point Arial font.

Whoever sent it had been careful about covering their tracks. No DNA evidence or prints were recovered from either the letter or the envelope it was sent in – or indeed from any of the ones that followed. It was sent from a postbox close to the scene of Rebecca Brown's abduction, and the ones that followed were always posted similarly from the town from which the victim had been taken.

When it was initially received, the first letter was assumed to have been sent by a crank. That was an understandable response; in my experience, even the smallest murder investigation attracts them. You get false confessions from lonely people looking for attention, and you also get more malicious communication from people who want to play games. If you're not careful, such correspondence can derail an investigation and send it spiralling off in an entirely wrong direction. It can cost lives. Although the letters were casually investigated, it would be several years – and victims – before their authenticity was finally corroborated and the contents taken seriously.

There were scans of all of them in the case file. While Emma curled up at the other end of the settee, reading whatever battered old paperback she was currently invested in, I logged into the department system on my tablet and loaded up the first of them.

I want to tell you a story about a girl named REBECCA. Rebecca was a BEAUTIFUL girl once, with long brown hair. She also had the most GORGEOUS eyes you will have ever seen. She cycled here and there and everywhere and her legs were very tanned and toned as a result of this. She was a very pretty girl indeed back then and was never wanting for male attention, which she encouraged and enjoyed. Despite being married, she had MANY lovers and her husband never knew.

She was cycling when she met me along that lonely towpath and it is true that I was later also to become her LOVER and that she would later also come to encourage and enjoy that. She stayed with me for two months and I want you to know that I was the last thing she ever saw and

that she was BEAUTIFUL when she was dying and that her
eyes remained GORGEOUS as they emptied. She is alas
not so pretty now but I will take good care of her remains
although the best of her is of course gone and washed
away in the RED RIVER.

Staring at it now, I felt like the words were crawling on
the screen. With the benefit of hindsight, the letter made for
disturbing reading, but it was understandable that it hadn't
been taken entirely seriously at first. Certain information about
the disappearance of Rebecca Brown would have been circulat-
ing in the media at the time, including photographs, and there
was nothing in this letter that suggested the person who had
written it had done anything more than watch the news and
read the local papers.

Washed away in the RED RIVER...

That final sentence had eventually given our killer his special
name, as each of the letters that followed made some reference
to the term. Each also began in the same way: *I want to tell
you a story...*

The letters had been taken far more seriously after the abduction of Melanie West in 2005. I turned my attention now to that
sixth letter, which had arrived a month after her disappearance.

I want to tell you a story about a girl named MELANIE.
Melanie was very BEAUTIFUL but not in a conventionally
attractive way and so she had to settle for marrying a man
who was UNWORTHY of her and did TERRIBLE things to
her. But she had an inner light that shone through her skin
and everybody agreed she was very kind and gentle. She
liked to walk and it was while walking home by the side of
that canal that she met me, a far more worthy man, and
now I can appreciate that glorious light AS I WISH.

Melanie remains with me still but she will know the RED
RIVER soon just as she secretly already knows it in her
heart. I have taken good care of her for as long as I can

and I will keep that special light aglow until the waters finally wash it to darkness. I return AN ITEM that she no longer needs, for in the eyes of the world she must now be seen as DIVORCED.

I tapped the screen, which changed to show a photograph of the item that had been returned with the letter: Melanie West's wedding ring, which she had been wearing when she went missing. A note in the file confirmed that her husband had identified it. Although no further tokens were received with subsequent letters, it was enough to confirm to investigators that the correspondence was genuine.

Why send the wedding ring?

Had Melanie West meant more to Blythe than the others? Or was it just another dig at the relatives? The allegation that Rebecca Brown had had affairs, for example, had never been substantiated; her husband denied it, and there was no evidence to suggest it was true. People have secrets, of course, but I thought the most likely explanation was a banal form of sadism: a little extra detail that would hurt the people left behind even more. Or perhaps he had sent the ring because he was worried the letters weren't being taken seriously, and that the barbs he included in them weren't getting through to the families and sinking in . . .

'What are you looking at?'

Emma had put the paperback down, splayed open on the arm of the settee, and was staring at me curiously.

'Just the case file.'

'You seem completely lost.'

'Do I? I'm sorry.'

She shook her head. 'Don't apologise. It was just strange. I don't think I've ever seen anybody look so absorbed in something. Even you.'

'I'm reading the Red River letters. Thinking about them.'

'Thinking what about them?'

For a moment, I couldn't answer. The truth was that I was

actually building up to something – steeling myself to read the one piece of correspondence that mattered to me the most, and procrastinating as I did so. Putting the moment off. I'd read that eighth letter before, of course – Anna's letter – and I wasn't sure why I wanted to do so again now, except that it felt important in some way. A kind of pilgrimage, perhaps. I was *in the room*, after all, and Anna was the reason I needed to be. It pained me that I couldn't explain any of that to Emma, but it was my burden to shoulder.

There was more to it, however, than simply dwelling on the past. Something about the letters actually *was* bothering me. They didn't seem to fit somehow. I was struggling to articulate what it was when Emma sighed, perhaps reading at least some of my thoughts.

'Look,' she said, 'you know where we stand. Ferguson made his play. He's handling that side of things. Let him worry about the letters, the victims, tying them to Blythe. All that. It's our job just to find him. And if there was anything in those letters that would help us, it would have been spotted long ago. Let's not go treading on toes.'

'I think you secretly get a kick out of treading on toes.'

'Only when those toes are in the way. And they're in the right direction.'

'Ferguson *did* say we all had to become experts on the case.'

'Yes, very good.' Emma shook her head. 'I just have this strange feeling that I'm going to have to watch you on this case, Will. Even more than usual.'

'Oh,' I said. 'You and your *feelings*.'

'Hmmm. Well played, I suppose.'

She didn't sound remotely convinced, but she picked up her book again anyway, and I turned my attention back to the tablet. Both of us, in our own ways, immersed in stories of horror.

But instead of heading straight back into the case file, I opened my email and read the message that was there.

From: Rob_P_828@yahoo.com

Will, you must have seen the news. You must know what's happened. I can't believe it. I don't know what to think or feel. And I'm sorry for everything, and I really wish you'd get in touch with me. I'm so sorry. I miss you, you know? You were my best friend, and it's been so long since we've spoken, and I could really do with getting back in touch with you again right now.

I wonder, do you ever think about that day on the Bridge? I don't know if you even remember, but one day we cycled there and I thought I saw a man. A man with a sad face. But there was nobody there really. Do you ever think about him? I think about him all the time. I think about *you* all the time too, believe it or not, and I'm so sorry we don't speak any more. Please talk to me.

I stared at the email for a long time, reading it through over and over again. It was impossible to know what I felt in response. Anger? Guilt? I'd done my best to forget about Rob. I hadn't even known my former friend still had my email address. I should have changed it.

You were my best friend.

I'm so sorry.

For a few moments, my fingertip hovered over the reply button. I almost pressed it. But what was there to say after all this time? And what would be the point?

Please talk to me.

It was far too late for that.

I'm sorry too, Rob. I moved my finger away from the screen. *But I've not got time to think about you right now.*

Beside me, Emma shifted on the settee, and out of instinct I closed the email down. But she was only adjusting her legs. I opened the case file again and took a deep mental breath, then clicked through the various screens until I found the letter I wanted to read. The emotions threatened to overwhelm me, but I forced them down, clicked on the link and began to read.

Immediately, the memories came flooding back. I might have been a teenager again, as deeply in love as it felt anyone could ever possibly be. The sadness followed swiftly after.

I want to tell you a story about a girl named ANNA...

Nine

'Good evening. Thank you all for coming.'

The young woman onstage had a microphone, but the volume was turned so far down that it barely made a difference. Sitting two rows from the back of the room, Jeremy Townsend thought that was probably deliberate. He had been to many meetings like this over the years. Everyone spoke softly at them, as though attempting not to bruise the other people present. The bond they all shared demanded quiet. These gatherings were more like church congregations than support groups.

'My name's Mary Cooper. I organise this group, along with my brother, Ben. I see a few familiar faces in the crowd tonight, but also some people I think are attending for the first time.'

As she spoke, her gaze moved around the room. It landed on Townsend and he felt a prickle of alarm. He was tall and angular, and the rows of seats were so narrow that he had to sit perched carefully, in a way that hurt his back. He imagined he looked as awkward and uncomfortable as he felt. Cooper's gaze seemed to linger on him. Was he going to be recognised? Singled out as an interloper and an impostor?

You have every right to be here, he told himself.

That wasn't true, though. It wasn't true at all.

But then Mary Cooper looked elsewhere.

'I want any newcomers to feel welcome,' she said. 'There is never pressure on anybody to take the stage here. But before we begin, I want to explain a little about who we are and what we do here.'

Relax, Townsend thought. It was foolish to worry. He had been to enough of these meetings by now to know that nobody was ever forced to speak. That would go against the support they endeavoured to provide. At places like this, you were always allowed to talk in your own time, or to not talk at all.

The meeting this evening was being held in the hall of a local primary school. It was a cavernous, echoing space. The floor was made of polished wood, and the bare brick walls were lined with folded-away climbing frames and ropes tethered by metal hoops. A pile of faded blue crash mats rested in the corner beside the stage. Over the years, Townsend had become used to places like these. School halls. Churches. Rooms in buildings that had more regular uses during the day, but which shifted their purpose come night-time. They might house a community meeting, or a local film society, or a children's karate class. Sometimes, like tonight, they played host to support groups.

Wherever he was in the country, though, the people who attended always seemed familiar, like the same cast of actors assembling in different locations. There were couples leaning together for comfort, their fingers intertwined; single people staring down at something invisible in their laps; the young and the old. And yet while they were all separate individuals, they were also all the same: lost souls; souls who had lost. Grief, Townsend had read once, was love without a home. It was grief that had drawn these people here, and it defined them far more strongly than any physical characteristic.

Townsend was only interested in one of them, and he could feel the man in the row behind him now, close enough to touch if he were to turn around and reach out. Tom Clarke had arrived so late that Townsend had been worried he might not show up at all. That would have been annoying, as he'd travelled a long way for this. But a minute before Mary Cooper took the stage, he felt a tingle on the back of his neck, turned slightly and saw him there.

He had been forcing himself not to turn around ever since.

On stage, Cooper took a deep breath.

'We founded this group because, several years ago now, Ben and I lost touch with our father.'

As she spoke, Townsend listened to the beats of her story play out. The details and characters were as familiar as the people here. There was the alcoholic father, the redundancy, the divorce. As adults, Cooper and her brother had discovered their father was living rough, because he had been too ashamed to seek help and then too proud to accept it when it was offered. He continued to live rough on the streets, and then, some time later, he disappeared.

All familiar. But then that was what stories did. They played out over and over again, in different places and at different times. The actors changed but the roles remained. Townsend had been a writer once. He wasn't any longer – not properly, anyway – but he still knew how to listen carefully enough to hear the refrains repeating in the world around him.

'To give an update,' Cooper said, running a hand through her hair, 'there's no news. We continue to look, of course. We've done some travelling this week. It seems impossible that our father can have just vanished, but that's exactly how it feels. Nothing changes. Except that we miss him more every day.'

More every day.

Townsend felt the pit begin to open up inside himself.

That's exactly what happens.

Over the following hour, members of the audience took their turn on the stage, each quietly telling their own story. As well as a congregation, the room reminded Townsend of a group of townsfolk meeting to discuss the existence of a monster nobody else would believe in – and in a sense, he supposed, that was exactly what they were. Everybody had lost someone, but for most people that loss was attached to a single moment, or perhaps a short string of them. There might be a car accident, a hospital stay, a week of slow deterioration – and then it was over. However devastating and horrible death was, the *fact* of it was finite. But everyone present here tonight was missing someone, and that was an entirely different thing. Here there were men and women whose friends, lovers, fathers, mothers, sons and daughters had not died but *disappeared*. And there was no closure there. Missing was not a single moment. It was never finite.

A disappearance raised a hundred ongoing questions. Was the loved one alive somewhere? What kind of life were they living if so? Where might they be? In the absence of a final explanation, the possibilities were limitless. As a storyteller, Townsend imagined it as a book with empty pages at the end. You could allow your mind to go in any direction and complete the story in any way you wished, but you'd never know for sure if your ending was a deviation from reality or a mirror of it. Dead and not dead; happy and unhappy. The missing existed in all states simultaneously, because you lacked the knowledge to narrow the possibilities down to a single definitive narrative.

As he listened, he felt the ache inside him widening. It was always there, but much of the time he managed to suppress it so it was just a background throb of pain and guilt. But it flared now, profound and hollow, an absence that carved him from the inside out. Loss and guilt. The two always stayed close together, like a dog and its owner, even if it was never clear to him which was which. He fought them with reason now. There was no taking back what he'd done. There never could be, however much he might want to.

The hour was nearly over before Tom Clarke took his turn to speak. Clarke was big and burly, with long, bedraggled hair. In his jeans and checked shirt, he looked like a trucker. Townsend recognised him well enough from the media coverage five years ago, but the intervening years had not been kind to him. Clarke looked weary and lost as he moved slowly to the stage, and when he spoke, his voice seemed too small for his frame.

'Hi, everyone. I think most of you know me by now, but for those who don't, I'm Tom. Several years ago my wife – my Ruby – went missing.'

Several years ago.

At meeting after meeting, Townsend had heard variations of that same phrase. It was minimising: the way you'd talk about something so insignificant that it was almost hard to remember. Or something so horrific that it had to be pushed away and kept at a distance.

'Nobody knows exactly what happened to Ruby. Not for sure, anyway.' Clarke took a deep breath. 'But it seems fairly clear now that a man took her. She was walking home one night. She always took the same route. I never worried; there were usually lots of people around. It should have been safe. But it wasn't, not that evening. She never made it home. It was as though she just vanished.'

Townsend found himself nodding at that. It was almost as though the man who had taken Ruby Clarke possessed supernatural powers: as though he could appear suddenly from nowhere, wrap his arms around a victim, and then blink away again without anyone seeing him.

'Not long afterwards,' Clarke continued, 'the police received a letter from the man who claimed to have taken her. They let me read it. It was... awful. So I suppose I'm not like many of you here, because I think I do know what happened to my wife. And I believe that she's at peace now. But at the same time, I don't know for sure.' He pressed his fist against his chest. 'Not in here. And I won't know for certain until she's found – if she ever is. So as stupid as it sounds, even with what I know deep down, I don't give up hope.'

Clarke looked around the room helplessly.

'Because you should never give up hope,' he said.

And this time, the ache inside was much harder for Townsend to suppress.

No, he thought emptily. *You should never give up hope.*

Despite travelling all this way to see him, Townsend hadn't been intending to talk to Clarke in person.

Which of course begged the question: why did he come to

these things at all? He always struggled to answer that for himself. Why did he drive miles and miles to sit in an audience, listening, waiting for one specific person to take the stage and share their particular loss? One explanation was that a part of him felt an urge to see the relatives of the other victims with his own eyes: to take them in and hear them speak. When he was a writer, he had always been thorough in his research. He never relied on the internet, instead getting out into the world, visiting places and talking to people. So perhaps it was partly just some leftover instinct from his old life.

But it wasn't only that.

There was a question he needed to know the answer to. On the rare occasions when he had spoken to one of the other relatives directly, he had never asked it out loud. To do so would mean revealing who he was and what he had done, which was impossible. But the truth was also that he had never *needed* to ask. The answer had always been obvious in their eyes; he didn't need to hear it out loud. And he couldn't bear the thought that, even in a room like this, where he *should* feel kinship, he was still utterly alone.

Tonight, however, when the meeting was over, Townsend hovered close to the door as people drifted slowly past him out into the night. Clarke had moved over to a table where coffee was set out in polystyrene cups. Townsend watched the man retrieve a hip flask from his coat pocket and top one of them up. If anybody noticed, nobody seemed inclined to say anything. Clarke downed the coffee in one, then picked a second and repeated the process with the flask.

And despite everything, Townsend found himself walking over.

Up close, he could smell Clarke. Not just the whisky in the coffee, but the wild smell of the man himself. His long hair was slick with sweat, and there was a sheen of dampness on his cheeks. He looked desperately unhealthy.

'Excuse me.' Townsend smiled awkwardly. 'I don't want to

interrupt. I just wanted to say … I suppose that I was really moved by what you said on stage. I'm really very sorry.'

Clarke didn't look at him. 'Cheers.'

'What happened … it must have been incredibly hard for you.'

'Harder for her, I imagine.' Clarke laughed slightly at that, then shook his head: a gesture of contempt directed towards himself.

This is a mistake, Townsend thought. He was about to step away when Clarke turned to face him. His eyes were red and bleary, and Townsend wondered whether the man had been sipping from that flask all night.

'You didn't speak tonight, did you?' Clarke said.

'No.'

'And I haven't seen you around here before, have I?'

'No.'

'Well, it can be hard the first time.' Clarke shrugged, then drained his drink. 'But it's supposed to help, letting it out. That's what they say, anyway. Bullshit, of course. Nothing helps. Not when you know they're dead. Not when you know what they went through.'

Be careful, Townsend reminded himself. *Be very careful what you say next.*

'I lost my wife too,' he said. 'Different circumstances, but … well, not so very different really.'

He swallowed. Why had he said that? Despite the alcohol, Clarke suddenly looked uncertain.

'Really?'

'Yes,' Townsend said. 'Sort of. You said the man responsible wrote a letter to the police?'

Clarke nodded. His gaze was intense and suspicious now, and the air between the two of them had become electric. Townsend wondered what Clarke saw when he looked at him. Because he too appeared much older than he really was. His own loss and the guilt over what he'd done had added years to him.

And in that moment, the question came out.

'Did he ever... write anything else to you?'

Immediately the answer was obvious in Clarke's expression. The question had baffled him.

'No.' He looked even more uneasy now. 'What do you mean?'

Townsend felt a trickle of sweat run down his back. What was he doing here? He needed to get away from this man before he said something he'd really regret. But at the same time, he felt a desperate urge to explain. And he was a storyteller once, wasn't he? He could still make things up.

'Mine did,' he said. 'The man who killed my wife, I mean. He wrote to me from prison. I don't know why. I think it might have been out of guilt. Like he wanted to apologise... or somehow take back what he'd done. As though he was pretending to himself that he hadn't meant to kill her. I had to talk to the officials in the end. Get them to make him stop.'

He realised he was gabbling and ground to a halt. Were those good enough lies? He thought they might be. The best lies were built around a kernel of truth, after all. Every story, however fanciful, must be tethered to the ground to stop it flying away.

Clarke continued to stare back for a few seconds, still evaluating him, still uneasy. Then he shook his head and turned away.

'The man who took my wife was never caught.'

He got out the hip flask again.

'I'm sorry for your loss,' Townsend said.

More sorry than you know.

He stepped away then, grateful that Clarke, lost in the act of preparing his next drink, didn't bother to return the sentiment. And as he walked towards the door, towards the blissfully cool night air, he thought:

I'm sorry that your wife is dead because of me.

Ten

When he'd first moved to the city, Simon Bunting had chosen his house for a number of very specific reasons, not all of which could easily be explained to an estate agent. One of them was the proximity to Blythe's own house, in this area of identical properties; Bunting had wanted to feel as close to his Monster as possible. Another was that the hedges to the side of the driveway and garden were high and overgrown enough to seclude him totally from his neighbours. Bunting valued his privacy. He stood in his driveway now, breathing in the cool night air, still trying to calm himself down.

Because panic wouldn't achieve anything.

After passing the scene at Blythe's house, he'd circled the neighbourhood, checking out his own street from both ends to make sure there were no police waiting for him. Everything seemed quiet, but as he'd got out of the car, he'd been expecting to hear megaphones crackling and to sense bodies rushing him from all sides.

Nothing.

He was safe for the moment.

Get inside. Watch the news.

That was exactly what he had done. He needed to keep calm, scope out the terrain and find out the exact parameters of the situation he was dealing with.

Inside the house, he'd listened carefully for activity and checked for any sign of disturbance. There was nothing. The back door was locked and bolted; the windows hadn't been tampered with; the cellar remained secure. Everything was precisely as he had left it. In the front room, he had turned on the television and flicked through to a news channel.

Blythe's face was right there, staring out of the screen at him. A woman's voice was talking loudly over the image, and Bunting almost laughed as he heard it. The Monster would be affronted by that, all right. He'd never have stood for a woman talking over him.

'Police are appealing for anybody with knowledge of John Blythe's whereabouts to come forward now. They are urging the public not to approach the man, but to report any potential sightings immediately. It is ... ah ... *urgent*, they say, that they locate this individual as soon as possible.'

He hasn't been caught yet.

Bunting had marvelled at that. He'd always been aware that Blythe possessed a certain degree of base, animal cunning, but the man was still a brute at heart, and Bunting had always seen himself as the brains of the operation. If it could be called that. But here was Blythe, apparently outwitting the authorities for the time being, while Simon Bunting sat in his front room fighting back the fear that his intelligence hadn't been enough. That he hadn't been *clever* enough.

How careful had he been?

You've been careful, he'd told himself. *Just watch the news for now.*

Yes – that was what he needed to do.

The basics of the situation soon became reasonably clear. Blythe was on the run, and the police didn't seem to have any idea right now where he might be. They'd released his name, photograph and details of his vehicle. Amanda Cassidy had been found alive in Blythe's house, but was currently in a critical condition in hospital. Other remains had been found within the property.

Those were his parameters, then.

Except not all of them. Not yet. Bunting had looked across

the room to his small dining table, where the laptop sat. Closed for the moment – always closed in the house, of course, precisely because he *was* clever and careful. And if he was going to extricate himself from this situation – if he was going to untether himself from the Monster and come away clean – then it was precisely that intelligence that he would need to rely on.

He had to keep calm. He had to stay in control.

Maintain frame. That was how they described it on some of the masculinist websites he visited. Obviously he only logged on to them so as to laugh to himself at the people who posted there – men like Reardon for the most part, he imagined – but he had to admit, you could sometimes find common sense there too. Maintain frame. Manage the conversation. Control what people were thinking. He liked that.

But in order to do so, he needed to know everything.

Bunting carried the laptop and the portable Wi-Fi device out to the car. He drove for about half an hour, avoiding CCTV cameras, until he found an isolated spot, where he parked up in the black space between two street lights. He was careful, clever. And so only then did he risk connecting to the internet, logging into his anonymous email account and checking for messages.

There were two, in bold, right at the top of the page. One from this afternoon, and one from this evening. As always, Bunting felt the touch of fear that came from being in contact with something that wasn't entirely human. In the past, there had also been the thrill that came with that, because he was safe and secure from the Monster – in control of it even – but not tonight. The door to the cage was open, and the animal was loose.

Steeling himself, he opened the most recent message. And despite himself, as he read what was there, the calm dissolved inside him and the panic took over.

Where are you you WORM?

Because I promise you you ARE going to help me.

Part Two

Part Two

Eleven

The next morning, Emma and I arrived at the city hospital early.

We had been told that Amanda Cassidy was in Room 211, but it would have been easy enough to find her on that floor anyway, as two police officers were stationed outside the door. We all knew that the chances of Blythe coming here were ridiculously slim, but it wasn't impossible. More to the point, it wasn't beyond the daring of some of the more repugnant reporters gathered outside to attempt to sneak in.

We showed our IDs.

'Any excitement?' Emma said.

'Nothing, ma'am. The doctors are in and out. One of them said he'd be with you shortly. The husband's sitting in with her.'

'Thanks.'

The husband's sitting in with her.

I wasn't relishing that. Normally I was good at talking to the relatives of victims; it was one of the few things that Emma usually left to me when necessary. She had only been half joking when she told me that my unnatural solemnity suited such encounters well. For some reason, I had no desire to do it today.

As it happened, the door didn't lead directly into Amanda's room, but into a kind of exterior viewing area. There was another door leading into the room itself, with a large glass window that ran along the rest of the wall. Through that, I could see Amanda Cassidy lying in bed. Her head was wrapped in bandages so that only a quarter of her face was visible, and there seemed to be tubes emerging from everywhere under the covers, connected to an elaborate arrangement of equipment behind the headboard. A man in his early thirties – her husband – was sitting on a chair by the side of the bed. He had his elbows resting on his knees, his hands clasped, his head bowed.

Was he praying? It looked that way. If so, I wondered what those prayers might be: whether he was asking for Amanda to come through this, or offering thanks that she had been found alive. Either would have made sense. She remained critically ill, and yet over the course of the last month, her husband must have given up hope and assumed that she was dead. I couldn't imagine what he had gone through in that time, and what he must be feeling now. Wrong, perhaps, to concentrate on *his* feelings in a situation like this. And yet, cocooned in the bed, Amanda looked so still and peaceful that he almost seemed the sicker of the two.

'Detectives.'

A doctor entered the viewing room behind us, then closed the door gently. He was tall and thin, with grey hair and a serious, hawkish face.

'I'm Dr Cleaves. I was told you were coming. I'm afraid it's not going to be a very helpful visit for you.'

'No,' I said. We'd been hoping to interview Amanda, as it was possible she might know something about where her captor had gone. A slim chance, admittedly, but we needed all the information we could get right now. It was obvious just from looking at her, though, that it wasn't going to happen this morning. 'What's her condition?'

'Our patient is very ill indeed,' Cleaves said. 'At the moment, she's in a medically induced coma. She's lost a lot of fluids and her body has been subjected to a significant degree of trauma. She's stable for the moment, but she still needs a great deal of care.'

'I understand.'

Cleaves stared through the glass at his patient.

'I've worked here for decades now, Detectives, and in that time, I've witnessed some horrific injuries. But I think I can speak for all my staff when I say we've never seen anything like what has been done to this young woman.'

When Amanda Cassidy had been brought in, he told us, she was severely dehydrated. She hadn't eaten or drunk anything for a number of days; she was also disorientated and traumatised, and lost consciousness soon after arrival. In addition to her general physical state, she had suffered a number of more specific injuries. There was evidence of a series of prolonged sexual assaults. She had also been tortured. There was clear indication of burning to her legs and torso, along with severe bruising all over her body.

I looked down at the floor as Cleaves spoke, trying to keep my face impassive. None of it was any real surprise; it was the reason men like John Blythe abducted women in the first place. But it was hard to hear. Hard to extrapolate from that to what his other victims must have gone through too.

They were downstairs now. I'd attended several autopsies at the morgue in the basement here. It was likely a coincidence that the bodies were stored down there, but it sometimes seemed that there had been a design to it, however subconscious – an understanding that the dead belonged under the ground, away from windows and daylight. That was where the victims were right now, just a few floors below us, and for a moment it felt like I could sense their presence in the soles of my feet. *Her* presence.

'Some of those wounds were open,' Cleaves said, 'and infection had set in. I'd say that if she hadn't been found when she was, there's a good chance she would have been dead within hours. As it is...' He shook his head sadly. 'Well, let's just say that we're still not out of the woods.'

I nodded to myself. *Out of the woods.* The expression felt right. It was as though Amanda had been stolen by some monster from a fairy tale and hidden away in the depths of a secret forest. We had found and rescued her, and so by rights she should now be safe, and yet a part of her remained there. Even though she was back here with us, it was still possible that the monster who had taken her would end up killing her. However many policemen we put on the doors, and however hard we hunted for John Blythe, nothing could change that.

I stared through the window at Amanda Cassidy lying bandaged and motionless, kept alive for the moment solely by the plethora of equipment that surrounded her. If she did survive, her life would be irrevocably changed – damaged perhaps beyond repair. My gaze moved to her husband. Not just her life, either. The lives of everyone who had known and loved the person she once was.

'Thank you, Doctor,' Emma said. 'Are we done, Will?'

I continued to stare at Amanda for another few seconds, then looked at Cleaves. Something about what he'd said was niggling at me, I realised, but it could wait for a moment.

'We're done,' I said.

Back outside the room, we walked slowly to the elevator.

'Well, that was disappointing,' Emma said.

She spoke quietly, with none of her usual breezy confidence, and it was obvious the details had got to her just as much as they had to me. *Disappointed* wasn't quite right, though. While it would have been good to get a lead of some kind, it also felt important just to have seen her. It was a reminder that, among the death and horror that Blythe had wrought, one woman had survived. For now, at least.

I said, 'I was thinking about what Cleaves just told us. That if Amanda hadn't been found when she was, she'd have died pretty soon after.'

'Right?'

'Well, does that fit with Blythe?'

'What do you mean?'

'Not with Blythe,' I corrected myself. 'With the letters.'

'Oh God. Not back to the letters again, please.'

'No, hear me out. Think about it. Blythe apparently goes on holiday and leaves her alone without food or water. She's injured. He must have known there was a good chance she wouldn't survive.'

'Maybe he wasn't thinking. Hard to imagine what goes on in the head of someone who'd do that.' Emma glanced behind her, back down the corridor. 'Or perhaps he was even counting on it. I mean, for all we know, that could be his preferred method of killing them. He just leaves them to die when he's finished with them.'

'Exactly. And that's at odds with the letters, isn't it? In the letters, he seems to talk about actively killing them – about being involved.'

There was more to it than that as well, I thought. The whole tone of the letters was strange. They seemed almost loving in places, albeit in a disturbing way, and that didn't seem to fit with the details of sexual assault and torture we'd just heard about. It also didn't seem to fit with just leaving his victims to die, discarded like pieces of trash he no longer cared about.

'Maybe he changed his MO with this one?' Emma said.

'Yeah, maybe.'

We reached the lift and stepped inside. But instead of hitting the button for the ground floor and reception, I hesitated, then selected the one for the basement instead.

'Will,' Emma said patiently. 'What exactly are you doing?'

'We're here anyway.' I shrugged. 'I want to see them.'

Except that wasn't true. The fact was that *want* didn't actually come into it at all: it was a sense of compulsion that was taking me down to the autopsy suites. And it worried me as the elevator began descending that perhaps just being *in the room* wasn't going to be enough for me with this case.

Because if that wasn't enough, then what would be?

Twelve

One of the worst things when a relationship ends is the way it makes you distrust everything that happened before.

You're forced to question it all – especially when the end is sudden, arriving unexpectedly and apparently from nowhere. When one day everything is fine and the next it's over, you know that it's impossible for your life to have fractured so completely overnight. So it's natural to work your way back through all those recent *I love you*s, all those *I couldn't live without you*s, and cross them out one by one in your mind, dismissing them as the lies they must have been at the time. You feel foolish and stupid. You were tricked. And that's what allows the hate and anger to come flooding in.

That was exactly how it felt when I lost Anna. And I did very much think of it as *losing* her when it happened, as though something I'd possessed had been taken away from me. When it was over, I went back through all the happy times and experiences, the secrets we'd shared with each other, and I drew a thick black line through each of them. I worked hard at negating her and everything she'd meant to me. That wasn't fair, of course. With hindsight, I came to believe that it wasn't a lack of love that had made it so sudden; more that Anna had been unhappy for a while but reluctant to hurt me. There had been no malice. It had made no difference at the time, of course. I was devastated and I was angry, and in my head I

82

rewrote everything that had happened between us and cut her out of my life.

The last time I saw her was before her second term at university, at the train station, when she was heading back after the Christmas we'd spent together. In hindsight, again, I realised that she had seemed a little more distant than usual over the break – slightly distracted, as though her thoughts had been somewhere else half the time. I'd put it down to the fact that her life had diverted along a new and interesting course. While I had stayed home and applied to the police, Anna had moved into a very different existence of studying and socialising. It was natural enough, I'd thought, for her to change a little because of that. I'd been too stupid to recognise that the path she was heading on was diverging quickly from my own, and that they would shortly be too far apart for us to hold hands over the divide.

As a teenager, I'd been convinced Anna and I would be together for the rest of our lives. I'd always imagined that she felt the same. When our relationship ended, I wondered if I had only ever been a stage to her, and if she'd known all along that she would leave me behind. If when I stood by the ticket barrier that day waving her off, she'd been thinking what a fool I was, and perhaps even – intolerable, this – feeling pity for me. We talked on the phone a few times after she went back, and exchanged emails. And then a few weeks later, in one of those phone calls, she told me that she'd met someone else at university and that it was over between us.

The last time I saw her – except not quite. We lived in a small village, after all, with only a handful of pubs and places to socialise, so I would sometimes catch sight of her on the other side of one room or another, and I'd always leave when I did. I couldn't bear to see her happy. I couldn't bear to see her at all. And so we became ghosts to each other, only ever half glimpsed from the corners of our eyes, gone when we turned to look properly. There was no dissection of what went wrong. There was never a need.

People change, of course. Feelings soften and bruises fade. I like to think that if I had bumped into Anna now, it would have been okay. We might have gone for a drink and laughed, and I might even have begun to look at all those blacked-out memories and uncross a few of them. But it never happened, and after 2008, it never could. So I hadn't seen her after that afternoon in the train station.

Today would be the first time.

In the basement, Emma and I passed the usual rooms.

There were several suites down here: all steel and porcelain, with square metal doors in the walls like ovens, and the pungent smell of antiseptic in the air. The bodies would be moved into those later today. But due to the scale of the investigation, it had been forced to begin elsewhere: the chief pathologist, Chris Dale, had arranged for a larger room to be used to house the barrels that had been removed from John Blythe's cellar.

There was a police guard waiting for us by the door at the end of the corridor. As we showed our IDs, I looked at the closed door behind him. There was a crawling sensation in the back of my head. My heart was beating quicker now.

'Detective Beck, Detective Turner,' Emma said. 'Is the good doctor in?'

The officer grunted. 'Dale is, if that's who you mean, ma'am.'

Emma nodded, with some degree of sympathy. Chris Dale was not particularly well liked by most people. He had a reputation for being blunt and sarcastic, and was allegedly none too forgiving of the staff who worked under him. He approached his interactions with the police in much the same spirit.

The officer opened the door for us, and Emma stepped into the room. I hesitated before I followed. It felt a little like moving forward into a strong wind, except it was a maelstrom of emotion and memory pushing back at me.

And then I stopped.

The scene before us was so incongruous that it was initially hard to make sense of. The autopsies I'd attended before had all been single victims, laid out on a gurney. What lay in front of us now was more reminiscent of something you'd expect to see in a war zone, where a field hospital had been hurriedly erected to deal with the bodies unearthed from some mass burial.

The room was much larger than I'd been expecting: long and wide, the floor almost entirely covered with polythene sheeting. The four barrels recovered from Blythe's basement were lined up at intervals close to one wall. The tops had been removed, and the contents were now laid out carefully on further sheets in front of them. There were metal grilles whirring close to the ceiling, but the smell was so strong that for a second I might have been back in Blythe's cellar.

'Shit,' Emma whispered.

I nodded, my gaze moving here and there, trying to take it all in.

'No,' Emma said. 'I mean Ferguson's here.'

I looked over. There were a number of people working in the room: men and women dressed in white protective clothing, moving solemnly around, some taking photographs, some crouched down measuring remains and even gently moving parts of them. Ferguson was at the far end, standing with Chris Dale.

For the moment, neither of them had noticed us.

'Oh,' I said. 'Oh well.'

I walked across to the sheet laid out in front of the nearest barrel. Emma followed tentatively. From what I could see further ahead of me, these must have been the remains of the earliest victims. The contents of the first barrel Blythe had used in building his collection were spread out over a seven-foot-by-seven-foot square.

When somebody dies, the remains go through various stages of decomposition. The body bloats with gases; liquid escapes from it; the organs break down and effectively dissolve. It eventually ends up skeletal, surrounded by something called a cadaver decomposition island. In many scenarios, that matter will be absorbed by the environment: soaking down through soil or bed sheets. But not here. The barrels had been sealed, and so the bodies had decomposed and deteriorated within them, and none of it had escaped.

It would almost have been an alien sight, except it was possible to make out numerous stained bones amongst the mess. My gaze moved over ribcages and thigh bones and the cupped peaks of skulls. At the far end of the sheet, the barrel that had held them was still partially full at the base.

'Lady,' Dale said, arriving beside us. 'And gentleman. Assuming that's the correct word for you, Detective Turner, and I'm not at all sure that it is.'

I gestured at the remains on the sheet.

'The oldest?'

'Yes.' Dale's bald head gleamed as he nodded once. 'For the moment, all I can really tell you is that you're looking at the remains of four people. The way the bodies have broken down, we can't be clear which bits belonged to whom yet, but hopefully we can attempt identification before too long.'

'Beck. Turner.' Ferguson had followed Dale over. 'What do you think you're doing here?'

I ignored him, still looking down at the bodies.

'We were just in the area,' Emma told him.

'What's that supposed to mean?'

'We came to talk to Amanda Cassidy. And while we were here, I figured we might as well pop downstairs.'

I glanced at her for a moment appreciatively. I had no doubt Ferguson would know full well it was my idea, but it was good of her to side with me anyway.

'Your job is to find John Blythe,' Ferguson said. 'I don't want to tell you how to do that job, but I think you're extremely unlikely to find him here, aren't you?'

'I'm surprised you're not at his house,' Emma said. 'I mean, the TV crews still are.'

Dale snorted at that. Ferguson glared at him for a moment, then back at Emma and me. It was obvious he wasn't going in for any kind of faux-friendly jousting this morning.

'What can I say, James?' Emma smiled. 'Like you said yesterday, I thought it was important for us all to become experts on the case.'

My line, that one, I thought. *I can manage them when I'm relaxed.* I looked back at the remains in front of me. There was something horrifically hypnotic about the sight of them, as though if I stared at them for long enough they would begin to form a pattern of some kind...

'What about you, Turner?' Ferguson demanded. 'Liking what you see, are you?'

I looked up at him, annoyed by that.

'Four victims here,' I said. 'The oldest ones.'

'That's right. They counted the skulls.'

I kept his gaze.

'Rebecca Brown,' I said. 'Mary Fisher. Kimberly Hart...'

I waited, still staring him straight in the eye, letting the silence pan out. He didn't look away, but I could see the frustration on his face. The anger, too.

He didn't know.

'Grace Holmes,' I said finally.

I walked past him. Dale and Emma followed me to the second sheet, Ferguson trailing behind.

'Barrel number two,' Dale told us. 'We face a similar problem here to the first, although the bodies are slightly more intact, and I think we've managed to separate them. These victims were more obviously in layers. Again, it's four bodies.'

'I can see that,' I said quietly.

As with the first barrel, there was a mess of material here, but Dale and his team had organised it into four roughly skeletal shapes, with the skulls resting on their bases at the top and bones arranged below. These remains were harder to look at than the last lot. That was partly because they were more obviously *human*. But it was also because of the maths.

I needed to keep calm now. Give nothing away.

'Sophie King. Melanie West. Chloe Smith.' Despite myself, I hesitated. 'And Anna Parker.'

My eyes moved over the bodies, the bones. Even with the victims separated, there was no way of knowing which of them might be Anna. I assumed that it would be the remains on either the left or the right, but I didn't know for sure how Dale had unloaded the contents, and didn't want to ask. The right, I guessed. My gaze moved over the bones there, up to the skull. There was nothing to differentiate it from the bodies beside it. The empty eye sockets were staring along the ground past my feet, long past seeing.

The first time since…

It would be too much to think about that now. I didn't want to stand there for too long, so I moved on to view the contents of the third barrel, conscious of the sudden weakness I felt in my legs. *Concentrate.* Once again, there were four victims laid out here – Blythe had clearly decided that was the limit to what the containers could hold, unless the number had some other significance for him. These bodies were much more clearly delineated than those stored in the previous two barrels. Two of them were entirely skeletal, and looked similar to the ones from the last sheets, but the other pair had retained patches of skin. We were moving from the past towards the present.

'Amy Marsh. Ruby Clarke. Olivia Richardson. Carly Jones.'

I tried to think back to the photographs of the victims from the briefing. In the hours that had followed, familiarising myself with the case as much as possible, I'd stared at each of them in turn, attempting to memorise them. Despite the level of decay here, I thought it should be possible to recognise at least one of the bodies, but I couldn't. In fact, aside from Anna, it was hard to recall the faces of any of them at all right now.

Until we reached the final sheet, anyway.

'Angela Walsh,' I said.

Discounting Amanda Cassidy, she was the Red River Killer's last known victim. Her body seemed mostly intact. Her hair was spread out in a wiry fan around her head, and her face was as taut as parchment but still clear enough to picture how she had looked in life.

I shook my head and turned to Dale.

'Which doesn't make sense. There was only one body in the fourth barrel?'

'Yes, Detective.' Dale nodded slowly. 'I know you all have a very low opinion of us here, but that's not something we'd have missed. Do you want to have a look for yourself?'

I ignored the sarcasm and glanced back down the line of sheets. Four bodies, four bodies, four bodies – and then one. I realised that, with the exception of Angela Walsh, any one of the names I'd recited might have been wrong.

Anna might not even be here at all.

'Thirteen bodies,' I said. 'That means we've got one victim missing.'

Thirteen

NO FLY TIPPING, the sign said.

Simon Bunting almost laughed as he heaved the first of the bin bags over the low wooden fence into the field. The council was probably worried about people dumping broken furniture, or unscrupulous builders getting rid of old timber on the cheap. For once, they were going to have some actual flies to deal with.

He checked around as he lifted the second bag, but the country lane remained completely deserted. Best not to hang around, of course. He had been to a tip on the outskirts of the city earlier, disposing of the more everyday items he needed to be rid of. The attendant had been checking his phone throughout, entirely uninterested, but these would have got him noticed even there. Bunting tossed the second bag over the fence and it landed on the far side with a wet thud. He grimaced. He was wearing gloves, but rubbed the back of his wrist under his nose without thinking.

Jesus. The stench of them.

There were two more bags at his feet. The white polythene was stained red, while the contents, only dimly visible, were black and lumpy. They stank of rot – an odd, burning smell. It was a bright, sunny day and the warmth seemed to have brought the bags to life, so that their surfaces were squirming slowly, the maggots within turning blindly in the heat. He picked one up in each hand and threw them over quickly, one after the other, then walked back to his car.

Another task completed.

There were two ways to solve a problem, Bunting knew: analytically, by applying careful reasoning; and creatively, by thinking outside the box. Neither method was necessarily superior to the other, and often they could work in tandem. And so, after reading the emails from John Blythe last night, he had allowed the panic to bloom for a short while, and then he had calmed himself down and returned home to begin approaching what he thought of as the Blythe Problem from both angles.

Thinking analytically, *was* it a problem?

Put simply, was it possible for the police to uncover the fact that he had been communicating with the Red River Killer for all this time? Over the years, he had to admit that he'd grown slightly blasé about his correspondence with Blythe. Yes, he tried to keep up to date with technological developments and update his own security measures accordingly, but it was impossible to take everything into consideration. The individual computers he'd used when emailing Blythe had all been purchased second hand and paid for in cash. He'd used a portable Wi-Fi device and he'd bought new SIM cards for it – again with cash – every time the credit ran out. The email addresses he'd used were, he thought, untraceable: run entirely through the dark net.

But none of that meant he had been careful enough. He *had* grown blasé, he was sure – perhaps even overconfident. And that was how it happened. That was how people got caught. They took every possible precaution to begin with, but over time, as the previously dangerous situation became normalised in their mind, they relaxed and then eventually messed up. He didn't think that was true in his case, but it was entirely possible that somewhere down the line he had made a mistake.

More to the point, he doubted Blythe had been particularly circumspect when it came to internet security. The man was cunning, yes, but also quite astonishingly insane. His areas of intelligence occasionally mapped over those of normal people, but not always and not consistently. Bunting had to assume that once the police had Blythe's computer, they would discover at least some of the email correspondence between the two of them, and that they would then attempt to trace the source of it. He didn't think they would be able to do so – but that didn't mean he was right. In addition, he might well have given something away in the content of his own messages that he wasn't aware of. At which point, he would be going to jail for a very long time.

In short – to be absolutely certain he was safe – he needed Blythe's laptop out of the picture.

This morning, he had called in sick to work. His manager had sounded disapproving, even though it was rare for Bunting to miss a day. And of course, there was that database to finish. Well, fuck him, Bunting had thought. If there were to be consequences later, there were far more serious ones to be worrying about right now. He had surprised himself – briefly – by hanging up on the man mid-sentence. The database. Reardon. How inconsequential it all seemed now, when his freedom was hanging in the balance. So he had put it all out of his mind and set about the far more important matter of the Blythe Problem and how to solve it.

To secure the laptop, he would have to meet Blythe.

That was the starting point, and there was no way of getting around it. It was a frightening prospect. Blythe represented the kind of power he'd always fantasised about having, and for a time he'd been able to pretend to himself that he'd harnessed it – that the Monster had been like a placid tiger, tolerating the leash around its neck as it hunted for more interesting prey. But it wasn't true. And he would have to face that tiger out in the wild soon.

He was in an extremely precarious position and time was not on his side, but it never paid to rush. When you rushed, you ended up with a database that needed something you should have planned for from the beginning. He needed to think. He needed to find the right story.

Back in his car, Bunting smiled to himself.

The right *story* – that was the phrase that had come to him this morning, as he'd considered the situation and his place in it and turned his attention to the creative side of matters. He had been writing stories since he was a boy, at first emulating those superhero tales he loved, and then moving on to far grander and more ambitious works as he grew older. His parents had discouraged him, of course. His mother told him he was too clever for such things, and that he needed to concentrate on his proper studies, while his father seemed to see it as just another in the long of list of unmanly embarrassments his son represented. But Bunting had never given up. And whatever the spurious and stupid reasons for the rejections he'd received from publishers over the years, he knew deep down that he could tell a story.

That was what he needed to do now. If the police found Blythe's computer and somehow traced their correspondence back to him, they would have a straightforward story laid out before them, one he would be unable to refute. What he needed to do was create an alternative narrative that held up even better.

And he had done so.

He had then spent most of the morning walking around his house, analysing each room and making notes of the various assets and obstacles that could either be utilised or needed to be dealt with to tell the tale he wanted. He wrote the tasks he needed to perform on an A4 pad by hand so that the list could easily be disposed of later.

Now, he drove a short distance away from the fly-tipping site, parked up again and took out the pad of paper. A number of items had already been taken care of, and he ticked off the latest one.

Off work ✓
Withdraw cash (£200 should be enough) ✓
Clean house ✓
Break and mend kitchen tap (wrench? – yes) ✓
Mental list of important areas of house ✓

Cover story for Moorton (use Marwood C? – yes) ✓
Disposal of various items (collected) ✓
Disposal of old meat ✓
Purchase tent (cash)
Clean car boot
Purchase newspaper (tomorrow??)

And so on...

The next thing he needed to do was head to the outdoor supplies shop on the edge of town. There was one nearer – on a roundabout he passed every day on the way to work – but even paying cash there was a danger that that could come back to bite him. Better safe than sorry. Dot every i and cross every t. Bunting didn't want to risk being caught on CCTV. And he had never bought a tent before in his life, and didn't want to be remembered for any hesitation in a place the police might conceivably visit if and when it came time to test his story.

His gaze moved all the way down to the last item on the list, and he wondered exactly what to do about that. Because that one was outside his control for the moment. He couldn't do anything about it for the next day or two. He had to let events pan out and see where they left him.

Bunting set off.

Jeremy Townsend would have to wait for now.

Fourteen

There was a café directly opposite the police station. Jeremy Townsend was sitting at a table by the window, with the greasy leftover swirls of a full English on a plate in front of him, watching the activity outside. He was on his third coffee now, and doing his best to make it last while he decided what to do.

The reporters lined up across the street seemed in good spirits. But then why wouldn't they be? None of this mattered to them except on the level of it giving them a good story. They kept coming into the café for takeaway drinks and rolls, all of them smiling and chatting happily away.

Each time one of them entered, Townsend kept his head down a little, wondering if any of them would recognise him: the tall, thin man sitting by the window, looking exhausted and empty. None of them had so far. It had been a very different story when Melanie disappeared. Back then, even through the fog of grief and guilt, the relentless attention had made Townsend feel like an odd kind of celebrity. But of course, none of it had ever really been centred on him as a person. It wasn't *him* they chased and photographed and clamoured at for a quote on what he was feeling and how he was bearing up. It was the grieving husband they were interested in – the character in the story, not the actor currently playing it. There was no reason for any of them to recognise him now.

The owner of the café came and took his plate away.

'Everything all right for you?'

'It was fine, thank you.'

She smiled as she cleared the table. She had been cheerful all morning – buoyed by the additional trade the journalists represented, he supposed. Either she didn't know the reason for their presence or she didn't care.

But then surely everybody knew by now.

It felt to Townsend that he must have been one of the last people in the world to find out. Last night, after talking to Tom Clarke at the missing persons support group, he had returned to his hotel room and opened a mostly blank Word document on his laptop. He hadn't been able to write for years – unless you counted his work on the short stories, which he refused to – but the compulsion to try remained. Writing was a deep-rooted *need* for him; it always had been, even as it had become so frustratingly difficult over the years. In Melanie's absence, though, the last vestiges of whatever decent material he'd been able to scrape out of himself appeared to have vanished altogether. The need, coupled with the inability, was a form of torture for him. One of many, he supposed. And he deserved them all.

Last night had been a similar exercise in frustration: a few bland sentences written then hastily deleted, followed by a feeling of emptiness and loneliness. He'd only turned the television on in the hotel room to give himself the illusion of company.

When he did, he'd sat very still for a long time, watching the news on the bright screen with a mixture of numbness and absolute horror. Some time before midnight, he had packed his few belongings, checked out of the hotel and driven home. He'd arrived back here in the city in the early hours, and hadn't slept since. The exhaustion was making him hazy now. Thinking back, it was hard to believe that an unbroken stretch of consciousness linked *him yesterday morning* with *him now*.

The horror remained, though. That was keeping him going, acting like adrenalin. Every time he thought about what was happening, his heart lurched. He took out his phone and opened the browser, looking again at the page that remained open there.

At John Blythe's face.

It had taken Townsend by surprise, the first time he saw it. It had appeared on the television screen without warning, and when he'd realised what he was seeing, he'd instinctively tried to blink the image away. Left to his own devices, he would have wanted to build up slowly and prepare himself for that moment, but the rolling news coverage had plunged him straight into the cold water of it. He had a name now, anyway, and a face to go with it. Staring down at the phone, examining the man, he saw all the hardness and cruelty he'd always expected to find. Was that down to expectations, though? People's faces were often ambiguous, the meaning of their expression shifting with what you knew about them. But what surprised him most of all was that he didn't recognise John Blythe at all. After everything that had happened, a part of him had expected to.

He put the phone down and sipped his coffee. It was almost too cold to drink.

Blythe was on the run. What did *that* mean? What were the repercussions? Townsend couldn't hold his thoughts together, couldn't think it through. He glanced out of the window again, at the police department across the street, and wondered what on earth he was going to do.

Whatever he did, it would doubtless be another mistake.

It felt as though his life had been defined by them. The first was in many ways the most unforgivable of all, although in the grand scheme of things it appeared small and insignificant now. But it was the nature of mistakes that there were consequences for them, and the more mistakes you made in response, the more those consequences accrued. That was how it worked. At first you might only take one step down the staircase into the darkness, but that step then led inevitably to the next – and then all the ones that followed. Mistakes had a velocity. Before you knew it, the light was a long way behind and above you.

The guilt threatened to overtake him now.

He put the coffee down, his hands trembling. Everything he had done was suddenly too much to bear. He closed his eyes and tried to gather himself.

The door opened, distracting him from his thoughts. He opened his eyes and saw a couple of men walk into the café, one of them rubbing his hands together as though it was cold outside. Reporters. He could tell. They had that air of importance about them. The stars of the show right now.

As they headed over to the counter, Townsend picked up his phone again and loaded a live page on a news website, scanning through to see if there were any new developments. There was little. Officers were still searching Blythe's house, but there were no updates on the man's location, or on the condition of Amanda Cassidy. The police had issued a brief statement, revealing that a number of remains had been removed from the property and post-mortems were due to be performed soon. There would be further statements later in the day.

None of which helped him.

So what are you going to do?

Deep down he knew the answer to that question. He had known it even before leaving the hotel room last night. He needed to find out what was happening. He needed to understand better what was going on here, and where that left him. If pursuing it turned out to be a mistake, then really, what did one more matter? He had to discover what the police had found. He had to know what they knew about...

Melanie.

They had met at university. Townsend was three years older than her, and had been starting an MA in English Literature when she arrived as an undergraduate. His talent for the subject, along with his passion for writing, found him already embedded in the department, and he had been asked to assist with first-year tutorials. Melanie had been in one of his groups. She was attractive – pretty and brunette – but what he recalled most of all was how inquisitive and confident she'd been. Most of the first years sat there in silence, sometimes out of laziness but more usually due to fear that someone might notice them. It took a while to shake away all the wispy insecurities from school; he'd been the same. But Melanie wasn't like that. Her natural pose – one he associated with her from the beginning to the end; one he could still picture in his head so clearly – was leaning forward in her seat, her knees pressed around her hands, her collarbones visible at the top of her shirt, *making a point*. She had brown eyes, wide and earnest. Her intelligence had captured him, but he would be lying if he said those eyes hadn't also played a part.

That his growing attraction to her was reciprocated was inexplicable to him. He'd been a shy, bookish teenager, accustomed to a lack of attention from the girls around him. He had average looks. He was good with language on paper, perhaps, but not so much in person. While he could write fluently, when speaking, the words failed him more often than they won. What could a woman as beautiful and bright as Melanie possibly see in him? And yet she saw something.

One evening, he'd shown her some of his fiction: a short story he'd written, or at least that he'd attempted to. He wasn't happy with it, and that was how he'd presented it to her: with an apology in advance; an excuse for its shortcomings. Giving her his permission to hate it. And yet she had loved it. Or rather, she had devoured it, those eyes of hers wide when she'd finished, and had seemed to look at him in a new light afterwards. She had told him how brilliant he was with words. She wasn't entirely uncritical, of course. *Your prose is great*, she'd said. *Really beautiful. But there's a lack of focus here, like you're not entirely sure what you're writing* for. *Or maybe why*.

Or maybe who, he'd thought.

She had been right, though. His work did lack focus. He'd had an easy, uneventful upbringing. Nothing bad had ever happened to him, and he hadn't seen enough of the world to gather subject matter inside him to use. As a result, his stories were empty. Graceful phrasings, yes, but with little in the way of substance beneath them. But he was almost drunk on the look on her face, and at that moment he'd resolved to change all that.

Hey, Melanie had said then, and he'd heard the same trepidation in her voice, the same nerves, that had been in his own. *I've never told anybody this, but I write poetry. Do you want to read some?*

Townsend shook his head now.

He didn't want to think about the poetry, or really about Melanie at all. This right now was about him; his descent had always been his own. He was damned, and he was damned alone. The mistakes, the guilt, the deaths on his conscience – they were all his. And if the suffering from that sometimes seemed impossible to bear, then the knowledge that he deserved it was always enough to keep him going.

I love you, Townsend thought. *I hope that somehow, wherever you might be now, you know that. And that deep down, you know that all the terrible things I've done, I did for you.*

Then he drained the cold dregs of his coffee, stood up and headed across the street to make another mistake.

Fifteen

Only thirteen bodies.

It wasn't our problem, of course; that was Ferguson's head-ache. Our job was simply to track down Blythe, not tie him to the victims or identify the ones that had been found. But even so, as Emma and I worked our way through the reports and interviews gathered by our team of officers, my attention kept coming back to it. We had a desk at one corner of the main operations room. At the far end, the images of the fourteen victims remained on display on the large plasma screen there. However much I tried to focus on the information in front of me, I couldn't help staring at their faces.

At Anna's.

We had Angela Walsh. She was certainly one of the bodies found in Blythe's basement, which at least proved that he was the Red River Killer. So who *didn't* we have yet?

Inevitably my gaze kept returning to Anna. I kept thinking *what if?* But until all the bodies were identified, there was no way of knowing which victim we were currently missing, or what it meant that one definitely was.

Emma reached out and clicked her fingers quietly in front of my face.

'Come back to me, Will. You're drifting.'

'I'm not drifting.' I turned back to the desk. 'I'm thinking. It's different.'

'No, with you it's the same thing. And I don't need you floating off right now.'

'I'm tethered. I'm grounded.'

'You're still bothered by the thirteen bodies, aren't you?'

'Yes.' I resisted the urge to look at the screen again, but it didn't help. I could feel the weight of Anna's gaze on me regardless. 'We'll have relatives calling in soon. They deserve to know.'

'And they will. But these things take time. Most of them have waited long enough.'

'Yes,' I said. 'That's the point.'

Survivors. When I thought of the word in relation to a case like this, it never just referred to women like Amanda Cassidy – people who had encountered a killer and lived – but also to friends and family of the victims. The men, women and children who were left behind.

Friends and family of the victims are always involved in an investigation to some extent. Cynically, there are things you want or need them to say, and things you need them not to. There are careful interviews to be conducted and tactful searches to be made. And as a case progresses, there are developments, or often the lack of them, to deliver.

Opinions vary amongst police as to how much to share with relatives and how to do so. Personally, I always told them as much as I was able. Everybody was different, but I could usually recognise the same aching emotional hole at the heart of those who had lost: the desperate desire to *know*. Some detectives preferred to pass that particular buck, either because they didn't care, or because they couldn't allow themselves to care, whereas others felt a responsibility to handle that side of things in person – to show that the loss and grief those people were feeling was being taken seriously.

Where possible, I was one of those detectives. With one exception, I would take on that role here too. But if Anna's parents came to the department, I would have to delegate that responsibility, that duty. I could still picture them very clearly in my head. While they had undoubtedly changed a great deal in the intervening years, there was no way they wouldn't recognise my name, my face, and I couldn't risk that connection coming to light.

Emma said, 'They'll understand we can't confirm anything at this point. It's too early. Too soon.'

'Maybe,' I said. 'Does it really not bother you, though? Thirteen bodies. We're missing a victim.'

'Thirteen – unlucky for some. In this case, Ferguson.' Emma shrugged. 'I don't mean to be flippant about it, but there's the rest of the house to take apart yet. Who knows what they'll find? There could be more than one. The wall cavities could be full of bodies for all we know.'

'I don't think so. It's clear from the way that Blythe stored the bodies that the method was important to him. It looks like he even slept down there from time to time. So why would he get rid of the missing victim in a different way?'

'You expect a guy like Blythe to make sense?' Emma said.

'Yes. On his own terms, absolutely yes.'

'You saw the inside of the house, Will. You saw what he did to those bodies. I'm not sure I'd be anticipating much sense there if I were you.'

'Okay, but I expect his behaviour to conform to some kind of pattern. If he's going to put thirteen bodies into barrels and keep them in his cellar, then that's clearly his preferred method of disposal.'

'It could be the first one that's missing.'

'Rebecca Brown.'

'Perhaps he disposed of her in some other way.'

'Maybe. But if not, then we're missing something. Either he deliberately changed his method, or something forced him to. And I want to know what.'

'You can ask him when we get him.' Emma looked at me. 'Assuming we ever do at this rate.'

'Yes. Okay. Point taken.'

I forced myself to turn my attention back to the reports on the desk in front of me. They made for depressing reading. It was our job to find Blythe, yes, and there was precious little to go on so far.

'Still nobody who seems to have known him at all,' Emma said.

'No.'

It was frustrating. As well as the practical side of the search, one of our aims was to build up a picture of Blythe, to see if there was anything in his personal or professional life that might indicate where he could be right now. But the picture we were forming was still little more than an outline, with nothing much in the way of content. We knew his name, age and profession, the make and registration of his car – all of which had already been released through the media – but it was proving difficult to colour the man in any further.

According to his work colleagues, he kept to himself. They described him as a loner, gruff and unfriendly, and none of them had ever socialised with him. They didn't know if he had any friends at all. If he did, he never spoke about them. His neighbours had told us much the same. None of them could remember even a single meaningful interaction with him, and most of them had only ever really seen him from a distance, leaving for work or returning. The woman in the adjoining house couldn't recall him ever having any guests.

A search of his home had so far revealed no address book, no landline, no computer. He *had* owned a mobile phone, as his boss at the garage had given us the number, but checking through records had given us nothing: his only calls had been to the work number on the few occasions he phoned in sick, and he'd never sent a single text message. The last known location the phone company had for the mobile was his house, a couple of weeks ago. We had a search out for it, of course, and the moment he turned it on we'd know where it was. But something told me he wasn't going to be that stupid. It wouldn't have surprised me if we found the mobile phone in his house before too long: shoved away and forgotten in some drawer.

Family had turned out to be a similar dead end. Blythe had

grown up in Moorton, a small village a couple of hundred miles north, close to the mountains. A single child to a single mother, who seemed to have been unable to care for him, he had bounced around a succession of more distant family members in that area. He had been a poor student, but as a teenager had never been in any kind of serious trouble with the police. No convictions on record. Almost unbelievably, his sheet was entirely clean.

'No word from Moorton PD yet on friends in that area?' Emma said.

'No.' I opened the file they'd sent, scanned down. 'We've got a list of random unsolved crimes there from way back when. I don't think they've even filtered it. It's just an info dump. Mostly burglaries.'

'Oh, how useful.'

'Tell me about it.'

We'd have to look through unsolved crimes eventually, but it was no help to us right now. What we needed was a name – someone he'd been friends with, or still had some kind of relationship with – and we wouldn't find that in unsolved crimes that, by their nature, had no names attached to them at all.

We had copies of his financial records, going back the last five years so far. Blythe hadn't used his debit card since withdrawing that two hundred pounds in cash close to home, which was disappointing. That would at least have given us a direction to start looking in. Searching vaguely for positives, I supposed at least it meant he was cash-limited. I expected him to ditch his vehicle soon, if he hadn't done so already, and public transport would be impossibly risky for him with his face all over the news. That meant that wherever he was right now, it would be difficult for him to travel very far away from it. All we needed was a confirmed sighting, a single concrete lead, and we could begin to close the net.

Nothing on that level so far.

I had been twiddling a pen as I worked. I put it down now

and stared at the plasma screen again. At the victims. Pressure was building in my chest. I still couldn't keep my thoughts away from the bodies we'd found, and the body we hadn't.

'Blythe moved here in 1998,' I said. 'A year before the killings began.'

Emma didn't look up. 'Yes.'

'That means he had his base before Rebecca Brown was abducted. He was here from the start to the finish.'

'Yes.'

'Meaning there's no reason we shouldn't have found all fourteen bodies in the house.'

'Oh God.' Emma looked up at me now. 'Leave it, Will. It's not our problem. Focus on *our* problem. Please.'

I was about to argue my case again, but of course she was right. Our problem was finding Blythe. I couldn't tell her about *my* problem, which was entirely separate and which I had to keep secret. Even the possibility of being removed from this investigation made that sense of pressure harden in my chest.

I switched windows on my computer and logged into my personal email. There – again – was that message from Rob. Another link to the past. I opened it and reread it.

Will, you must have seen the news. You must know what's happened.

I think about you all the time.

I'm so sorry we don't speak any more. Please talk to me.

The emotions rose up inside me – anger; guilt; a profound sadness at how things had changed – and once again I wanted to click on reply. But there was nothing to say after all this time, and no point in even trying. Talking to Ferguson before the briefing yesterday, I'd felt that the distinction between *then* and *now* made little sense, but while sometimes that was the case, it wasn't always true. Time can build bridges, but it can also destroy them. Sometimes the ones you wish you could repair are too distant, too far away. Some things, once left behind, slip very quickly out of reach.

The phone on the desk rang. I picked it up.

'DI Turner.'

It was the desk sergeant from downstairs. 'Got someone here to see you,' he said. 'A relative.'

The pressure tightened again. *Anna's parents*. I was convinced of it. I shut down the email with a single click. If only it was really that easy to push the past out of sight.

'Who?'

'Jeremy Townsend. Melanie West's former husband.'

'I hope he's out of earshot for that description.'

'Don't worry.'

The desk sergeant's voice was loud enough that Emma could hear him.

'Go,' she told me. 'If anything, it'll be helpful for me.'

There was some relief that it wasn't Anna's parents who had arrived, but it was short-lived. There was still so little I would be able to tell any of them who came here.

They'll understand, I thought. *It's too early. Too soon.*

'Okay,' I said. 'Bring Mr Townsend to my office.'

Sixteen

'Please. Come in.'

The office Emma and I shared was little larger than a cupboard, with barely enough room for a desk and two chairs, and no natural light. I'd at least managed to clear away the piles of paperwork. And I supposed any of the people I ended up talking to in here during the course of this investigation weren't going to care too much about the decor. They would have far more important things on their minds.

Jeremy Townsend certainly appeared to.

He was tall and thin, and was dressed in a crumpled white shirt, which he'd left untucked from his old black cords. His hair was greying and unkempt, and his beard was scratchy and uncared for. The clothes looked like he'd had them for years and no longer fitted properly: his upper body was bird-thin beneath the shirt, and the trousers looked in danger of falling down. He hesitated in the doorway, glancing around the room nervously, his gaze not meeting mine at first, and then seeming bleary and unfocused when it did. If I hadn't known why he was here, I might have assumed he was a derelict of some kind.

'Please.' I said it more softly this time. 'Come in.'

Townsend nodded once, then stepped inside and closed the door behind him. I shook his hand over the desk as he approached it.

'Detective Will Turner,' I said.

'Jeremy Townsend.' His grip was as tentative as the rest of him. 'My wife was Melanie West.'

Melanie West was the sixth known victim, abducted in 2005, but looking at Townsend now, it might as well have happened yesterday. I wasn't sure I'd ever seen someone look quite so tired; not just in the everyday sense, but something deep inside him: an exhaustion of the soul, perhaps. But it was stupid to judge. Even if he had moved on in the intervening years – buried all the sadness and grief – the news from yesterday would have disturbed the soil, turning it over and bringing all those terrible memories back to life again.

'Thank you for seeing me,' he said quietly.

'Not at all.' I gestured to the other side of the desk. 'Please. Have a seat. And can I get you a drink? Coffee? Tea?'

Townsend shook his head as he sat down.

'No, I'm fine, thank you. I'm sorry for the way I must look.'

'You certainly don't need to apologise.'

He closed his eyes and rubbed at them, and I noticed the wedding ring on his hand. Even after all this time, he still wore it. It was possible he'd remarried, I supposed, but I suspected he hadn't. There was something about his manner and his clothes. He looked as if he'd been trapped in the time of his wife's disappearance and had somehow stepped straight over a decade to see me now.

His hands moved back down to his lap.

'I don't really know what to say, now that I'm here. I just knew that I had to come.'

'I understand,' I said. 'You can ask me anything you want. You'll appreciate there are limits to what I can say right now, but I promise I'll do my best to tell you what I can.'

'Thank you. There was so much that I wasn't told before. Back when it happened.'

I nodded sympathetically, casting my mind back – and yes, of course. It was Melanie West's abduction that had brought the investigation together. Hers had been the Red River letter that had included the wedding ring, confirming the veracity of the killer's correspondence. That development had flipped everything on its head. With the police involved distracted and excited, it was sadly very likely indeed that Townsend had ended up feeling sidelined from the investigation.

I also knew that his wife's wedding ring had been retained as evidence and never returned to him. It would be stored downstairs somewhere. And yet he still wore his own.

'I'll try my best to rectify that,' I said.

'He hasn't been caught yet? This man, Blythe?'

'No,' I said. 'Not yet. This is confidential information, but we believe the suspect left on holiday, and we don't as yet know where. I can tell you, though, that this is one of the biggest manhunts we've ever launched, and that we're co-ordinating with several departments around the country to trace him. And we will. We will find him shortly.'

'He's still somewhere in the country?'

'We believe so. And obviously, his details are in the public domain now. It's impossible for him to lie low forever. We'll find him, I promise you.'

'Alive?'

Townsend looked directly at me for only the second time since entering the office, and I was taken aback by the sudden urgency in his voice. The answer was clearly important to him.

'We hope so,' I said. 'I want to make sure this man faces justice for the terrible crimes he's committed. Obviously there are no guarantees, but we'll be doing everything possible to take him alive. In an ideal world, he'll turn himself in. In this one . . .' I spread my hands.

Townsend stared back at me for a few seconds longer, as though my answer wasn't sufficient. The look in his eyes was unnerving. Why did it matter to him so much? But after a moment, he looked away and swallowed.

'I understand you've found . . . remains.'

'Yes.' There was no point in sugar-coating this; it was all over the news, and in my experience, relatives of victims ultimately preferred that you were straightforward with them. 'Again, this is completely confidential. It appears that Blythe kept the bodies of his victims in a cellar below his house. They have been there for some years, and so the remains we've found are severely decomposed. It's going to take some time to identify the victims. But we will, I promise.'

'So you can't say for certain if you've found Melanie?'

'No. I'm sorry. We can't say that right now.'

Townsend shook his head and looked down, as though he couldn't make sense of what I was telling him. Despite the uncase at his manner, I felt sympathy for him. With his wife's abduction linking the cases, he would have been the first survivor who had understood early on what had happened to her, and so he wouldn't have been able to hold out hope in the way the relatives of earlier victims perhaps could. But of course, he would have done so anyway. That's what people do. Until we know, we hold out hope. Even if it's the smallest of possible flames, constantly fluttering, we cup our hands around it and do our best to protect it from the breeze. Yesterday, that hope must have been all but extinguished. And yet, at least in his head, I'd just given him the slightest hint of it back, because I couldn't tell him for certain.

The situation demanded more.

'I understand what a distressing development this must be.' I leaned forward, speaking gently. 'I can only offer my sincerest sympathies for the loss you've suffered, and how this news must affect you. The remains are being carefully handled, I promise you that, and we'll identify them as soon as we can. I also promise that we will do our best to find this man and bring him to justice on behalf of your wife and all his other victims.'

There was a moment of silence. Townsend's shoulders were moving slightly. I wondered if he was crying. If so, I would let him do so quietly. But then he looked up at me, and instead of the hope or sadness I'd been expecting, I saw bewilderment and confusion on his face – desperation, even. And there was *fear* there too, I realised. The tickling unease at the back of my mind intensified. Because I understood on an instinctive level that something about this man wasn't right.

'How many?' he said.

I blinked. It wasn't surprise at the question so much as the sense of things suddenly clicking into place in my subconscious – the sensation that my unease, even if I couldn't explain it logically, had been justified in some way I still didn't understand.

'I'm sorry?' I said.

And again that urgency in his voice as he stared directly at me.

'How *many* bodies have you found?' he said.

'Which is a strange question to ask, don't you think?'

It was later on in the afternoon, and I was back in the operations room with Emma: both of us in our secluded corner, working our way through the various reports and interviews that still kept coming in, and which still – so far – had given us nothing to go on. I'd been telling her about my encounter with Jeremy Townsend, focusing on the question he'd asked me.

Engrossed in a report on the other side of the desk, or perhaps just pretending to be, Emma shrugged.

'Is it?'

'I think so.'

'Well I don't,' she said. 'He's seen the news, so he knows we've found remains. You told him yourself you can't confirm if his wife's among them. And it's not like we've even publicly confirmed that Blythe *is* the Red River Killer. Maybe that was just his way of figuring out if the media reports were true.'

'Maybe.'

I supposed she had a point. Townsend knew we'd found Amanda Cassidy, who was *presumed* to be the latest victim of the Red River Killer, along with other remains on Blythe's property. But he didn't know for certain that Blythe was the man who had taken his wife, and I hadn't been able to confirm it for him. Perhaps that was what his question had been getting at. We couldn't identify the remains yet, but did the numbers at least match?

But the unease I'd felt while speaking to him remained. If anything it was stronger than before. It wasn't just that his question had tied into the discovery at the morgue – that one body *did* appear to be missing – it was the fact that something about his whole demeanour had struck me as odd and off kilter. He'd seemed nervous and apprehensive from the very beginning, but not in the way I'd expect from a grieving relative.

'I wish I'd recorded him,' I said.

'Yeah, that would have been a great idea. I'm deeply sorry for your loss, now let me read you your rights.' Emma shook her head. 'What on earth would you want to do that for?'

'So that you could have seen what he was like. There was something off about him. It was almost as though he...' I trailed off, thinking.

'Almost as though he *what*?'

'Almost as though he knew something.'

Emma raised an eyebrow. 'Seriously, Will?'

'*Suspected* something, then. I don't know. Like there was something he wasn't telling me. Like he was thinking about things from a different angle than he should have been.'

'Jesus. Maybe you *should* have dragged him to an interview room. It sounds like you wanted to.'

'Not quite.'

'What was his name again?'

'Jeremy Townsend. I'm so glad you've been paying attention to everything I've been saying.'

'I can't follow your every flight of fancy, Will. I'd never touch the ground.' She frowned. 'The name rings a bell, though.'

'Probably from the case file.'

'I don't think so. It's a big file. No, it's from somewhere else.'

'I'm sure it will come back to you.'

She shrugged again, then looked at me more seriously.

'Don't mess this up for us, Will? Okay?'

I looked back at her, and reminded myself that the case

meant just as much to her as it did to me, if for entirely different reasons.

'I won't,' I said.

'Good.'

She turned her attention back to the reports. Which was understandable. Aside from the fact that I was trying her patience severely today, she hadn't been in the room with Townsend and seen him face to face. And we both knew she was right about the flights of fancy. With this case especially, I had to be careful not to let them overshadow things. I was too invested here; I needed to be involved. There was a real danger that investment could cloud my judgement, and so I had to make sure I didn't do anything that pushed me – pushed both of us, in fact – out of the room.

It doesn't have to be you that gets him.

But as I glanced at the far wall for what must have been the hundredth time that day – at Anna's face, smiling out from the past – and felt the guilt and sadness and the *anger* inside me, I was no longer sure that was true.

My computer pinged. Emma's did too – a report coming through electronically, delivered to both of us. I turned to my screen and started to read it, but Emma got there first.

'We've got a sighting of Blythe,' she said. 'He's in Moorton.'

Seventeen

The old Grief House has been abandoned for as long as John Blythe can recall.

It stands more or less in the middle of nowhere, on top of a short embankment by the side of a rarely used country lane. There is a possibility that he explored it as a teenager, but a lot of these old buildings in the wilds between the village and the mountains are the same: hardy stone monoliths from another era, most of them only ever glimpsed in the distance while driving along the isolated roads out here. Any doors and windows are long gone, and the walls and floors within are bare stone. Some parts have collapsed, and the rooms are cluttered with piles of rock and fractured timber, open to the sky above. In other places, trees have burst through the floor to grow inside, their branches stretching out through the holes in the walls, so that they appear to be wearing what remains of the building like a stone suit of armour.

The Grief House is relatively intact internally, but still freezing cold at night and utterly inhospitable. Nevertheless, it has been a decent enough home to him for the last twenty-four hours, and it feels relatively safe. It's dangerous to think that, though. Don't get complacent, he reminds himself; don't fall into traps. In his situation, a day is too much time to stay in one place.

Always keep moving.

Blythe goes to the window that looks out over the road. It's little more than a hole in the wall, with what remains of the sill blanketed in moss. He breathes out into the night air, and watches the steam cloud before him.

He feels the trickle of excitement in his abdomen: that familiar sensation that comes from being alone and hidden. There is nobody out there. The road is empty; the landscape is totally dark; the world is completely silent. He might well be the only thing alive for miles.

That won't last.

If you were to believe the online reports, there have been no developments in the hunt for him. Blythe does not remotely believe that. While there is no way of knowing for sure, he feels certain that the petrol station attendant has come forward by now, and with this being where he grew up, they will begin to concentrate their activity in this area soon. They will find his jeep at the campsite. And they will draw a line between the two sightings that will point more or less directly here, towards the old Grief House and then to the mountains beyond. Which of course was the destination in his original plan.

He is changing that plan now.

The time he has spent in the Grief House has been adequate but far from comfortable, and he has to face certain facts. He can live off the land, yes, but that's no long-term solution, and the further he travels into the wilds, the harder it will be to escape the area. Ultimately, he needs to get away from Moorton, which will become more and more difficult if he heads north and buries himself into the landscape like a tick. So he needs a different solution to his problem.

He needs the Worm.

Blythe has no idea exactly who his mysterious email correspondent is, or how much knowledge of the area the man might have, so he needs to suggest a pick-up place they both know. And he can think of only one spot the Worm knows for absolute certain...

Suddenly he realises that, lost in thought, he has been scraping the tip of his knife against the stone wall below the window. He shakes his head. Must stop that immediately. Another mistake. He might not have a chance to sharpen it again in the near future.

He moves back to the centre of the room, and turns on the laptop and Wi-Fi device. Beyond a three-green-bar display, currently on two, there is no way of judging the charge on the latter. The laptop is presently at 68 per cent. Which is another reason not to leave escape too long. Within days, and certainly within weeks, he will lose all contact with the outside world, and he will be alone.

But he is not alone yet.

Blythe logs into his email. The Worm has still not replied to his messages. He suppresses the anger he feels at that. It's of no use to him. Except... well, he allows himself a small amount. Because it's time to pile on the pressure.

He imagines that, over the years, the Worm has come to believe that the two of them are friends, but that is certainly not the case. They have been in contact for fifteen years now, following the first anonymous email Blythe received from the Worm, explaining what he knew and how. At first, Blythe was annoyed to learn he had made a mistake, although it had never occurred to him to deny it: clearly no point. He'd spent time attempting to track the Worm down, but it had proved impossible. And so, over time, he had begun to tolerate the man's intrusions. In the early days, the Worm had insinuated that if he didn't get what he wanted, he might go to the police with what he knew, but that intention had clearly disappeared. And he didn't ask for much really. He wanted photographs and details of the women; he wanted to know *what it was like*. Ultimately, it was no skin off Blythe's nose to comply, and it had never before been worth calling the Worm's bluff.

It is now.

He begins typing.

I said where are you? You little shit, you runt, you nothing. You WORM. After all this time you think you can just WALK AWAY from this and go on with your life as normal? You will have

117

some HONOUR and you will come and help me or believe me you will suffer for this, I can promise you that. They don't have my computer yet but they will if they find me and they won't take me alive I can assure you. So it will be YOU left to carry the consequences. YOU that's still alive to be paraded through the media as I AM NOW. That's assuming you don't have the courage to kill yourself because that will be your only way out UNLESS you help me. Let me assure you you are NOT safe. You might think you have been careful but you know deep down that isn't true. They have more technology than you can dream of and they WILL find you. Your only choice is to help me. Reply to me NOW or I will not be held responsible.

Good enough. He clicks send.

While he needs to conserve the battery life on both devices, he's also certain that the Worm will be checking his emails as constantly as possible. After all, *he* doesn't need to save power, and the man is clearly a coward. Incapable of killing for himself, he's spent years enjoying Blythe's actions from a distance. While the Worm might want to pretend all this isn't happening, he will be too scared not to be checking his emails. He does not possess Blythe's inner strength or his ambivalence towards consequences. Blythe can imagine the Worm panicking now, feeling small and frightened. When he sees an email has arrived, he will probably piss his pants in abject terror.

It's another mistake to stay logged in, though. Blythe is still staring at the email when he hears a noise on the road outside.

A car.

Slowing down.

He closes the laptop immediately, and the room goes dark. That sudden difference tells him everything he needs to know: the light from the computer must have been visible from the road, even if just as a faint glow, and whoever is driving the car has seen it.

The police?

It's possible. He listens carefully, and can still hear the engine.

It's a little further away now, but the sound is constant. The driver has pulled up a short distance down the road and left the engine idling.

He's not going to risk looking out of the window. Instead, he picks up the knife and creeps quickly down the open stairs at the back of the property. The night-time breeze hits him, but for some reason it feels warmer outside the old house than in. The thrill of the hunt, perhaps. He reaches the far corner of the building and peers carefully around the edge. Nobody can see him here, but he can see the car: an oasis of shining light in the darkness, about twenty metres down the road.

He lowers himself into a crouch, then moves swiftly through the heather along the ridge of the small hill until he draws roughly level with the vehicle. The driver doesn't see him, he can tell; after all these years, he's developed a knack for invisibility. He lies on his stomach now, and begins crawling carefully down the embankment through the undergrowth.

He stops just a few metres from the road, the grass here tickling his face, and then lies immobile. The car is clearly visible, and it's not police, which makes things easier. There's only one occupant, in fact: a man in his mid forties, talking into a mobile phone. Blythe holds his breath and listens, but can't hear the conversation. Every now and then, though, the man glances around nervously, either back towards the Grief House, or at the dark, empty countryside surrounding him. At one point, he looks directly at where Blythe is lying just a few metres away, his knife ready in his hand, but Blythe doesn't react, doesn't move. He hasn't been seen. He's just been *sensed*. The man's spine is telling him there is a monster out there in the night, perhaps even nearby, and he is afraid.

As he should be.

The question, as always, is what to do about this development. If the man hadn't been on the phone, Blythe might have attempted to kill him and stop a call taking place. Too late for that; nothing to be gained. If the man gets out of his vehicle, though, he will gut him. He can be up and on him in two or three seconds at most.

He waits.

The man finishes his call and continues to look around. He reaches out to the side, as though to open the car door. Blythe tenses. But the man pauses. A moment later, he faces forward again, nodding silently to himself. Then he drives off down the road.

Blythe watches him go before standing up at the bottom of the embankment. He has a few minutes at most. That's the worst-case scenario, and so it's the one he has to work with. He runs quickly back to the old house, no longer concerned about being seen, and gathers his stuff together. There's too much spread around, but he shouldn't need most of it. He gathers the bare necessities into his backpack, and in less than a minute he's out of the old house and heading away into the night.

Time to put his new plan into action.

Your only choice is to help me. Reply to me NOW or I will not be held responsible.

Eighteen

'Aha!' Emma appeared in the doorway to our front room. 'I *knew* I recognised the name from somewhere.'

'Who?'

'Jeremy Townsend.'

I shook my head. It seemed as though we'd somehow swapped roles. I hadn't forgotten about my encounter with Jeremy Townsend; it still niggled at the back of my mind, something about it not sitting correctly. But since getting home, I had been trying to distract myself from thoughts of the bodies we'd found. Instead, I had immersed myself in the hunt for John Blythe.

The sighting hadn't turned out to be the huge breakthrough we might have hoped for. But it was something. A worker at a petrol station close to Moorton, where Blythe had grown up, claimed to have seen him a few days earlier. For the moment, that couldn't be fully corroborated: the station was some old, ramshackle affair out in the wilds and wasn't fitted with CCTV, while the staff member himself didn't know Blythe directly and was basing the ID on TV reports he'd seen. But the customer had paid cash, which fitted, and it was in an area that made sense. It did *feel* right.

Local police were following it up, searching various possible areas in the vicinity, and DCI Reeves had swung it for Emma and me to head up there first thing in the morning if there were any further developments. So far there had been nothing major, but I was following what little there had been on my laptop.

Whereas Emma, it seemed, had been occupied with my earlier concerns. When I looked up at her, she seemed pleased with herself. She was holding a hardback book.

'I told you it rang a bell.'

'What's that?'

She walked over and handed me the book. The jacket looked tattered and old: Emma kept almost everything, but never bothered much about taking care while reading them. The cover of this one was mostly black, with a small cluster of trees, almost childlike in conception, in the centre. They had chunky dark brown trunks and muted green leaves bushed up overhead, and seemed small and shadowy, as though the darkness of the rest of the cover was intruding into them. Or perhaps the reverse – as though some inherent blackness from amongst the trees was extending out and infecting the rest.

The title and author were above and below the image.

'*What Happened in the Woods*. Jeremy Townsend.' I looked up at Emma. 'He's a novelist?'

'I guess so.' She inclined her head and frowned at the cover. 'I can only vaguely remember it, to be honest. I'm sure there was some kind of buzz around it at the time, but I can't have liked it all that much.'

I turned the book over. The back of it was taken up with a large photograph of Townsend: an austere professional head-and-shoulders shot that I thought was very much an 'author photo'. It was recognisably him, but it was astonishing how much younger he looked here: confident, cultured and far less troubled. I wondered when the book had been published. Turning it back over and flicking to the copyright page gave me the answer: 2003. Two years before his wife's disappearance. It was dedicated to her, as well: 'For Melanie, with all my love.'

There was a synopsis on the inside flap of the cover.

You know the past is the past...

The day that sixteen-year-old Jonathan Jameson found the body of his best friend in the woods, his life was torn apart. In the years that followed, he built himself back up. Now a decorated homicide detective, that traumatic event has defined him, even as he's done his best to leave it behind.

You know the present is safe...

When a new murder draws Jameson back to his home town, he must confront the girl he left behind, a vicious killer in the present day... and the secrets of his own past. Because everything he's ever taken for granted is about to be overturned.

You know what will happen...

The clock is ticking. The secrets are coming out. The body count is rising. And if Jameson can't unravel what *really* happened in the woods on that terrible day, he and everyone he loves might not have a future at all.

You think you know...

YOU DON'T.

'So... he's a crime writer,' I said.

'Yeah. Hey – maybe *that's* the reason you took against him.'

I gave Emma a look for that. She was only joking, of course, but it did seem to be exactly the kind of book I wouldn't like, whatever she said about escapism and happy endings. Reading and writing this kind of material seemed like an unpleasant form of play to me: making entertainment out of pain that some people suffered for real. Looking at the photograph on the back of the book, I was struck again by how confident Townsend appeared. At that point, his life had presumably not been touched by the kind of horrors his work focused on. The contrast with the hollowed-out man today could hardly have been more pronounced.

I set the book aside and turned my attention back to the laptop, opening a fresh window and loading up Amazon. A quick search for 'Jeremy Townsend' produced an unedifying page of results. He had written three novels, with *What*

Happened in the Woods the last chronologically. If there really had been some kind of buzz around his final book, it couldn't have come to much. He hadn't published anything since, all three books were currently out of print, and second-hand copies appeared to be changing hands – or not – for pence.

'I don't think your copy's worth much,' I said.

'That's a shame.'

'And I think he's given up writing.'

'That's a shame too.'

'Is it?'

'Yeah,' she said. 'Of course.'

I could imagine a number of reasons he might have stopped. Perhaps he'd simply found it too hard to continue when the whole subject was no longer as far from home as it had been. Or maybe he'd simply been too broken, too desolate, to write anything at all. *For Melanie, with all my love.* Perhaps with her gone, he didn't have anyone left to write to.

Either way, I supposed Emma was right.

But my interest had been piqued now. I spent a while checking back through the old news reports on Melanie West's abduction that were available online, and only found a couple of mentions of Townsend's profession. On one level, that seemed surprising. If he'd achieved at least some minor success as a novelist, that was the kind of detail the press were usually keen to latch on to. Then again, it wasn't like he was a household name, and it was possible the detail had just been missed. There was a lot for the media to keep track of. After a while, with a case like this, the quantity of information begins to swamp the finer details. And at that point, they'd just had the confirmation of a serial killer to run with.

But that didn't mean the connection had gone entirely undiscovered. Searching more generally took me to a writing website that had a forum devoted to obscure and forgotten authors, and I found a thread from a couple of years ago discussing his work.

THREAD: Anyone remember *What Happened in the Woods*
by Jeremy Townsend?

#1: writer_at_heart
This just came back to me. I remember reading this book
a few years ago, but then there's been nothing since? No
new releases available on pre-order or anything. The guy's
got no website either. Anybody know What Happened to
Him? (Sorry...)

#2: crimefan_33
Yes, I remember that. I think it did quite well from what I
recall? The cover looks familiar. He wrote two others before
it but I don't know anything about them. Looking at the
listings on Marketplace, I'm not sure they were crime.
Think he was a literary-style writer and *WHITW* was a shift
for him and maybe it didn't work out.

#3: writer_at_heart
You said it did quite well?

#4: crimefan_33
Well, maybe not well enough! I don't know, I don't have
access to the sales figures. But we know full well from this
forum that loads of good writers slip through the cracks.
That's why we're here, after all!

#5: writer_at_heart
True, true. But it's surprising he hasn't published anything
since in any capacity. I'm going to do some digging.

#6: writer_at_heart
Okay, I turned up something potentially interesting? (I
mean, I'll leave it up to you to decide whether it is.) His
name is mentioned in this article here. It's a news piece
about those abductions. The Red River case? Melanie

West was apparently the fifth known victim, and Jeremy Townsend's name is given as the husband. Not sure if it's the same guy?

#7: crimefan_33
Holy shit, yes. It doesn't say what he does for a living, but from the bio it's the right geographical area. I wonder if that's really him? If so, that might explain why he hasn't published since. Imagine that. You write a crime novel and then something like that happens to you. That's fucked up. Holy shit indeed.

#8: writer_at_heart
tumbleweeds Is it only you and me that are interested here, by the way? I've got an evening free tonight. I'm going to look into this some more . . .

#9: writer_at_heart
Okay, I've got something. Not sure what to make of it so far, but I think it's definitely him, although it's a bit weird. I did a search for his surname and her name, and I found some more news reports but none of them mention he was a writer. But I also found a bunch of other links too, and this is where it gets interesting and strange. Buckle yourself in, my friend. There's a writer called J. S. Townsend, and he's published a series of short stories online. See the link *here*. And look at the titles. 'Melanie 1'. 'Melanie 2'. So Melanie West was the woman abducted. Her husband was Jeremy Townsend. And now we have a J. S. Townsend writing stories with that name? Couldn't be a coincidence, I thought, and when I read them, I was sure of it. Click through and see for yourself. I think we've found our boy.

#10: crimefan_33
Holy fucking shit! You're totally on the money. It *has* to be him. I don't know enough about the circumstances of the

Red River case, but once you've read a couple of them, it's obvious, isn't it? They're all about his wife and what might have happened to her?

#11: writer_at_heart
Yes. I haven't read them all yet, but they all seem to start off from her going missing, and then each one is different – spinning a different story about what might have happened to her. Like he's imagining all the different possible scenarios. But then, I guess he didn't know, did he? I think (???) the abductions hadn't been connected at that point, had they? Maybe they had. I'm not sure. But maybe he was just exploring all these different possibilities.

#12: crimefan_33
That's really quite sad.

#13: writer_at_heart
It is, isn't it? It's very sad indeed. Maybe that's why he published them under the initials? To keep them separate? It's similar, so maybe it was a personal project for him, something he was compelled to do for some reason, but at the same time he didn't really want other people to know it was him?

#14: crimefan_33
(Plus, they're not very good, are they?)

#15: writer_at_heart
Hmmm. I don't know about that. They're certainly different, though!

#16: crimefan_33
Yeah, definitely that. Because *WHITW* was quite good, from what I remember. We all know that writers disappear for

all sorts of reasons, but this is very sad. It's like he lost everything at that point, and these are an attempt at getting some of it back, but they're just not very good. Like he's flailing around trying to do what he always used to do, but he lost his writing talent when he lost her.

#17: writer_at_heart
I'm beginning to wish I hadn't started this thread . . .

#18: crimefan_33
Agreed. I think we should be circumspect here actually. It's possible that he could read this thread at some point, and so we should be careful what we say. Possibly a bit late for that (oh for an edit function, mods . . .), but I'm not sure he would have wanted this to be made public. I think we should move on from this now. What do you think?

#19: writer_at_heart
I agree. Although the name change wasn't too extreme, was it? Maybe it was more like 'I'm a different person now'? But I'm sure he could have capitalised on his original success if he wanted to, and he clearly chose not to. I think we should respect that. Vote to close and lock for further comments? (I'm not sure what we'll do if you say no!)

#20: crimefan_33
Agreed.

#21: writer_at_heart
Cool. And Jeremy, if you ever do read this: I'm really sorry for what happened to you and your wife. I only started this because I remember liking your book and was wondering what had happened to you. That's what we do here! But all the very best, and I hope you're okay.

So it seemed that Townsend *had* published more fiction, albeit under a slightly different name, and in what sounded like a less professional capacity: just stories posted online. Although from the discussion on the forum, there was some argument as to whether they could be considered stories at all, or even fiction.

I clicked on the link in the forum.

A moment later, a new site loaded – an anonymous BlogSpot address. The title at the top of the page read:

THE MELANIE BOOK
J. S. Townsend

I wondered why he'd changed his name. Was it like those posters had guessed: an attempt to differentiate his life now from the one prior to his wife's disappearance? Or was it out of shame because he knew that the work was inferior, even though he still felt the urge to publish it anyway? If so, why that need?

The menu at the side of the screen listed the story titles, just as the posters had described: 'Melanie 1', 'Melanie 2', etc. Scrolling down, I saw there were fourteen of them altogether.

I clicked on the fourth one at random.

As soon as the page loaded, and I read the first line, the unease I'd been feeling about Townsend since meeting him bloomed again, larger than ever now. I remembered the Red River letters and my chest tightened.

I want to tell you a story, it began, *about a girl named Melanie.*

Nineteen

Sitting in his car, parked up between two different street lights from the night before, Simon Bunting prepared himself for what he was about to do. There was no fear now, helped partly by the fact that he was exceedingly tired. It had been a long twenty-four hours.

But a productive one.

He'd spent most of the last few hours working his way around the house, ticking items off his plan as he went, and occasionally – disappointingly – finding new ones. But he was as ready as he could possibly be. The house was prepared, he had disposed of anything that might incriminate him, and aside from the newspaper, which he would have to buy in the early hours tomorrow, everything he needed was in the car with him right now. When he set off from here again, he wouldn't be going home.

He'd plotted his story carefully. Now it was time to start writing it.

He opened the laptop and loaded up the anonymous email program. There was one new message. Last night, he'd been afraid when he'd seen those two bold lines at the top of the screen, and had hesitated before opening them. Now, though, he felt completely in control, and he opened the message immediately.

I said where are you? You little shit, you runt, you nothing. You WORM. After all this time you think you can just WALK AWAY from this and go on with your life as normal? You will have some HONOUR . . .

He read the rest of it, and then forced himself to read the whole thing through again. Despite his intention to remain calm, the ferocity of the message was still startling, and he tried to approach the text as dispassionately as possible. *His grammar is appalling*, he told himself. But then it always had been. When he was finished, he read the email a third time, this time analysing it for additional information he might have missed. There was nothing.

Blythe was correct about needing to keep the laptop out of police hands, so at least they were superficially in agreement about that, but the animosity was otherwise clear enough. If Bunting had ever allowed himself to believe that they were partners of some kind – kindred spirits, even; that the Monster was under his control – then that illusion was well and truly shattered. The man clearly despised him.

Bunting picked up his notepad, with its columns of assets and obstacles, and considered the matter for a moment.

He wrote JOHN BLYTHE in both columns, then set it aside again and looked back at the email.

You little shit, you runt, you nothing. You WORM.

Anger flared inside him then, and he allowed it to. How dare Blythe look down on him? Blythe was a man who tortured and murdered *women*, for God's sake. Bunting knew that he was none of the things he'd been accused of. And he was much smarter than Blythe, of course. Smarter than *most* people. Smart enough to take control of the situation.

He'd prepared impeccably. There were still a huge number of practical considerations to be dealt with, of course, and it would be very difficult indeed. Taken together, the obstacles seemed almost insurmountable. But a story was only ever just one word after another, and that could be done. He would need a degree of luck, and there would certainly be some nervous moments ahead of him. It had been a busy day, and he had a busy night to come. But if each part of the story he was building clicked neatly into place – or even just slotted in eventually with a nudge – then it would work.

You little shit, you runt, you nothing. You WORM.

His eyes scanned down to the bottom.

Your only choice is to help me. Reply to me NOW or I will not be held responsible.

Worm, he thought.

You'll see.

They're all going to see.

And then, still smiling to himself in the darkness, he began to compose his reply.

Part Three

Twenty

Emma and I set off early the next day.

Just before nine o'clock in the morning, we were driving along the winding country lanes towards Moorton. The wilds around us were thick with purple heath, the grassland in the distance dyed in patches of yellows and browns. As we crested the top of a hill, the land fell away and the village appeared below us.

From a distance, it looked beautiful. The miles of land around it were dotted with farms, and in the far distance, beyond the village itself, I could see the dark spread of the woods. The river that curled across the land here was silvery and still, and the whole scene seemed misty and sleepy in the morning sun: a place that would yawn and stretch and wake up slowly at its leisure. If we'd stopped the car and got out, I doubted we'd have heard anything apart from the wind.

'So this is where Blythe grew up,' Emma said.

'Yes.'

'It seems a little incongruous, don't you think?'

I didn't reply. I knew what she meant, though, and as we drove into Moorton itself, that impression of incongruity became even stronger. The narrow cobbled streets were picturesque, and the shops all looked like small stone cottages, nestling between the houses. With the window down I could hear the quiet rush of the river a few streets away. The church we passed looked to have been in place for centuries. Beside it, a war memorial stood fenced off, still festooned with garlands of poppies, the red bright against the sunlit grass at the base. All in all, it seemed so peaceful that it was hard to imagine it had spawned a man like John Blythe.

But, from experience, we both knew that life didn't work that way. Moorton might have looked tranquil, but you didn't need terrible social conditions, economic deprivation and grim buildings to create a killer. All you needed was a closed door; all you needed was other people. While there are no absolute certainties in the formation of psychopaths, there are warning signs you find in a high percentage of their childhoods: the lack of a coherent home life; neglect; domestic or sexual abuse; household alcoholism; head injuries; petty violence; poor academic performance; animal cruelty. We knew Blythe had suffered at least some of those things. Monsters are made, not born, and the truth is that they can be made anywhere.

Today, of course, there was an additional incongruity. As we drove slowly through the centre, it was impossible to ignore the scale of the police activity in the village. Further to the sighting of Blythe at the petrol station south of here, there were now two additional scenes being investigated, both of them to the north of Moorton itself, both discovered overnight. At the first, Blythe's vehicle had been found at a makeshift campsite down a dirt track half a mile from the nearest main road. There were the remains of an old fire and a half-eaten meal, along with marks on the ground that suggested a tent had been pitched there. The tent, along with any clothing and belongings he'd brought with him, was not present at the scene.

A search team was currently scouring the area, but the evidence suggested he'd left the site some time ago, possibly even as the news of the findings at his house had broken. At that point, he would have known that he was a wanted man and his vehicle was compromised, and he must have decided to fit as much as possible into a backpack and go on the run.

The second scene was less clear cut, but it was further north, much closer to the woods and mountains, and all the evidence so far suggested that was where he was moving to. This location was the present focus of the search, and where we were meeting DI Warren, our counterpart here in Moorton.

In the meantime, the police presence in the village itself felt overpowering. There were numerous vans and cars parked up along the roadsides, with officers ambling along the pavements in pairs, many of them armed. A house-to-house search was presently taking place, although I doubted it would yield any results. In reality, this was all for reassurance more than anything else.

'Seems a little heavy-handed,' I said.

'Public relations,' Emma replied. 'Although I guess, for all we know, Blythe *could* be holed up somewhere here.'

'No, I think you were right the first time.'

It didn't seem like a productive use of resources to me. I thought about that dark spread of woods beyond the village, and remembered what Ferguson had said outside the incident room on the first day. *I think he's going to kill himself. Bet you.* He'd probably said it just for the sake of disagreeing with me as much as anything else, but even so, I wondered if he was smarting slightly at the developments overnight. Blythe appeared to be on the run, so I had been right and he had been wrong, and I imagined that would bother a man like Ferguson. For my own part, I just felt apprehensive. We had been hunting Blythe down metaphorically for two days. Now, knowing that he was out there somewhere in front of us, we were about to start doing so literally.

I tried to weigh up how difficult that was going to be.

Although I didn't know Blythe, I had already formed a mental picture of the man. He was big and strong – physically quite formidable. An outdoors type, certainly; I could imagine him fishing and hunting. He had grown up here in Moorton and presumably knew the countryside well, which meant he had the knowledge and endurance to live off the land. The search area was large and awkward.

At the same time, our own resources were formidable.

Logistically, we would soon have more than fifty armed police officers in the vicinity, along with many other casuals. They weren't all locals, of course; the department here had become stretched massively overnight and had drafted in units from several other areas. There were five armed response vehicles and numerous officers, including two sniper teams, on their way, along with a helicopter fitted with infrared cameras that was being readied to aid with the search of the extensive woodland.

And Blythe was only one man.

Sometimes that could work to a fugitive's advantage, of course; it's harder to spot a speck than something larger. But Blythe's face was all over the news. He was presently the most wanted man in the country, and almost anyone he encountered would recognise him. His only real chance of evading capture lay in living – and staying – off the grid, but even then, if we concentrated and worked methodically, we would find him eventually.

We will get him.

I watched the village through the passenger window, imagining him somewhere close by and fighting down the urgency that came with that.

We will.

As well as the police, the media had – of course – already descended on Moorton, and I saw several news vans parked up, with crews filming on the pavement, the cameramen slowly turning, gathering establishing shots of the beautiful village around them. Even passing in the car, you could sense the excitement amongst the reporters: the feeling that something was going to play out here, and that the endgame for the Red River Killer was in sight. Every reporter would want to be there when it happened. They would cross cordons, push boundaries, get in the way. In the meantime, they were busy recording footage for the endlessly rolling news channels. There would be people safe in homes across the country right now watching developments play out in real time: a real-life horror reduced to the status of the last thriller they watched on DVD.

At the far edge of the village, we reached the tail end of traffic caused by a checkpoint that had been set up. Looking out to the right, I saw the local primary school: a surprisingly large building, with a peaked roof and a spacious playground. It looked very old. I wondered if Blythe had attended there. Right now, five armed police were stationed at the various gates. More overkill; more wasted resources.

The playground was thick with parents and little boys and girls arriving for lessons. Today would be a very different day for the children, I imagined. Many of them were far too young to understand what was happening in their village, but it would certainly be something to talk about and remember. To spread ever more frightening and exaggerated stories about as the years passed. Perhaps, I thought, wherever Blythe was found would acquire a name and become a landmark on those obscure internal maps that children use to navigate their villages and towns. When we name things, we give them power. In children's minds, the Red River Killer, and what happened to him out here, would undoubtedly become part of the village mythology.

After we had edged forward and passed the school, I glanced at the playground in the wing mirror and caught sight of two little boys running together slightly apart from the other children. They were dressed in different uniforms from the others, too, and seemed as though they didn't belong.

Best friends forever, I thought. *That's what I'm looking at here.*

A moment later, I lost them in the crowds, and then Emma drove forward again, and the school disappeared from view. Even so, I felt a kind of existential *thump*. I picked up my tablet and read the email I'd received from Rob again.

You were my best friend.

I'm so sorry.

I closed the message and instead opened the browser, loading up the link I'd saved last night.

THE MELANIE BOOK
J. S. Townsend

And as we headed out towards the wilds beyond the village, ever closer to John Blythe himself, the feeling of tension and urgency within me was replaced by one of dread.

Twenty-One

The last sighting of Melanie West, aside from a few grainy CCTV images from the town centre, was as she left her office in the English department at the university a little after five o'clock in the evening.

According to the reports Townsend had learned of, she'd called in at the main office to drop off some files, and said a breezy goodbye to the secretaries there. She'd been in good spirits. He could imagine all that easily; his wife had always been a friendly, down-to-earth woman, much liked at every academic level within the department. After leaving, she had then walked a short distance through the edge of the city centre, down to the wharf, where the canal and the river came together in a weave of interlocking waterways.

The home they'd once shared was three miles away. She hated the gym, and usually walked home along the banks of the canal, for exercise but also for enjoyment. On summer evenings, she generally dawdled, taking longer than she should. The surroundings were very pretty, and in the years before her disappearance she had taken up photography – strictly at an amateur level, she insisted, although to Townsend's eye the images she captured always seemed unusually beautiful and well composed. He was pleased. She seemed to have given up writing prose and poetry, and he was glad that the spring of creativity inside her had found a new outlet. The camera he had bought her the previous Christmas disappeared along with her. Like Melanie herself, it was never found.

Some mornings or evenings – when the light was identical – Townsend took the bus into the centre and walked the same route that she had. He was never sure exactly why. Was it a kind of pilgrimage? Or was it in the hope that he might catch something in the air – that past and present might come together in some impossible way and reveal a glimpse of her? Ridiculous if so. But it was a romantic idea, and it appealed to whatever remained of the storyteller within him.

He stood now on the solid mossy blocks of stone at the wharf, gazing over the flat expanse of green water at the tall brick wall on the far side. The curls of graffiti scrawled there were reflected in the water below. This was once the heart of the city, but while the area remained heavily industrial, everything seemed run-down or derelict now. There were a few barges, but none of them looked like they had moved in years. The enormous factories beyond the far wall were mostly abandoned husks, their corrugated-iron walls thick with rust.

Gathering himself, he set off along the towpath.

For a time, the canal stayed relatively close to one of the main roads out of the city centre, and for the first mile or so he could hear the morning traffic a little distance away. Across the water, the broken-down factories continued for a time, before giving way to impassable banks of undergrowth and trees. The canal curled gently along. Every now and then, he stopped to peer into the water, occasionally catching sight of an old bicycle frame or shopping trolley lying in the silt below the surface. It was generally too murky to see much. The water was as swirled and foggy as it must have been when they dredged it, searching for Melanie's body. But there were clearer patches. At one point, he even saw a shoal of small, thin fish darting about in unison. They formed a strange black language in the water, but were gone too quickly for him to decipher it.

The further he walked, the more the main road and the canal diverged. The land to the right now seemed as wild as that on the far bank. For the most part, the path was eerily silent, although he did see a few people, most of them cyclists coming from the opposite direction, heading to work in the city centre. In the evenings, it was the other way around: an exodus of people from behind. Because Melanie was walking, she would have been overtaken by a great number of people. Townsend wondered if she had been blasé about that – if the familiarity of the surroundings had created an illusion of safety. Certainly, he recognised many of the sights he passed from her photographs, and could easily picture her paused at the side of the path, concentrating on capturing the moment, oblivious to what was happening around her.

I doubt she was scared.

It was a thought he'd had many times before. She was never a fearful person anyway, and despite the silence and solitude, there was nothing particularly threatening about the walk along the canal. Without knowing what had happened here, it would seem tranquil and idyllic. It felt safe.

So, no. Melanie would not have been scared.

Not then.

But of course, it was likely that none of the other victims had been worried either – that was partly why the Red River Killer had managed to be so successful in his abductions. Townsend had also thought about that often. In reality, it was very difficult to kidnap someone in public in broad daylight, even if you were significantly stronger than them, or even armed. You needed a confluence of circumstances – an alignment of factors. You needed them alone; you needed them vulnerable and unaware; you needed a lack of witnesses. Perhaps more than anything else, you needed a degree of luck. And yet Blythe had got away with it again and again. And that was because every place, no matter how safe it felt, had a window of danger: a moment when a cloud passed quickly over the sun and everything went dark. Blythe had always been good at being there when it did. Townsend remembered what he'd thought the night before last, listening to the husband of Ruby Clarke speak on stage. It was as though Blythe could blink suddenly into existence and then disappear away again without being seen.

Would he manage the same trick in Moorton?

Townsend had slept badly, and he'd woken early to the news reports that Blythe had apparently been spotted in his home town. He believed those sightings. In fact, he could probably have told the police exactly where the man was heading. He still could, of course, although not without consequences that were impossible to calculate right now. At the same time, he had to do something.

You know what you have to do.

See this through to the end. Make amends for everything he'd done.

The thought terrified him. For now, he kept walking.

The police could never confirm the exact location of Melanie's abduction, but Townsend felt sure he knew where it was, and about two miles along the towpath, he reached the spot. A little way ahead, there was a bridge over the canal, and there was something wrong with it.

It was difficult to say precisely what. Maybe it was because there didn't seem to be anything obvious on either side of the water for it to lead to or from, or because it seemed so old and strange. Its ancient stone was scorched almost entirely black. It always reminded him of some malignant creature perched there over the water. Looking behind him, he saw that he was alone now, just as he always seemed to be when he arrived at the bridge. The world was entirely silent apart from the dripping sound from up ahead.

He kept walking.

The area beneath the curve of black stone felt like a small portion of an entirely separate world. It was dark and cold here, and the quality of sound was different. The ground to the side of the path was littered with large rocks, with dirty litter spread amongst them: old cans, bent at the centre; cigarette butts; scrunched-up pieces of dirty tissue. There was what appeared to be the remains of an old fire. The underside of the bridge was covered with graffiti, but whatever language it was written in was impenetrable. Townsend looked up. From between the metal struts and girders that underlined the dark rock, water was dripping. It hadn't rained in days, and he wondered where the water came from. It seemed like it must have been absorbed from the canal beside him, sucked up like moisture through the roots of a tree, and was now dripping steadily back down from the stone. The sound echoed: constant, deep and rich.

This was where she was abducted.

Nobody could know for sure, but Townsend did.

He had researched the area extensively in an attempt to discover what this bridge was for and how long it had been here. It felt like a place this ominous should have a name, even if just a colloquial, local one, but his investigations had found nothing.

As always, he didn't linger. The bridge was only about eight metres wide, and he emerged quickly into the sun again. Approaching it, he always felt trepidation, as though moving towards something alive and dangerous. With it behind him now, there was a feeling of relief, but also an itch at the base of his spine. It was a strange, childhood sensation. *There is something frightening behind you. You should run.* Instead, with his heart beating hard, he forced himself to keep walking. There was no danger. Blythe had been here once, and his presence had poisoned the place forever, but he wasn't here now.

As Townsend walked the remaining distance back to the village on the outskirts of the city where he lived, he was lost in thought, his mind circling the decision he had to make. The decision that he knew deep down had already been made.

When he reached the metal barrier, he stepped through, and then walked down the hill, crossing a different bridge, this time over the river. He leaned on the railings for a moment and stared down, smelling the flaking metal beneath his forearms and watching the rush of the water below. It was the kind of bridge you could play Poohsticks on. He remembered doing so with his mother on a different bridge, standing on tiptoes to see over the railing and watching the sticks dipping quickly away out of sight. Racing away together for a time, side by side. Then separating. And then lost.

He walked back to his house. Without going inside, he got straight into his car and began the long drive to Moorton, to John Blythe, to the Red River.

Twenty-Two

Emma drove us into the countryside along increasingly narrow lanes. It was farming and walking country out here; the village's tourist trade generally came from ramblers and fishermen, while most of the local work was done in the fields we passed. There were large industrial sheds filled with tractors and ploughs, and dusty car parks with corrugated-metal signs advertising eggs, meat and vegetables for sale. I could see the beginning of the woods in the distance. In the real world, rather than just on a map, the scale of them looked daunting.

What I didn't see was many police.

'Not a van,' I said. 'Not a car. Not an officer. Oh – there are two.'

But they were just wandering slowly along the roadside, paying us little attention. Moorton had a much smaller department than ours, but even so... They seemed to have far too much going on in the village, where Blythe was unlikely to be, while the rest of their resources were presumably stretched out further north. It was a gamble, and it made me nervous. We needed Blythe quickly. We certainly couldn't allow him to get away.

'Playing the odds,' Emma told me. 'And they're waiting for reinforcements to arrive.'

'And here we are.'

She laughed. 'What are you looking at?'

I glanced down at my tablet, open on *The Melanie Book*.

'Research,' I lied.

While we were not remotely in charge here, I knew I should still have been concentrating on the hunt: checking maps, reading reports and thinking about angles. Predictably, my lie was not remotely convincing. Emma knew me too well.

'You're reading those stories again, aren't you?'

'No.' I put the tablet down. 'Yes.'

She sighed. 'I think you should let that go.'

She was probably right. I'd shown her the one I'd opened yesterday evening, with that familiar first line: *I want to tell you a story about a girl named Melanie.* Checking the beginnings of a couple of the others, I discovered that all Townsend's stories began like that. With the exact same phrasing that all the Red River letters did.

Emma, of course, had pointed out the obvious: all the relatives, including Townsend, had seen the letters the killer had sent about their loved ones. Beginning his own tales that way proved nothing beyond the fact that the words had stuck in his head and he'd decided to use them in the tales he wrote. She had then, perhaps a little pointedly, curled up at the far end of the settee and started rereading *What Happened in the Woods*, while I sat at the opposite end and worked my way through all the stories Townsend had uploaded to that website.

It was hard to disagree with what had been written on the forum I'd found. Not only were the stories not very good, they could barely be described as *stories* at all. They all began with the same opening line, and each of them then continued with a description of Melanie West walking home along the canal on the evening of her disappearance. At that point, what amounted to the plot diverged, exploring a number of different scenarios that might have happened afterwards.

In one story, Melanie tripped and fell into the water and was somehow washed away. In another, she travelled a long distance from the scene and committed suicide in a lonely, secluded spot where her remains would never be found. In a third, there had been an ongoing affair, and she met and ran off with a mysterious, superior lover. One scenario found her living anonymously in another part of the country – beginning a new life – as a punishment for some slight on Townsend's part.

There were abductions too, of course, especially in the later stories. In some, she escaped and wandered, her memory occluded by trauma. In the hardest stories to read, she was vividly tortured and murdered, cursing her husband's name either for failing to save her or else for something he'd done.

That was another common thread, I realised now. In every story, Townsend had written himself as the bad guy. Not always explicitly so, but he was invariably presented as pathetic and weak. Inferior. Deceitful. A failure.

A man who had done something wrong.

I found it hard to comprehend how he'd managed to write even the less visceral stories, never mind the ones describing Melanie suffering and dying, and what must have been going through his mind when he had. It was awful to realise that the horrors described in those later stories in the series were likely close to the reality of what the women Blythe had taken had undergone.

I should have been leaving it alone and concentrating on the matter at hand, but the disturbing effect of reading the stories remained. There was something about Townsend that bothered me. He was like an itch at the back of my mind that I needed to scratch but couldn't quite reach.

'I just can't figure out why he would want to write things like this,' I said.

'Oh God, maybe he didn't *want* to.' Emma took her hands off the wheel in exasperation for a moment, then quickly grabbed it again. 'Whoa there, cowgirl. What I mean is, maybe he just felt like he *needed* to.'

'Why would he need to?'

'Christ, Will. His wife had gone missing. Disappeared. Does it not make sense that somebody in that situation might begin to imagine all kinds of things? That's what people do. And they blame themselves, too; they feel guilty, even when it's not their fault.'

Yes, I thought. *Yes, they do.*

'And Townsend was a writer, so it really doesn't surprise me that he went and wrote all that down.' Emma shook her head. 'He was grief-stricken, Will. Still is, from what you said.'

She was right again, I supposed. There was a progression in the stories that hinted at that not-knowing – the exploration of different possible scenarios, all of them hopeful in terms of her fate, but negative about Townsend. The abduction of Melanie West rested at the pivot point of the investigation. Before her wedding ring had verified the letters and officially connected the disappearances, the relatives of the first few victims wouldn't have known for sure what had happened to them; they might have been able to hold out hope. Perhaps Townsend had been able to as well, even after the letter arrived, but had gradually come to accept the truth about what had happened.

And yes, it was natural that he blamed himself. I understood that, not only because I felt it myself, but because I'd seen it many times before. *If only I'd done this, everything would have turned out differently.* The story might have taken a different course. It isn't rational, but in the absence of an obvious perpetrator, thinking like that is one way for people to make sense of the world and attempt to process the pain they're feeling.

It didn't quite fit with the way Townsend had seemed, though. Nervous and awkward, fine. But I had also got the sense that he was hiding something, and that impression had not gone away.

How many *bodies have you found* . . .

'We're here,' Emma said.

She pulled up on what barely amounted to the roadside. Looking around, we seemed to be in the middle of nowhere now, with the only real signs of life being the three vans parked up ahead of us. They were police vehicles, but unmarked. While the discovery of Blythe's tent was already on the news, this more recent scene was being kept under wraps for as long as we could manage. Assuming Blythe was following the coverage

– and I was certain he would be – we wanted him to know as little about what we were doing as possible.

Perhaps that was even an explanation for the fact that most of the activity was being concentrated back in the village – that Blythe might think we hadn't realised the direction he appeared to be heading in. If so, there was a slim chance that he might relax slightly, make a mistake and give us the edge we needed. But that was all slightly more charitable than I was prepared to be.

It was cold outside the car, despite the sunshine. The air seemed damp, as though it was raining but the drops were too small to see, and the wind felt bitter against my face. It was also profoundly silent out here. If you shouted, it was easy to imagine the noise would echo for miles before anybody heard it.

I pulled my coat around me and looked up the embankment.

The old farmhouse stood at the crest, about a hundred metres away, its base obscured by overgrown grass and heather. It seemed so ancient that it might have been here for centuries, and although worn down, with its windows and door missing, there was still something solid and guard-like about it. It gave the impression that it would still be standing here in centuries to come, more a natural feature like a rock face than something man-made.

Various officers were standing around it at the top of the embankment, and one of them began making his way down to us now, waving a hand overhead in a casual greeting. He was early thirties at most, good-looking, and he was wearing sunglasses and a pink shirt with a black tie that the wind was wrapping over his shoulder as he approached. No coat, but not remotely bothered by the temperature – or not showing it, at least. The perks of growing up acclimatised to the environment, perhaps. Which would apply to Blythe too, I thought.

'Detective Turner? Detective Beck? I'm Dave Warren. I spoke to your DCI on the phone first thing. I'm in charge of the search, at least out here.'

Up close, Warren was short, but also looked toned and strong. His smile was friendly enough, but when he shook our hands – or mine, at least – his grip was overly firm, and I thought deliberately so. It was a handshake that emphasised *I'm in charge* and the overall message was obvious enough: Emma and I had no real authority here; he was the one who would bag John Blythe and get the credit for it. Fine, I thought. I didn't care about the latter so much. I wasn't so sure about the former, though.

'Nice to meet you,' I said.

'Likewise. Okay, to fill you in on the scene, over there is the man who got in touch with us.' Warren gestured to someone standing with officers by the side of one of the vans. 'Stan Maguire. He's a good guy. Owns a farm over yonder. You want to speak to him?'

'I don't know,' I said, ignoring the undertone in the question. Whatever the hierarchy of authority here, I didn't think we needed permission to walk a few metres and talk to someone. 'What's his story?'

'Not a long one.' He pointed up the embankment. 'That's the old Grief House. Don't ask: I have no idea why it's called that. Has been for years, since long before I was a boy.'

The Grief House.

'Kids pass names down,' I said, almost to myself.

'Yeah, I guess they do.' Warren cocked his head, considering the idea. 'Anyway, it's been empty for as long as I can remember. There are a bunch of them around here. Old fortified farmhouses. Stan's an unofficial warden, I guess. There's never any trouble, but he'll drive past every now and then just to make sure everything's still standing. With the news and everything, he drove past last night. He saw a light in one of the windows and called us.'

'He didn't investigate himself?'

'No, he didn't want to scare off whoever was inside. Plus... well.' Warren looked slightly awkward. 'You know.'

I nodded. Stan Maguire didn't look a particularly imposing

type, and while John Blythe was only a man, he loomed much larger than that in everybody's minds. He was the Red River Killer, after all, his identity bound up in the terrible, inhuman crimes he'd committed, which meant the danger he represented was exaggerated to similarly monstrous proportions. Confronting him would actually be the same as confronting any comparable human male, and yet it would *feel* different, as though you were standing face to face with something far more terrifying than just a human being.

Which was rubbish, of course, but the idea was potent. I remembered reading that during the serial killer Jeffrey Dahmer's autopsy, the doctors – men of science and reason – had kept his corpse shackled at the feet. What he had done in life was so awful that even in death he caused fear. And Blythe, of course, was not dead.

'I think he did the right thing,' I said. 'How long until you arrived?'

'We had officers on scene within half an hour.' Warren seemed to bristle slightly, as though I'd been accusing him of something. 'I mean, we're on high alert here, obviously, but we're undermanned – for now, anyway. So, half an hour. By which point he was gone.'

'You did well,' I said. 'Blythe probably thought the road would be relatively unused, but then he heard the car. I'm guessing Maguire at least stopped for a moment?'

'Yeah, he phoned it in from the roadside. Doors locked. Said it was the scariest few minutes of his life. It felt like he was being watched the whole time.'

'He probably was,' I said.

Still looking up at the old farm, I could imagine how frightening it must have been. This place was isolated and desolate enough even in daytime. At night, with nothing but the darkness and silence for company, it must have been unnerving as hell: staring out into the dark, expecting to see a figure emerge from the undergrowth at any moment.

'But Blythe will have been gone quickly,' I said. 'He wouldn't have hung around and taken any chances.'

'Stupid of him to have a light on, if he's being that careful.'

Yes, I thought. It was. So there must have been a reason for it.

'How strong was the light? What colour?'

'I don't know what colour. Stan said it was soft, though. Not flickering or moving about, so not a torch or anything. But it's pitch black out here at night, so any light travels.'

'Maybe he was checking a laptop,' I said.

'What?'

I shrugged. 'Or whatever it is he's using to communicate with the outside world. He saw the news coverage somehow, after all.'

Warren looked at me, curious again.

'You think he's *communicating* with someone?'

I didn't reply for a moment. What I'd actually meant was that Blythe was observing the outside world somehow – and yet that particular word had slipped out. As though he might be interacting with someone. From our investigation, it didn't seem that Blythe had a single living relative to turn to, and it seemed odd to think that anyone else might be prepared to help or shelter him given what had been revealed. At the same time, I found myself unwilling to take the word back.

'I don't know,' I said. 'I just think we should be prepared for anything. Anyway. We don't need to talk to Mr Maguire for the moment. I would like to see inside the property, though.'

'Why? There's not much to see.'

I shrugged again. 'Just because.'

The embankment was steep and the ground was uneven. I've always been a little uncoordinated, so I worked hard not to go over on an ankle in front of the other officers. The grass wavered around my shins. Beside me, of course, Emma managed the short climb with cool aplomb.

As we reached the top, the old farmhouse came properly into view. It was separated from the embankment by a dry-stone wall with a wooden stile in it. The house was two storeys and made of old stone, coated in moss, with an open doorway at ground level and a rough set of steps that ran up the front towards another open doorway on the first floor. An empty window stared out from above. The roof had long since fallen in, but two triangles of stone remained at either end. When we reached the stile, the wood looked as old as the building itself, and one of the struts felt warm, as though it was somehow alive: a tree grown into a strange shape.

Warren was with us, but I showed my ID to the officer guarding the stile anyway, and he nodded, stepping to one side to allow us through.

'What are you expecting to see?' Emma asked me quietly.

'I really don't know.'

I couldn't say anything more than that, because the truth was that I didn't know exactly what I was expecting. Blythe had been here, but he had left yesterday night. There was nothing to *see*. Perhaps the truth was actually something different. I didn't expect to see anything; I expected to *feel* it.

And as we walked through the downstairs doorway, it happened immediately: the same strange sensation I'd experienced when walking into Blythe's house for the first time two days ago. The interiors couldn't have been more different. Blythe's house had been his home, and it had reflected his fractured mindset: the odd arrangements of possessions; the sheer disturbed functionlessness of the rooms; the mishmash of material, nothing apparently thrown away and everything stored at random, or according to some unfathomable mental plan. Whereas the downstairs of this old farmhouse was entirely empty. A hollowed-out husk. And yet I felt him there regardless: a presence that lingered in the air as potently as a recently smoked cigarette. It was only because I knew he'd been here, of course, but the sensation was real all the same. We were gaining on him. I could sense him in the distance, like the thud of a heartbeat that was becoming quicker and heavier the closer I got.

'We think he slept upstairs,' Warren said.

I looked up at the ceiling and nodded to myself.

The internal stairs were at the far side of the room. I walked over, drawn to them – not caring whether the others followed, but dimly aware that they did. Open to the elements, the first floor was freezing cold. The stone floor was scattered with a handful of belongings: ragged clothes for the most part; a small portable gas stove lying on its side in the corner. I looked around. No backpack. No sign of a phone or laptop, either. Blythe had clearly left in a hurry, but he still had his wits about him.

Four SOCOs were working the room, but I ignored them for the moment and walked over to the window instead – if a large square hole in the wall could even be called that. Close to, the bitter wind whipped in. I wondered whether Blythe had been here since abandoning the campsite after he'd heard the news. If so, he was made of sterner stuff than me.

I stood there for a few moments, staring out of the window, thinking. The view was quite something. I could see the road below, with the line of police vehicles; beyond that, angled shades of green stretched ahead for miles, shadowed by clouds drifting overhead. The window faced in the direction of Moorton, although the village itself was too far away to be visible from here. There was little in the way of civilisation in view. I could imagine Blythe standing here, looking out and feeling completely safe and alone – king of all he surveyed. I was at home in the city. Out here in the wilds was Blythe's natural territory. He wouldn't feel unnerved by this isolation; he would welcome it. Not only did it suit his purposes right now, it suited his nature.

'What are you doing?' Emma asked.

I glanced behind me and saw that both she and Warren were looking at me strangely. I'd been completely lost in thought. Looking down, I realised I'd been absently stroking the wall below the window ledge – a slow, repetitive upwards motion – and stopped immediately.

'Nothing,' I said.

But when I moved my hand, I saw the marks on the stone. They were too pronounced to have been made by me. I crouched down, inclined my head slightly and peered at the dusty white lines that had been carved into the wall. It was as though somebody had been moving a knife against the stone as he stood by the window, contemplating the scene before him. With the woods and mountains behind him, and Moorton somewhere in the distance ahead…

I stood up.

'Nothing,' I said again.

Twenty-Three

Blythe sits on the bank, calmly eating a leftover sandwich as the river rushes past.

It is still quite wide here – about twenty metres to the far bank. The water flows down from the mountains to the north, narrowing as the course of it snakes and curves along the contours of the land. Here, the ferocity and force of it remain. By the time it runs through the centre of Moorton, it is about half this size. There are old bridges where you can stand and watch it tumble past underneath you, frothing and folding over the rocks and then disappearing away into the distance. He remembers as a boy watching the slick black rats darting in and out of a hole under the bridge. The world beneath the world.

He must have been very young then, he thinks, taking a bite of the bread and ham. His early childhood is mostly lost to him. Although there are a handful of dim memories here and there, they are random impressions more than anything else, as though someone took a little boy's life and smashed it on the floor, and only a few pieces were ever deemed worthwhile enough to salvage, most of it swept away instead. He is sure there was fear there once, because all children feel fear to begin with. And there was occasionally a great deal of pain, but you grow used to both things in time. They become ordinary, acceptable, just the way things are. Ultimately, whatever happened to him, pain and fear were not notable or unusual enough for his mind to have bothered imprinting an actual memory of them.

There were lots of stripped-down homes, and men and women he thought must have been relatives but could never really identify. Everybody was an aunt or uncle, but most likely not even that. There were bruises. Bad nights he won't think about. Not all of it was terrible, of course. One place he thought was a farm at the time, until a boy at school made fun of him for that, and Blythe broke his nose. Whatever random uncle it was just kept chickens, pecking around in the dirt at the front of a house that was little more than a one-room shack. There were wire mesh cages full of them round the back. One day, Blythe killed a chicken: put a broomstick on its neck, then stood on either side, rocking his weight back and forth while he watched the thing blink up at him stupidly. Women blink like that too eventually, he found out later. He was never caught for killing the chicken, and that memory is a little keener than others. There was a feeling of power there, to the extent that there was a feeling of anything at all.

But the strongest memories are of the wilds – the campsites and countryside and woodland in which he spent so much time as a child and then a teenager. His isolation seemed the best course of action for everyone. As he grew, he became too strong for the other children to bully, and so they all simply steered clear of him, and that was fine; he neither had friends nor wanted them. His family life was fractured and indifferent, and nobody really noticed or cared when he disappeared for days on end, sleeping rough and teaching himself to hunt. It suited him deep down too. The concentration and patience required to build traps and snares, to start a primitive fire, to fashion a shelter – these were things he could become lost in and not have to think. Just as he could when taking apart the old cars in one of his uncle's garages, methodically stripping them down and building them back up again, already dimly wondering what it would be like to do the same to a human being.

This spot by the river was one of the places he used to come. It was one of the few areas along the bank north of the village where there was enough space to pitch a tent, and it was secluded enough for him not to be disturbed. Or at least, rarely so. As a boy, he would sit here for hours on end, watching the water roar and roll past him, listening to the unchanging noise of it, his mind entirely empty of thought. The power of the river had always felt endless and uncaring. Sitting beside it was like being dangerously close to a stampede of animals charging past, completely oblivious to his presence. He related to it on a deep level. The world was angry and violent. It didn't care about people at all, and the river was a visceral reminder of that truth.

Of course, he had to stop coming here after what happened.

That makes him think of the Worm again now. Blythe finishes his last mouthful of sandwich and turns his attention back to the laptop. The signal is weak here, but good enough for a steady connection. No emails yet. But he's confident there will be soon. The last communication said that the Worm would be on his way to Moorton this morning. It's an act that must go against every desire in his feeble little body, Blythe is sure.

Because that's why he's stayed in the darkness all this time, isn't it? The Worm – burrowed in the moist earth beneath the feet of better men, trailing them while always remaining hidden, desiring to join them in the sun but being too frightened of the light. It still annoys Blythe that such a weak and timid individual has had any amount of power over him. But it was his own fault. He made a mistake a long time ago – right here, by the river – acting on impulse, imagining he was alone and that he hadn't been seen. But he had, and so the Worm has been with him ever since. He is nothing but a parasite. He's too scared to cause any pain of his own, but still black and dead enough inside to want to feed safely off the pain created by others. Well, Blythe imagines that he isn't feeling too safe right now. Even though he's never seen the Worm's face, he can easily picture the man's hands on the steering wheel as he drives here now, and they are *trembling*.

As they should be.

Over the years, Blythe has spent a handful of idle moments wondering about the identity of his correspondent. His mind has formed a picture. The Worm is a pudgy, ineffectual man: the sort who would endure the beatings and loneliness of a pitiful childhood rather than take himself off into the wilderness and grow into something more self-sufficient. Hating the world, but too weak to turn his back on it. Not stupid – which in fact Blythe is counting on to get him away from here – but hardly exceptional. Vulnerable. He will have few if any friends, as he will no doubt be a figure of disgust, revolting those who encounter him. And certainly no wife. No, the Worm will live alone, in an average and unremarkable house.

All of which put together means that few people will notice when he goes missing, and fewer still will care. Assuming Blythe can get away from here, back to wherever the Worm lives, he will have a place of safety and security until he works out his next move. Money, too: the Worm will no doubt have savings squirrelled away, and he can get the details out of him before killing him. The next few hours will obviously be crucial, but if Blythe comes through them then the future is already looking considerably brighter.

Any number of things can still go wrong, of course, but he remains completely calm. The river has that effect on him. In a hundred years, everybody will be dead, but this river will still be flowing, still ferocious and uncaring. The water is constantly changing, and yet somehow it always stays the same.

So for now, Blythe sits with the laptop open and waits.

There will be a message soon, he is sure. In the meantime, he watches the river. It's so long ago now, but out of all his memories, it's the keenest and clearest of them all. He remembers the way her hair was pulled away towards the village by the currents at the edge of the water. And the blood that trailed from her head, briefly staining thin and insignificant tendrils of that ever-changing river red.

Twenty-Four

The main command centre directing the investigation was based in the department back in Moorton. We'd passed it when driving through the village: a small building, currently bursting at the seams with officers struggling to co-ordinate everything. It would be the focus of the search in the village itself, and the central hub to which reports were returned and actions issued. But authority had been delegated to a handful of other local bases of operations. The one directly handling the manhunt itself was basically the three large unmarked vans parked up on the road by the Grief House.

Warren directed us to the first of the three, where the sliding doors were open across the middle.

'Welcome to our humble abode,' he said.

The van was very long, and the interior was as complex and carefully designed as the inside of a canal boat. There were banks of computers and monitors, microphones and control panels. Several officers sat hunched over, their faces illuminated by the screens before them.

'This is Detective Turner, Detective Beck,' Warren called out. 'They're up here from down south. Obviously John Blythe is back home with us now, but they're along for the ride as a courtesy. We've got a couple of spare screens, so we might as well make use of them.'

'The more the merrier.' That came from one of the nearest

officers. He had a shaved head and a thick neck, and he didn't bother to turn around.

'This is Detective Carling,' Warren told us. 'If you need anything, give him a shout.'

Carling just grunted. I glanced at Emma, and she raised an eyebrow at me but said nothing. It was clear enough from both men that we were not expected to bother anyone by needing something any time soon.

We edged our way towards the back of the van, where two stations were free.

'Friendly,' Emma whispered as we sat down.

I didn't reply. She was more attuned to the territorial issues than I was – or at least she cared more than I did – but we both knew how things worked. If the situation had been reversed, she wouldn't have been as bad as Ferguson or Warren, but she'd still have wanted to keep a tight hold on things. Instead, I turned my attention to the screen, clicking through until I found details of the search. From a satellite image of the area, it was even more obvious how small and isolated Moorton really was – the village itself just a tiny spread of beige and brown towards the bottom left corner of the monitor, with a few roads spreading out around it. At the top of the screen, above the woods, the mountains began. Between here and there, we were looking at thousands of acres of undergrowth, wilderness and dense woodland.

Three waypoints had been marked on the map. The first was to the south-west of the village, along one of the few major roads. This was the petrol station where the owner had identified Blythe. The second point was to the north-east, at the campsite where his abandoned vehicle had been discovered. The third was our present location, the farmhouse, which was further north-east still, much closer to the woods. A line drawn through the three locations would run roughly diagonally up the screen.

From his camping and hunting experience, and from his apparent trajectory so far, it was natural to believe that the woods, and possibly even the mountains, were Blythe's intended destination.

I clicked an option on the screen, which overlaid live GPS updates from all the officers out in the field. Small green arrows were moving steadily away from our current location in a fan shape that mirrored Blythe's most likely path. There was a heavy concentration in the village itself, of course, and a few more spread over the network of roads between here and there. Still not enough for my liking. Regardless, it was clear how constrained Blythe's options were. If he'd headed west from here, he would begin to meet main roads and heavier traffic. If he'd moved south instead, he'd currently be caught in the fields and woodland between the officers on this road and the ones in Moorton itself, an area that would be searched as additional officers arrived on the scene.

Assuming he was intent on flight and escape, heading northeast was his best option.

I watched the green arrows slowly update, and it was difficult to escape the sensation that the officers were corralling him – forcing him onwards. I could imagine a marker for Blythe himself on the screen, only slightly ahead of his hunters, stumbling awkwardly on.

I hoped that was true.

But something was bothering me. The feeling remained that we were missing something. Perhaps it was simply because of how much this case meant to me, but I didn't think so. I thought again of the knife marks that Blythe appeared to have made in the farmhouse behind us, presumably as he stared out of the window, over the fields and woods, in the direction of Moorton.

I looked at that particular area on the screen now. It was roughly contained by officers, but not presently being searched.

Blythe wasn't stupid. You didn't stay unidentified for so many years without a degree of cunning, and however good he was at surviving outdoors, he would know that with our resources he couldn't stay ahead of us forever. Despite being caught on the hop with the news, he'd had twenty-four hours to regroup, gather his thoughts and make a plan.

But what was it?

My gaze stayed on that area between here and Moorton. There were a handful of small roads – little more than trails by the look of it. Patches of woodland, thicker in some places than others. The river curled through before reaching Moorton. *The river*, I thought. Even though it was just a word, and there were rivers everywhere, I found myself tracing the course of it. About halfway between here and the village, it turned parallel with the road we were on. At one point, in dense woodland, there seemed to be a separate body of water a short distance away from it, connected to the sparse web of roads by the thinnest of trails. It was too small to be a lake. But it was something.

'What about this area?' I called over to Carling.

He didn't turn around. 'Which area? I'm not psychic.'

'South of here, back towards Moorton.'

Carling sighed heavily, then unhooked his earpiece and made his way over, crouching slightly. When he reached us, he leaned on the back of my chair more heavily than he needed to, and peered over my shoulder at where I was pointing.

'Frog Pond,' he said.

I felt a tingle: that familiar itch at the back of my head. Words. Words and titles confer power on people and places.

'Frog Pond?'

'It's always been called that.' Carling leaned away; my seat rocked slightly. 'There's nothing really there. There are the woods, and there's the pond and the river. Some of the local kids go up there sometimes. Get up to usual kinds of kids' stuff. Why?'

'We're not searching there?'

'Not yet, no. We've got more feet on the ground than we're used to, but you'll have noticed there are still limits to what we can do. We'll get to it.'

'I'm not criticising you.'

'Aren't you? All the evidence suggests he's heading north, north-east, doesn't it? And besides...'

Carling reached over my shoulder and gestured at the GPS signals around the screen. The implication was clear enough. If Blythe had headed in that direction, he would effectively be trapping himself. He'd be contained in an area that *would* be searched within a day or two. And he would know that.

And yet it continued to bother me.

'What are you thinking?' Emma asked me.

'I'm not sure.' I turned to Carling, who was moving away from us now. 'But we're a spare wheel here, aren't we? Just getting under your feet a bit.'

He didn't deny it. 'So?'

'So.' I turned back to the screen. 'I was thinking maybe Emma and I might as well have a drive down there. Check it out.'

Twenty-Five

Bunting drove slowly through the centre of Moorton.

The village was swarming with reporters and police. Despite his attempts to keep calm, he was having to fight down the panic. He was in the belly of the beast here. *Good line, that*, he thought. But it was of little consolation right now.

What was the correct way to act in the middle of all this? He forced himself to analyse the situation rationally. On the one hand, it was impossible simply to ignore the heavy presence of police and media on the streets, and so surely the normal, everyday response was to show some interest in all this unusual activity. On the other, he didn't want to draw attention to himself. He didn't want to risk staring in case somebody stared back and noticed him. As calm as he was trying to be, he imagined the nerves he was feeling – that anybody would be feeling, to be fair – would be painfully obvious.

So that was the choice: try to blend in, or try to remain invisible. He'd always been better at the latter, of course. He kept his eyes fixed on the traffic in front of him, driving carefully, trying to give the impression that he was just passing through – aware of what was happening, but not all that interested. *Prurient*, he thought. That was what all this was. He tried to project that through his body language and behaviour. *Let's just all keep moving, please. I don't know about you, but I find it most distasteful to gawp.*

There was no need to panic.

Easier said than done, that – especially given the way the situation had developed overnight. When he'd begun formulating his plan yesterday, there had already been a long and complicated series of obstacles to overcome, and while meeting Blythe was a terrifying prospect in itself, it had actually been a fair way down his list of problems. Out of all the parts of the story he was creating, it had seemed like one of the easiest to orchestrate. The man would be in hiding somewhere, and Bunting would go there. The inherent danger of the encounter aside, that was really all there was to it.

Except that it hadn't worked out that way. Blythe had been spotted, his location narrowed down, and the net was closing around him. Bunting felt like he'd just swum quickly in through one of the holes, and now he was part of the haul shifting steadily upwards. Somehow he needed to get them both out before the net reached the surface. The belly of the beast, indeed. *The lion's den.* Maybe that was better. Regardless, the point was that he hadn't envisaged having to meet the bastard directly under the noses of what appeared to be about two hundred police officers, all of them focused intently on finding him. And right now, he wasn't quite sure how he was going to manage it.

No choice, though. Blythe and his laptop were out there somewhere, and he couldn't allow the latter, at least, to fall into the hands of the police. Realistically, it was all or nothing. If he didn't succeed in what he was doing here, he was likely to fail somewhere down the line anyway.

The traffic came to a standstill again. Bunting yawned. That was another problem – he was so tired that it was hard to think. It had been a busy evening and night, and sleep had taken up very little of it. There had been the long drive to Moorton itself, stopping at various roadside bins to dispose of the last-minute items he needed rid of. Pitching the tent several miles south of here, and then the two hours spent traipsing through woodland and undergrowth in the dark, at huge personal risk to himself.

None of it had been an edifying experience, and he could only hope it would end up being worthwhile.

It had all worked out perfectly so far, but he was suffering for it. He was normally smart and sharp, but his mind was foggy right now, and just at the point when he needed to be confident and in control.

To concentrate...

The traffic moved forward, but only one car length. Bunting put the handbrake on and wound the window down, peering out and around the cars in front to see what was happening.

Then tucked his head back in quickly.

The police were checking cars.

For a moment, he couldn't think at all. He stared through the windscreen, hardly seeing anything that was in front of him. His hands were gripping the steering wheel, and his knuckles were white.

Calm down.

The car in front edged forward again, and then stopped. Bunting moved his own vehicle to keep up. There were cars behind him, so it was too late to back out now. Looking ahead, he was now two cars away from the checkpoint. An officer with brown hair and a thick moustache was leaning on the driver's side of the vehicle at the front, chatting to whoever was inside. It seemed an amiable enough conversation, but Bunting felt like his chest had been filled with ice.

Which they will realise, he thought.

Because how could they not?

The conversation finished, and the car at the front set off. Bunting edged forward again, and the officer began talking to the driver directly in front of him. He couldn't hear what was being said, but again, it looked easy-going enough. And crucially, the policeman didn't seem to be checking the boots of any of the vehicles.

If they looked in his, it was all over.

But they won't look, he told himself. Not unless he gave them a reason to. So what he needed to do was stay calm.

Maintain frame. In fact, for his eventual purposes, it wouldn't be the end of the world if an officer *did* remember encountering him here. That might work to his benefit. But it had to be in hindsight. So there was a balance to strike here. Behave in a way so that he'd be remembered, perhaps, but not enough to prompt a full search of his vehicle right now. Because if the latter happened, he would be going to jail for a very long time.

As the car in front pulled away, and the officer beckoned him forward, Bunting realised that what he actually needed to be right now was himself. Simon Bunting. Small, ordinary, ineffectual. Naturally intimidated by the big man in the uniform. The kind of socially awkward and isolated man, in fact, who seemed a little bit intimidated by everyone.

He could do that.

He pulled up at the checkpoint. The officer leaned down on the edge of the window and smiled. Up close, Bunting could smell his aftershave, potent and manly.

'Good morning, sir. I'm very sorry about this hassle.'

'That's okay.' Bunting forced a smile. 'What's happening?'

'Ah, it's nothing really. We're looking for someone we believe might be in the area, and we're just checking vehicles as a precaution.' The man glanced briefly into the empty back seat. 'Can I ask if you're a local, sir?'

Bunting was about to say where he was from, but of course, that was the same city that Blythe lived in. Not an ideal answer to give.

'No,' he said. 'I used to be. I grew up here. I'm just here visiting my parents today.'

'Right. And whereabouts are they based?'

Bunting looked through the windscreen, and did his best to let a little of the anguish he was feeling appear on his face, hoping that the officer would misinterpret it and put it down to something else.

'Marwood Cemetery,' he said quietly.

*

A couple of minutes later, he pulled into the car park, his tyres crackling over the neatly turned gravel. Marwood was a prestigious final resting place. He didn't give a shit about his dead parents, of course, but it was as good a place to go as anywhere for the moment. The gates were open, and there were two other vehicles parked up, but nobody else was in sight. No police around, either. They seemed to be focused on the village itself, which vaguely cheered him. Perhaps he could do this after all.

He took out the laptop.

While he waited for it to acquire a signal from the Wi-Fi device, he peered out of the window at the tall, arched cemetery gates. His parents were buried somewhere in there, but he had no idea where. He hadn't attended the funeral, and had never bothered visiting the graves. He'd learned of his father's death from his mother, and then his mother's some time later from a council worker, and while there had been letters since, and attempts at phone calls – presumably to sort out the house and belongings – he'd left all of them unopened and unanswered. There was money probably, but it wasn't enough to balance out revisiting the past. He'd realised long ago that Moorton held nothing but bad memories for him. Let the house gather dust and collapse. Let the pair of them rot in untended patches of ground he wouldn't be able to find even if he wanted to.

The laptop came online.

He hadn't logged into the account since last night. Before setting off, he'd messaged Blythe and agreed to help him. Blythe had replied telling him to come to Moorton and let him know when he arrived. It was obvious he wasn't prepared to tell Bunting exactly where he was yet, even though it surely made no difference to his safety whether he did so then or now. That was the point about Blythe's intelligence. It didn't always bolt clearly on to the real world. That would be his undoing.

Bunting typed a message.

I'm in Moorton. Where are you?

He waited.

He was confident Blythe would be online constantly at this

point, checking for updates, and it amused him slightly to imagine the man's impatience and anger. Dangerous, of course, to poke a loose tiger. But it would at least begin to teach him a lesson for the Worm comment. He wondered where Blythe had spent the night, and where he was right now. He had a reasonable idea about the latter. He could see it very clearly in his mind whenever he closed his eyes. The sight of her remained so vivid, even all these years later.

A young couple came out of the cemetery, heads bowed, walking a short distance apart from each other. The woman glanced at Bunting for a moment, and he put on a sad expression and nodded once at her. That would help too. He could be remembered here.

The list of emails rolled down the laptop screen, with a new one at the top arriving in bold. He clicked on it.

You know where I am.

Yes, Bunting thought. He had been right. It would be there, wouldn't it? It would have to be.

He got out of the car and walked around to the boot, checking what was inside. It was all fine. Everything was still going more or less exactly according to plan for the moment. He took out a pile of blankets and placed it on the back seat of the car, then stood there for a few more seconds doing nothing at all – not even thinking right now, just allowing the peace and silence of the surrounding area to drift around and through him. *The calm before the storm*, he thought. If that wasn't a good line then he didn't know what was.

Things would become difficult now. But he could do it. And if he succeeded, there were going to be some truly great lines ahead.

He got back in the car and started the engine, wondering how long his luck would hold out. Then he drove out of the car park and headed north, towards Frog Pond.

Twenty-Six

'Why do you think it's called that?' Emma said. 'Do you think there are going to be lots of frogs there?'

'Kids give places names,' I said.

'I hate frogs.'

I didn't reply, just stared out of the passenger window, watching the scenery flashing past: identical stretches of grassland and hedges, differentiated only by the occasional farm vehicle pottering steadily along in the distance. Life – at least in this part of the area – seemed to be going on as normal. I supposed that many of the locals had read the news reports and come to the same conclusion as Warren and his team. The Red River Killer might have been here for a time, but now he was heading north, further into the wilds and towards the mountains.

Emma said, 'Do you want to tell me what you're thinking?'

'I'm not thinking anything in particular.'

'Not *thinking*,' Emma said.

'Feeling, then,' I said. 'Yes. Perhaps.'

Out of the corner of my eye I saw her shake her head. It was hard to blame her for that. She hadn't been happy about being dragged away from the main search, where at least we'd have been a more integral part of the investigation, and there was no real logic to heading out here. Blythe had grown up in the area and presumably knew these haunts, with their passed-down titles, but it made no sense that he was navigating on that level. It just reminded me of Rob, that was all – of my own childhood places. A confluence of circumstances that didn't mean anything.

'We weren't doing any good back there,' I said.

She didn't reply. I watched the empty road ahead of us.

'There aren't enough police out here,' I said.

'They're doing their best, Will. And they're playing it the right way for now. It's just that you think they're missing something, right?'

'I think we all are.'

'You don't think Blythe is heading for the mountains?'

'I don't know. Maybe he is, but it wouldn't work out for him in the long term. I think he's got a different plan.'

'That involves him moving dangerously close to the village?'

'Maybe.'

'For reasons unknown?'

'Exactly that.'

'Except *not* exactly that.' She looked at me. 'You actually think somebody's helping him, don't you?'

For a moment, I was about to disagree. Because on one level, the idea was ridiculous. When you had a hardened criminal on the run – an armed robber, say, or a gangster – you might expect them to rely on a support network of some kind. They would have friends and associates who hated the police and were prepared to take the risk of helping them out of sympathy or loyalty. But Blythe was in an entirely different category. Even friends – assuming he'd ever had any – wouldn't want to help him after what he'd done.

And yet. There was something to it on a subconscious level. A *feeling*. And I didn't think we could, or should, discount anything right now.

'I just want to cover all the bases,' I said. 'But actually, on that subject, I'm still not sure about the letters.'

'Oh for fuck's sake, Will.'

'No. Something about them feels off to me. They don't strike me as the kind of thing that Blythe would have written, given what we know of him. The language. The content.'

'*Given what we know of him.*'

'Be honest, Emma. Don't you think that too?'

She shook her head, turning the wheel to take us along a smaller country road.

'We know they're legitimate. And that Blythe didn't end up with barrels full of women in his cellar by accident.'

We know they're legitimate. That was true, but only because of the corroboration in the letter about Melanie West. Which brought me back to Jeremy Townsend again. But it was all just feelings, hunches, and Emma was clearly exasperated enough with me that I knew not to bring Townsend and his stories back up again.

And I needed to be wary of following hunches and feelings too far, because I was way too close to this case. I needed to be careful. Because of Anna, it meant too much to me. I could feel the tension in my chest from that right now. There had been a low-level anxiety from the very first day, and it had only increased with every passing hour. I was in danger of making a mistake.

'Well, we're not far off now,' I said. My voice sounded far tighter than I would have liked. 'And it's probably nothing.'

But I felt a chill inside me. And the distant heartbeat of Blythe's presence seemed to be growing stronger, so that now I could almost feel the pressure of each heavy thud in my ears. Despite what I'd said, and even though there was no reason for it, a part of me really wasn't sure that it was *probably nothing* at all.

Warren had insisted we were both fitted with GPS trackers, the same as the other officers in the field. Anyone looking at a screen in the vans outside the Grief House right now would have seen a pair of overlapping arrows slowly and steadily approaching Frog Pond.

And then driving past it.

The countryside around us had gradually condensed into woodland, until all I could see out of the passenger window was a wall of trees. They had thin trunks, but they were packed together so tightly, and the grass was so overgrown around them, that the whole area looked impenetrable. As the marker on our own GPS device reached the trail, I caught sight of the briefest break in the undergrowth, and then we were past it almost immediately.

'Back there,' I said.

'I saw. We'll never get the car down that.'

'Parking area.' I pointed back. 'Just by it.'

It was more of a passing area than a parking one, with space for two or three cars at most, but it was empty right now. Emma turned the car and pulled in. When we got out of the vehicle, I was struck again by the profound silence, although it was different here than it had been by the farmhouse. The land there had been open, whereas here it was contained. This was the silence of seclusion, of a place packed away from the world. When I closed the car door, the sound seemed to echo off the trees and go nowhere.

As Emma pinned her GPS tracker to her jacket, I walked around to the back of the car. It had been a long time since I'd carried a baton on my belt, but I felt like doing so today. I took mine out of the boot and clipped it on.

'Are you serious?' Emma said.

'Don't you want one?'

She looked at me incredulously for a moment, then round at the trees, clocking how utterly silent the woodland was. Even the breeze, moving the branches and leaves ever so slightly, produced no sound at all. It was eerie. But at the same time, it didn't feel like we were entirely alone.

When Emma looked back at me, she didn't seem quite so incredulous any more.

'Actually, yes,' she said. 'I do.'

Twenty-Seven

Right then, Bunting thought.

He drove past the vehicle that was parked up by the entrance to the footpath leading to Frog Pond, risking a glance into the car as he did. Empty. But he had little doubt that it was a police vehicle, and that meant they were already on their way to where Blythe was hiding.

Well, it had surely been impossible for his luck to hold forever.

After leaving the cemetery, he'd been surprised again by the lack of police activity on the roads directly north of Moorton. The search seemed to be based entirely in the village itself, as though they were confident that was where Blythe was hiding out. Which meant that if Bunting could get to Frog Pond, he had a decent chance of slipping through whatever tatters of cordon there might be out here.

Worry about the route you'll take in a minute, he'd told himself.

First of all, get Blythe.

And he had begun to feel confident that he would manage that until – slowing the car slightly as he rounded the corner to the Pond – he had seen the car parked there.

He sped up now, then drove around the next corner and stopped. There was no parking space here; he just pulled the car in against the undergrowth, but not in it – he didn't want to leave any tyre tracks. Which was good, he realised, as it meant he was still thinking. His heart was beating hard, in fact, and he felt more awake than he had in hours.

Somehow, the police had discovered where Blythe was hiding.

But actually, was that necessarily the case? For one thing, he couldn't be sure it really was a police vehicle. And surely, if they'd known that Blythe was in there, they would have set up proper cordons around this area immediately, and there would have been more than one car at the scene. Could it be someone was following a hunch? Maybe they'd just made an association with the pond and decided it was worth checking out.

Either way, he had very little time. If the police found Blythe, it was all over. And if they stopped Bunting right now, he was in deep trouble. One look at the contents of his boot and his story was in tatters. He would be finished.

He took the laptop off the passenger seat and opened it. After the cemetery, he'd left the wireless connected, so he got into his email within seconds. There had been no further messages from Blythe since the one he'd already seen, and he could only hope that the man had his own laptop open and ready for updates.

His hands were trembling as he typed; his fingers kept jabbing the wrong keys. But aside from the physical shaking, he was surprised at how level-headed he felt. *This is what it must be like*, he thought. This was how it felt to be someone like Blythe: someone who simply didn't care. After a while, the fear of it all diminished.

Looks like police car at the entrance road. On way already. Not sure if they know or it's a search on spec, but no way I can get to you there. Get back to the main road somehow and follow the road NORTH. I'm about two minutes away if you run. Bring laptop, leave everything else.

Bunting glanced in the rear-view mirror. The road remained empty in both directions. No traffic at all for the moment. He prayed it would remain so.

After a moment's hesitation, another thought occurred to

him. Whoever was going to Frog Pond had no real idea who they were facing in there. *What* they were facing. Because Blythe was far more powerful than just a man, wasn't he? He was the Red River Killer. He was the Monster. Violence was what he did, and that suggested another way out of the situation for them both.

Although there are probably only a couple of them, Bunting typed quickly, and then sent the email.

Twenty-Eight

The trail to Frog Pond was about a mile long, and only about ten feet wide. The ground beneath our feet was dry and hard; it was churned up, but by the tread of boots not tyres.

If Carling was right, and kids did come down here, they must have done so on foot. As Emma and I walked, the trees tall and silent around us, I could picture them in my mind's eye: groups of teenagers, walking in twos and threes, carrying plastic bags full of cans, torchlight sweeping back and forth over the undulating ground. Warm summer days, the air thick with midges; and then cooler nights, someone perhaps lighting a fire. There were places like this I remembered from my teenage years. They were subtly distinct from the more innocent maps of younger childhood, albeit sometimes sharing locations: a slightly different but overlapping web of connections laid over the neighbourhood.

The two of us remained silent as we walked. Presumably Emma still had whatever doubts had been there on the drive, but there was always something about heading into woodland this thick that was unnerving, and we both tried to walk quietly and carefully, making as little sound as possible. The silence containing us was oppressive – so complete that it was almost a presence in itself. It was hard to see very far between the trees to either side, but easy to imagine yourself being watched from among them.

When we were about halfway there, I felt a chill on my back and stopped.

'What?' Emma whispered.

I didn't say anything. I just stood very still, staring into the woodland to my right. The undergrowth between the trees was waist-high here, and it was impossible to see very far, but now that I'd stopped moving, I could hear the tiny clicks and cracks of nature. My heart was beating quickly, and my ears started ringing as I strained harder to listen. I felt something on a primal level: some deep-set genetic response to a presence that was sensed rather than seen, but no less real for it, and no less convincing.

There is a monster nearby in this forest, it was telling me.

And you need to run.

That was the last thing I was going to do, though. Instead I continued to stare intently into the woodland. Nothing was moving there.

'I can't see anything,' Emma said.

'But you can feel it?'

For a moment, she didn't answer.

'Come on,' she said.

A minute further down the path, I heard a noise.

At first it wasn't obvious. It was more like the ringing silence was somehow growing louder. But then I recognised it for what it was: a rush of water away to the right beyond the trees. The river. It remained out of sight for the moment, but it was clear that we were getting closer to it, and it sounded more and more relentless as we did: much wilder and less constrained out here than it had sounded while driving through Moorton itself. By the time we reached Frog Pond a couple of minutes later, the noise was a constant roar to the right-hand side, so loud now that I almost felt nervous turning my back on it and facing the pond.

'Well,' Emma said, standing beside me. 'I can sort of see how it got its name, anyway.'

I nodded. The pond was much larger than I'd been expecting.

There was an area of grassland off the left-hand edge of the path, and then the water expanded away in an oval shape until it reached a far bank of trees about thirty metres away, their branches hanging down in a sweeping curtain. Everything in sight was green. The sunlight cut through from above, rendering the whole scene vibrant and bright, and the air misty. Where we were standing, enormous fronds of grass lined the edges of the pond, and most of the surface was coated with light patches of leaves and darker green algae – so much of it that it must have accumulated over many years, all of it layering over and forming a crust on the water. It seemed much warmer here than it had on the trail, as though the water was steaming. It felt like the pond should be bubbling slightly, but the surface was entirely still. Breathing in slowly, I could smell the heady aroma of the overgrown vegetation.

'He's not here,' Emma said.

I looked around. There was no sign, in fact, that anybody had been here for quite some time. I caught sight of a few old cans, the metal bleached clean by the sunlight and tangled in grass that had grown around it, but other than that, the place seemed completely undisturbed.

But the sensation I'd had on the trail remained. I still felt *watched*. It was that kind of place, of course; a hidden spot of silent natural beauty always feels alive – always feels as though it somehow has eyes of its own. Blythe wasn't here, and there was no indication that he had been.

But I still felt it.

Emma kicked a stone from the bank. It landed on the surface of the water and rested there for a moment before sinking down out of sight.

'Can we go now, Will?' she said. 'It stinks here.'

'In a minute.'

I turned around slowly and stared at the wall of trees that separated the trail behind us from the angry noise of the river beyond. A little way past the entrance to the pond, there was a break in the trees. Not large. But wide enough for a person to move through.

I walked across to it, the sound of the river growing louder. And that *thud* of Blythe's presence, fast and heavy now.

'Will?'

Emma hadn't shouted, but I held my hand out behind me, indicating for her to keep quiet, then beckoned with my head. *Let's check this out.* I didn't wait for her to reply – just stepped carefully off the trail and between the trees.

Thud.

It was a path of sorts. The undergrowth had been worn away, and the ground was overlaid with a thatch of thin sticks and branches that looked to have been pressed down over the years into a kind of carpet. The foliage to either side remained overgrown, pushing gently at my waist as I moved through.

Thud.

As I stepped through a proper break in the trees, there was the river.

I found myself standing on an open bank of mud and stones, with the wide body of water tumbling violently past in front of me: sleek and fast at the centre, but crashing and flicking up at the edges, a bright white churn of froth and foam, with droplets saturating the air.

Thud.

I looked down. The bank beneath my feet was sodden. My shoes had sunk slightly into the mud, creating a perfect imprint...

Thud.

Amongst all the others.

Thud.

Amongst the flurry of footprints that were already there.

Thud.

And then that heartbeat fell silent.

I looked along the bank to the right, and there it was, where it felt like I'd somehow been expecting to see it all along. A tent. It was pitched close to the woods, the camouflage colours blending in with the pattern of the trees behind. The front flaps were peeled back and pinned into the mud, and clothes were strewn in front, as though whoever had camped here had left in a hurry.

Left very recently.

And then I was moving. Past Emma, who had her baton in one hand and her phone in the other, her face pale. Back towards the trail itself, and then running with all the strength I had towards the main road.

You won't get away, I told him in my head, my own baton in my hand now, my legs moving as fast as I could make them. A desperate *need* in my chest. Not fear at all now; not remotely. Just the knowledge that I was so close to him – the man who had killed Anna; the man who had killed all of them – and that he wasn't going to escape.

I won't let you, I thought.

I can't.

Twenty-Nine

Probably only a couple of them.

How *typical* of the Worm, Blythe thinks as he runs along the dirt track. How typical to suggest violence as an option, so long as he's not the one dirtying his hands or making the effort. The message has confirmed his expectations of the man. If there were only two of them, why didn't the Worm take care of them back at the road? The answer is obvious – he's ineffectual and weak, and relies on Blythe to do the killing for him, just as he has all along. He will no doubt present as an adult male, but the two of them might as well be from different species.

Blythe pounds down the old footpath, running as fast and as hard as he can.

He's completely out in the open, but that's fine: there's no point in hiding any more. This is a straight race, and trying to work his way through the surrounding trees will only slow him down and negate the benefit of his head start. The two police officers will have found his campsite by now, which means they will have called the scene in and there will be backup on the way. One or both of them may well also be in pursuit somewhere behind him. He doesn't look back to check – what will be will be. And he is fast. A good strong runner. He has the knife ready in his hand if he needs it, his arm pistoning back and forth as he runs. If it comes to it, he will take one or both of them down.

And despite his derision for the Worm, that was actually

a tempting option before, when he was hidden away in the depths of the undergrowth and saw the two of them walking along the path. A man and a woman. The man stopped for a moment and stared into the treeline, as though he could see him. He couldn't, of course; Blythe was too careful for that. But he had *sensed* him, just as the man in the car at the Grief House had last night.

Blythe crouched there, entirely still, and felt the power coursing through him. The power that came from the fear he engendered in others. The man looked weak and sensitive, and was obviously no physical match for him. The woman was just a woman. And so it was tempting to emerge from the undergrowth right there and then, or else to wait for them to move a little further on, then come out and attack them from behind. But he weighed the situation carefully. Despite how they appeared, these were trained police, armed with batons and radios, and he wasn't confident he could take them both down together. So he waited for them to pass, then came out on to the path and started running as hard as he could for the road.

There will be time for hunting in the future. What he needs to do right now is escape.

The trees create a cocoon of dark green around him, but up ahead he can see a bright, shining rectangle of sunlight. He runs faster, and the light judders around, growing larger – and then he reaches the road itself, sprinting straight out into the centre of it and curving north without even pausing. He has no choice now but to trust the Worm will be where he's said he will be and see what happens. There's an empty car parked up at the side of the road by the footpath, though, and Blythe slows just long enough to plunge the knife into the back tyre of the vehicle. Probably not much use, but he still feels a rush of pleasure as he sets off running again.

He is exhilarated, actually. The mostly empty backpack bounces on his shoulders as he sprints. There is a good chance he'll be caught within the next few minutes, and yet he feels truly *alive*. Not remotely calm, for once, but not panicked either. *Excited*. He runs straight up the middle of the road, in plain sight, and it feels good, powerful. He's spent the last few days hiding in the darkness, and it's strange to be out here in the sun now, so blatant and obvious, yet there's nobody around to see him. No traffic at all. It feels like he can do anything he wants, and they'll never catch him for it.

There's a bend in the road up ahead. As fast as he's running, he speeds up. The slapping sound of his footfalls on the tarmac comes quicker and quicker, then he rounds the corner and sees the car up ahead, and he accelerates again. It has to be the Worm. He's left his hazard lights on, as though the vehicle has broken down: two red lights blinking dimly in the afternoon light, wheeling around in Blythe's vision as he runs towards the car, then hits the boot hard with his open hand, the impact on the metal hurting his palm.

Out of breath now.

He reaches down and tries to open the boot. It doesn't work.

He moves around to the driver's side, and although he knows the Worm is in there, he can't see him right now. The sunlight fills the glass with a reflection of the trees at the side of the road. He taps on the window with the tip of the knife.

'Open the boot.'

The window slides down an inch, and he catches a glimpse of unkempt brown hair.

'No. Get in the back.'

The voice is stronger than he expected.

'Don't be stupid. I'll be seen.'

'There are blankets there. Get in the footwell, pull them over you.'

You fucking idiot. But Blythe looks back down the road, and he knows that they don't have long. No time to argue. The police at Frog Pond will be reaching the road soon, and there'll be more joining them – pouring in from all directions. So he opens the back door of the vehicle instead, then folds himself inside. There is indeed a neat pile of blankets on the other side of the back seat. He closes the door and ducks down, beginning to gather them over him as best he can.

It's ridiculous; there isn't room.

But the Worm is already driving. Blythe feels the car pull away, then senses the world moving more and more quickly underneath him. A few seconds later, while he's still working on the blankets, the car slows and he hears the click-click-click of an indicator, and then everything turns slightly and the car starts moving quickly again.

'Why not the boot?' he calls angrily.

The Worm doesn't answer.

Thirty

'We've missed him.'

I shook my head. It felt to me like I'd been shaking it more or less constantly for the past hour, ever since Warren and a handful of his officers had arrived at Frog Pond. As soon as Emma radioed in the scene, Warren had claimed to be setting up roadblocks in the vicinity, but when he turned up, he seemed sheepish. They'd stopped a couple of vehicles, he told us, sounding almost apologetic, but so far there was no sign of Blythe.

I'd hardly been able to bring myself to look at him.

The desire to grab hold of him and slam home the obvious truth had been strong: he hadn't had enough officers, and the ones he did have had been either stupidly concentrated in the village itself or else searching the wrong places. But there was no point. Instead, I had leaned against our car and stared down at the tarmac as he walked past me. But out of the corner of my eye I'd caught the glance he gave me. *How did you know?* In contrast with the combative tone he'd adopted when we first met, he appeared slightly nervous around me right then, as though I might be some kind of magician.

I wished I was.

I stared out of the windscreen. We were sitting in our car, still parked up by the entrance to the footpath that led to Frog Pond. We'd been joined now by several other police cars and vans, and the path itself had been cordoned off. Groups of officers were standing around slightly aimlessly, still achieving nothing. They should have been spreading out through the network of roads surrounding the area, and it frustrated me that they weren't. Many of them seemed in good spirits. Watching them, I had that urge to grab someone again. All of them, in fact. Make them recognise the weight of the horror that had been brought here. Force them to feel the shiver that walking in the shade of it deserved.

I wanted them to care as much as I did.

'He won't get away,' Emma said.

'He already has.'

'Not necessarily. They're filling the whole area with uniforms. Tightening the perimeter. And if he's on foot, he can't have got far.'

'He's not on foot.'

'You don't know that, Will. We've got absolutely no reason to think anybody's helping him.'

No, I wanted to say, but there had been no reason to think he'd be at Frog Pond either, and yet I'd been right about that. But I remained silent. I wasn't about to start claiming psychic powers, and intuition can only take you so far. When I'd reached the car after running back down the trail, there had been no sign of any other vehicles. I'd stood very still, listening intently, and heard nothing: just the quiet sounds of nature around me. The world had felt empty. Blythe had been here, and now he was gone. How he had got away, I still couldn't say for certain, because it *didn't* make any sense for somebody to be helping him. But I wasn't sure how he could have disappeared so quickly without a car.

And more than that, it just *felt* right.

But if someone was helping him, who? And why?

My phone bleeped in my pocket, but I ignored it. Sighing to herself, Emma took hers out instead and read whatever report had just been sent through to us.

'We've got a couple more IDs on the remains from the house,' she said. 'Emily Bailey and Anna Parker.'

She said it so casually that for a moment I might not have

heard it. It took the few silent seconds that followed for the information to settle in my head and my heart.

Anna.

She was there.

'Look, Will,' Emma said, putting her phone away, 'I think you just need—'

I bunched up my fist and punched myself in the thigh as hard as I could. The pain didn't appear until a second later. And then it flared. I did it again, and then again, contorting my face.

'Will!'

Emma grabbed my arm.

'What the fuck are you doing? You're scaring me!'

I looked at her. Her eyes were wide. From the expression on her face, I might as well have just grown a second head right in front of her and started baring my teeth. She looked not just shocked but terrified of me.

Calm down, I thought. *For God's sake, calm down.*

'You're losing it, Will.'

I looked away and nodded slowly. The muscle in my thigh was radiating pain outwards, with a slowly spreading centre of numbness where I'd landed the blows. As quickly as the emotions had overwhelmed me, they faded away. I'd lost control. I had it back now.

'I'm sorry,' I said.

'You should be. Jesus Christ. You shouldn't do that to yourself.'

'I know.'

'What the fuck is going on with you?'

'I'm frustrated,' I said. 'I'm angry.'

'Yeah, I am too. But that doesn't explain *that*.' She looked out through the windscreen and ran a hand through her hair. 'The past few days you haven't been yourself at all. You're always weird, but I've never seen you anything like this. I mean it. You're scaring me.'

'I'm sorry.'

'That's it? You're sorry? Don't you think I deserve more of an explanation than that? You're going to get us thrown off this investigation. Do you think nobody else saw that, for Christ's sake?'

I looked out of the window. The nearest cluster of Warren's officers were watching us, but turned away quickly when they saw me looking back at them. I stared at them for a moment anyway. *The weird guy from out of town just went nuts.* Well, at least I'd given them something more appropriate to be smiling about.

'I don't care,' I said.

'Well, you fucking *should* care.' Emma shook her head. 'You're too close to this for some reason. I don't know what's going on, but you need to tell me, Will, because you know what? This is no good right now. No good at all.'

I didn't answer. Eventually she sighed, and we sat in silence for a time. I stared out of the windscreen, watching the undergrowth moving gently at the edge of the woods, not knowing what to say.

Because the truth was, she was right about all of it. The case meant far too much to me. And Emma wanted to be in the room for this one just as much as I did: for the sake of her reputation, her professional advancement. I didn't begrudge her that. She deserved better than to spend her career stuck with me. But even though she was right, and I really did owe her an explanation for my behaviour, I just couldn't tell her. I'd be removed from the case. We both might be. And yet without an explanation, things were going to become very awkward between us, and I didn't want that. Right then, I had no idea how to square that particular circle.

The frustration at having missed Blythe was burning inside me.

We had been *so* close to him. *I* had been so close. And yet he'd managed to slip away. Whatever Emma said about the search area tightening, I had absolutely no faith in Warren and his men – or maybe I just had more faith in Blythe himself. He was working to a schedule none of us could see, and there was something we were all missing. It seemed that pretty much everybody else in the room right now was staring at the wrong wall entirely.

God, I wanted him.

I understood now that it had never been enough to be just peripherally involved – a part of the investigation, but only a tiny cog in the overall machine. And in a strange way, it was almost like I wasn't *supposed* to be sidelined. I'd felt it for the first time at Blythe's house, and I felt it again now, more strongly than ever. This was about him and me. This was a chance to make amends, as much as that was possible. Back at the pond, I had chased him as fast and hard as I could, and I realised now that one of the reasons it hurt so much to have missed him was that a part of me had also felt like I'd been chasing myself.

'Talk to me, Will,' Emma said. She was quieter now. 'Let me know what's going on. I don't like this. You owe me an explanation.'

I looked at her, feeling helpless. She was right, of course. She deserved to know what I was thinking and what lay behind this. Why it meant so much to me – far more than was healthy for the investigation as a whole.

'I...'

And I really was about to tell her everything just then. I really would have done. If I hadn't heard a car engine in the distance. Instead I fell quiet, looking in the mirror, and saw a car approaching from the north. It was a civilian vehicle by the look of it, and it seemed to slow a little as it came closer.

I glanced out at the groups of officers standing around. Most of them had noticed the car. As far as I could tell, none of them seemed obviously inclined to do anything about it.

I looked in the mirror again as it reached us, then out through the window as it went past.

And I saw who was driving.

Thirty-One

Townsend still had no idea what he was going to do.

He'd been thinking about it on the drive to Moorton. He wasn't a man who was built for heroics; he never had been. As a tall, skinny child, rarely found without a book in his hand, he'd loathed the sports and physical activities that so many of the other boys took to with such apparent ease. He rarely exercised, and whatever meagre shape he might once have been in had declined badly during the years of Melanie's absence. He was insubstantial now, his body bordering on the frail. No match for a man like Blythe, if it came to a confrontation.

So what on earth was he planning to do?

Heroics, he thought bitterly, both hands gripping the steering wheel. Though that was the wrong word, wasn't it? There was nothing remotely heroic about the things he had done in the past, and nothing he did now could redeem him. There were many words he could apply to himself, but hero wasn't one of them.

So, no: this certainly wasn't an act of heroism. It was more an act of duty. A taking of responsibility. For so long now, he had shouldered the guilt and shame of his actions, and he'd borne them because of Melanie. He'd punished himself over and over, battering himself with self-hatred until there were no edges left to him. The result was this. He had to be there for the conclusion. To be part of the story's end.

He blinked.

It really was that simple, he realised. That was all it came down to. It didn't matter what he was going to do; it only mattered that he was present for whatever occurred. Whatever happened to him at Frog Pond would just be the final punishment in the long list of pains he'd endured over the years.

Nearly there now.

He hadn't grown up in the area, but he had visited the village on several occasions, and had even gone to Frog Pond itself once, walking the path to it and taking photographs. He was struck by the contrast between the still green surface of the pond and the raging torrent of the river so close by. It was a haunting place in many ways. But he wasn't so familiar with the roads around Moorton that he hadn't gone slightly wrong today. Aware of the police activity, he'd deliberately avoided driving through the centre of the village, but as a result he had ended up circling round too far, only figuring out a turning or so back that he'd overshot the pond and would need to approach it from the north.

It should be somewhere around the next bend. From what he could recall, it was easy to miss, so he slowed the car slightly as he reached the curve in the road . . .

Immediately, he saw all the police activity up ahead.

Keep calm, he told himself.

Impossible, of course, but what overtook him wasn't panic so much as a curious kind of emptiness, in which his mind froze and became incapable of making any decision at all. It felt like he'd forgotten how to drive, and his body wouldn't respond at all. His car coasted slowly past the gathering of officers by default, by accident, because he was unable to do anything else.

He couldn't stop himself from looking as he went past.

There were a number of cars and vans parked up, and a bunch of officers standing by the entrance to the footpath. They watched him without much interest. Surely they were going to stop him? And yet they didn't. He looked into one of the cars he passed and recognised the man sitting there. The suspicious detective from yesterday. Turner.

Staring right back at him.

Townsend faced forward immediately and sped up a little. Not a lot – not a guilty amount – but enough to leave the cavalcade behind him. *Damn, damn, damn.* He watched the scene in the rear-view mirror the whole time. As he reached the next bend in the road, he saw the indicator light on the detective's car.

Round the bend, he sped up again, accelerating as much as the tight country lanes would bear. *Damn.* He slowed only slightly as the car reached the humped bridge over the river, and the chassis jolted as he hit the flat road beyond it. He needed a turning, but it was just woods to the left and hedgerows to the right. A cemetery. Then fields. He was trapped, with Moorton only a mile or so ahead now.

He checked the rear-view again.

Nothing for the moment.

But the detective *had* seen him. Presumably he was here to help with the hunt for Blythe, and he would obviously have recognised Townsend from their encounter yesterday. It was impossible to imagine that Turner wouldn't come after a man just happening on the scene who had such a clear connection to the case.

You can justify it, though.

Yes, he could. He was a victim, after all – a survivor of the Red River Killer's violence. It was only natural, wasn't it, that he might have seen the news and be drawn to Moorton, to watch first hand as the hunt for his wife's killer unfolded. Frog Pond – well, that was a coincidence. He didn't know the roads well. He'd taken a wrong turning.

All explicable.

Or else you could give in, he thought.

Tell them everything. Finally.

There was a moment when that seemed like an actual possibility. What would it feel like, after all this time, to explain everything that he'd done? The guilt could never be taken away, but perhaps it would ease slightly. It would be like passing on a terrible gift. Here: I've carried this for so long; it's yours to take care of now.

But it was only a moment.

He owed Melanie better than that.

Another bend coming up. Townsend glanced in the rear-view and finally saw the car coming after him, a light blinking on the roof. He rounded the corner and it disappeared from sight.

But looking ahead, he was descending towards the village. It was inevitable that he'd be stopped there. He didn't have long. As he drove, his thoughts turned to what it all meant. He couldn't process this new information – couldn't work out the repercussions of what he'd just seen back at the path to Frog Pond. Had they found Blythe? Had they captured him alive, or was he dead? Or had he somehow managed to blink away from the police, the same way he'd so successfully vanished with his victims in the past?

A moment later, he hit the tail end of a short line of traffic on the outskirts of Moorton and came to a halt. There were traffic lights a few cars in front where the police had set up some kind of checkpoint and were inspecting the vehicles entering and leaving the village. But it was clear that he wasn't going to have to wait – an officer with a thick moustache and sunglasses was already moving up the line of cars towards him. Turner must have radioed ahead. *I'm a VIP now*, Townsend thought. *I'm jumping the queue.* He wound his window down as the officer reached him.

'Mr Townsend?'

'Yes.'

'Can I ask you to turn off the engine and step out of the vehicle, please.'

'What is this about?'

'Just do as I ask, please.' The man turned his head and stared up the road away from the village, then sighed to himself. 'Ah. Here comes Hopalong Cassidy.'

Townsend opened the door and got out. Looking up the road, he saw immediately what the officer was referring to.

The car that had followed him from Frog Pond was listing badly, one of its tyres flapping angrily out to the side, and it arrived with a clattering sound. When it pulled to a halt behind Townsend's own vehicle, he thought he could smell something burning.

A woman got out of the passenger seat and began circling the car, running her hands through her hair. Turner got out of the driver's side, and if he was aware of the damage to the vehicle it clearly didn't bother him. He headed straight for Townsend.

'Jeremy,' he said. 'You might remember me. Detective Turner? We met yesterday.'

'Yes.'

'What the hell are you doing here?'

While the officer who stopped him had clearly been issuing orders, at least he'd been polite about it. There was none of that with Turner right now. Yesterday he'd seemed kind to start with, but that had changed as the meeting had gone on. Townsend knew he was a bad actor, and that Turner had seen through him almost immediately – that he was hiding something. There was nothing but animosity on the man's face now. Turner might not have known anything for certain, but he suspected. And of course, he was entirely right to.

Keep calm.

'I saw the news,' Townsend said. It had seemed so natural and easy in the car, but he struggled to find the words now. 'The man took my wife. I wanted to be here.'

'Not sure I believe you, Jeremy.' Turner was staring at him intently. 'Just happened to be passing Frog Pond, did you? Were you a bit surprised to see us there? You looked it.'

'I lost my way.' Christ, he was on the verge of stammering. And had he just given himself away there? 'I don't know what Frog Pond is. I was trying to get to the village but I ended up on the wrong road.'

'Bullshit.'

Townsend couldn't speak. He'd never been great at talking at the best of times, never mind when facing down naked aggression. And he understood now that there was no way he was going to convince this man with lies; he would see straight through them. Turner took a step closer, bringing them face to face, and Townsend almost flinched from the force of the anger coming off him.

'I think you're *lying*, Jeremy,' Turner said quietly. 'You're hiding something. You *know* something. And you're going to tell me what it is.'

'I...'

But he couldn't think what to say next. Couldn't come up with a falsehood. A decent story. Turner's manner was simply too intense, and whenever he tried to think, it was as though somebody was clicking their fingers repeatedly in front of his face to distract him. He was going to have to tell him. Confess it all.

'Will...'

The female detective was beside them now, her hand on her partner's arm. Turner seemed completely unaware she was there. His gaze was locked on Townsend's own.

'I...'

'I read your stories, you know.' Turner took a step back and nodded to himself. 'Pretty sick stuff, if you don't mind me saying so. I'm not sure what to think about the kind of man who writes stuff like that.'

The stories.

And just like that, the spell was broken.

The guilt, the shame, the self-hatred – it flipped in Townsend's head, and suddenly, rather than being intimidated by the man in front of him, he was *angry* instead. Turner had dipped a bucket into a deeply personal well of pain and misery, one he couldn't hope to understand, and had just triumphantly slopped the contents at Townsend's feet. It was too much.

'My *stories*,' Townsend said quietly.

'Yes. The ones about your wife.'

'They're my way of coping. My way of dealing with things.'

'Seems a bit weird to me.'

'I don't care how it seems to you,' Townsend said.

He stared back at the detective, more confident now. Anger had a way of doing that, he knew. Never a fighter, perhaps, but he'd still felt it on occasion – the way fear could roll over inside you, revealing anger on its underside. And for him, there was that whole weight of guilt and pain behind it too, pushing the anger forward. To hell with this man. A moment ago Townsend had felt feeble and had been ready to tell Turner everything. Now he felt ready for a fight.

How dare he?

'Will, please.'

The female detective spoke quietly. She still had her hand on Turner's arm, but the man was ignoring her, still staring at Townsend.

'I don't *care* how it seems to you,' Townsend repeated slowly, letting the anger surface. And didn't it feel just a little bit good? He'd been trampled underfoot for so long that it was almost surprising to feel some sense of validation. 'You don't know what it's like to lose somebody the way I have. You don't know how it feels. I'm not apologising to you.'

Turner stared at him for a moment longer, but Townsend met his gaze implacably now. *To hell with you.* Each of those stories had ripped him to pieces. The detective couldn't possibly understand the pain they had caused him.

Turner broke the stare first.

'You won't mind me checking your car, will you?'

'Not at all. I'll open the boot for you.'

'*Will.*'

But the woman stood helplessly as Turner moved away from both of them, around to the back of the car, waiting. As Townsend took his keys from his pocket, he glanced across the street and realised what she was so concerned about. There were reporters on the pavement there, and cameras pointing their way, eagerly filming every second of this encounter.

Thirty-Two

Later.

Much later.

'Why are we here, Will?' Emma said quietly.

I peered through the windscreen at the building I'd parked up outside. It was two storeys tall and looked very old. The roof was peaked in places. Whenever I visited here, it always reminded me of a mansion in the countryside, although we were only a few secluded and leafy roads away from a town centre. There were many windows. Most were dark right now, but a few were softly illuminated behind peach-coloured curtains.

'Why are we here?' she repeated.

After my encounter with Townsend, Emma had – understandably – torn shreds off me, wanting to know what was going through my head and what the fuck I thought I was doing. She was right: I'd lost it. The mistake I'd been so worried about making had happened. It would no doubt be all over the news by now, and there was a danger we'd end up removed from the investigation as a result of it. I was erratic at the best of times. This was anything but the best of times.

My mistake. My fault. And although I hadn't answered Emma at the time, and hadn't explained, I'd known deep down that she deserved better than that. When we'd finally got the tyre fixed and left Moorton, I'd told her that I was going to drive.

Why were we here?

'To see a friend,' I said simply.

'Bullshit.' Emma sounded uneasy. 'You don't have any friends.'

Normally, she might have said that as a joke, but tonight I didn't smile. She was more right than she knew. And I understood the doubt I heard in her voice, because the truth was that the last few days had begun to change things between us. However much we'd butted heads in the past, it had usually been playful at heart, and there had always been a tacit degree of trust between us. We had shared a flat for long enough that she had perhaps thought she knew me as well as anyone. Right now, it must have felt like I'd suddenly opened a door and revealed a secret room that I'd kept from her all along. When that happens in a friendship, whatever the content of the room itself, it changes how you feel about someone. It's enough to discover it exists at all.

'What is this place?' she said.

It's not too late, I told myself.

I could turn the engine back on, reverse out of the gravel car park and drive away without explaining. Even if Emma came back, she wouldn't get a definitive answer to her question beyond the obvious: that it was a hospital of some kind. An institution. That wouldn't tell her *why* we were here, though, and as good a detective as she was, I doubted she'd be able to find out on her own.

But she deserved better.

I opened the car door before I could change my mind.

'Come on.'

Emma hesitated.

'They're not going to let us in at this time of night.'

'Yes,' I said. 'They will.'

The nurses' station inside was occupied by a woman I recognised from previous visits. I showed her my ID.

'We're here to see Rob Parker,' I said.

Even at night, a regular hospital has a kind of life to it. There's a sense of activity – the presence of doctors and orderlies and patients. But in this place, everything was deathly silent. The hall lights were dimmed and the atmosphere was more akin to a chapel of rest. Just walking along the corridors, you understood immediately that nobody who moved into one of the rooms behind the closed doors you passed was expected to move out of it again.

'It's very expensive here, you know,' I said absently. 'I looked it up once. I can't remember the exact figure any more, but it must be costing them the earth.'

'Who?'

'My friend's parents.'

Rob's family had always been wealthy. It had been one of the few differences between us as children. My mother, a single parent, had struggled every month to make ends meet. But it had never mattered. Rob's parents might have been rich, but they had never been stand-offish or snobbish with me or my mother. They were good people, and had always welcomed me into their home. There had even been trips and holidays abroad, where I'd been invited along and treated as part of the family, and as far as I knew, the issue of money had never been raised. I think they'd worried that their small, shy, sensitive child would have trouble fitting in amongst the other boys and would never find a friend. In me, he had practically found a mirror.

'Will—'

'We're here.'

I stopped outside the familiar door. Over the years, I'd visited every few months, and the sight of it was indelibly stored in my memory. When I closed my eyes at night, I could picture every detail of the walk in my head.

'Who is this friend?' Emma said.

'You'll see.'

I turned the handle and opened the door.

Although softly lit, it was not what could be said to be an intimate or comfortable room. It was dominated by technology. An intricate nest of machinery rested behind the headboard of the bed, with tubes hanging down from racks above and several monitors mounted on supporting poles. The bed itself was elevated at a slight angle, with equipment around the sides: things that always looked to me like old-fashioned computers and printers.

And lying there in the bed, the focus of all this attention, was Rob.

I stared at him. Whenever I visited here, I was never entirely sure what to expect. On one level, Rob never really changed. After a period when his weight had deteriorated and his muscles had slackened and loosened, his body had seemed to settle into a form that never really altered. There were small changes – his hair varied in length, for example, or his head might be turned one way or the other – but they weren't substantial. And yet he always seemed different. Perhaps it wasn't him that changed at all – maybe it was more that I ended up viewing him through the prism of my emotions at the time, and so any changes I saw came from inside myself.

He looks young today, I thought.

It was partly because of how small he appeared in the bed. The covers were rolled down to his waist, with his bare fore-arms resting on the top of them to either side, and his head seemed almost lost in the pillow supporting it, the way a body looks in a funeral casket. But it was more than that. His face was unlined – almost serene. Aside from the plastic tube that fed into his mouth and the wires connected to the bed and his arms, he might have been a child sleeping.

'Hello, Rob,' I said quietly.

'Can he hear you?' Emma asked.

'I doubt it. You hear all these stories, though, don't you? People in comas – their relatives playing them their favourite tunes over and over, and they remember it when they come around.'

'He's in a coma?'

'Yes. But according to the doctors, he doesn't have much remaining brain function. And it's really only this equipment that's keeping him alive now. He's never going to come round.'

'Who is he?'

I took a deep breath, knowing that the answer I was about to give was insufficient and wrong, but also still deeply true.

You were my best friend.

That was what Rob had told me in the email he sent me. The email that I'd kept over the years and still read occasionally. The email that I still sometimes thought about replying to finally, despite the fact that there was nobody alive now who would ever read it. Pointless, perhaps. A meaningless gesture. But then, as I'd just said, people play music to people in comas, don't they? They visit graves and talk to the patches of ground as though someone might still hear. It wouldn't be so very different.

Rob and I. Once upon a time, as boys and then teenagers, we had been inseparable. Although we gathered friends around us over time, the two of us had always seemed distinct from the other boys: quieter; more sensitive and introspective; each of us likely destined for a childhood of alienation but for the sheer fortune of finding each other. We seemed to look at the world differently from other children. No, more than that, I think we actually *saw* it differently. I have never felt closer or more attuned to anyone. Not even Anna, I think.

It's been so long since we've spoken.

Our relationship changed over time, of course, because everything does. In the end, it was two things that separated us. The first was geography. Rob went to university to study English, while I remained at home and joined the police force. Those choices were in keeping with both our natures, I thought – the same introspection and sensitivity manifesting itself in different ways. Rob had always been happy lost in the words, thoughts and emotions of others. For him, it was about empathy and caring. And in my own way, that was what drove me into the police. Rob graduated three times, eventually achieving a PhD in literature. By the time I moved cities and made detective, he was married, teaching and publishing academic papers of his own, and we were long estranged.

Because the second thing that separated us was Anna.

I'm sorry for everything.

I still remember the phone call I received from Anna during that second term after she started university, when she told me that she'd met someone else and that it was over between us. At the time, she didn't tell me who that person was, and I hadn't thought to make the connection. I even spoke to Rob about it – crying down the phone at him – but he was either too nervous or too ashamed to tell me the truth. It was a few weeks before I found out.

And after that, I never spoke to either of them again.

Will, you must have seen the news. You must know what's happened.

Yes, of course I saw the news when Anna went missing, and I understood what it meant. Everything changes, and what I felt when I learned what had happened was an immense, crushing sadness. I understood how easy it can be when you're hurt to cast aside things that once meant so much to you. I imagined how it might have been to meet Anna accidentally some day, and how, with enough time passed, I might have been able to look back on our relationship with quiet affection rather than pain. Impossible once she was gone. But then you often figure out what's important after it becomes impossible to do anything about it. Regret clarifies many things.

Not everything, though. There's always room to make more mistakes.

I could really do with getting back in touch with you again right now.

Please talk to me.

I never did reply. Looking back now, I knew I should have overcome the long-dead anger I'd felt and reached out to him. We had been best friends once, and we had loved the same woman, and I was one of the few people alive who could understand what he was going through. I remember picking up that snail on the Bridge that day. It was a stupid act, perhaps, but it had been done out of a childish love for my friend, a recognition of how he felt about his sister dying, and a desire for him to feel safe and okay. But I found I still couldn't swallow that old pain and resentment. I couldn't bring myself to do it. And again, I only understood the mistake after it became impossible to change it.

I wonder, do you ever think about that day on the Bridge? I don't know if you even remember, but one day we cycled there and I thought I saw a man. A man with a sad face. But there was nobody there really.

Do you ever think about him?

Yes.

I do now.

Every single day since.

'How did he end up like this?' Emma asked.

She sounded reluctant to ask, as though the question might be inappropriate or an intrusion. Or perhaps because she was worried what the answer might be.

'He took his own life.' I corrected myself. 'Tried to, at least. Although I suppose to all intents and purposes he succeeded. You can't really say he's alive any more, can you? The life he was living at the time – he ended that.'

'I'm sorry.'

'It's been a while now. Going on seven years.'

'God. He's been here that long?'

'Yes,' I said. 'There was a bridge. Near where we grew up.'

The Bridge. It had been a key waystation for me as a child, but the memory of it had faded over time, and it had become just a bridge, any bridge. We leave these things behind. But yes, I still remembered the day Rob and I had gone there together and everything had felt slightly off kilter, as though the world had somehow folded over and a dreadful moment from the future had been briefly juxtaposed over the present.

A man with a sad face.

I could picture Rob standing there, years later, alone in the darkness. His hands on the rough stone, hoisting himself up on to the wall and then sitting there for a while, maybe staring at the night sky and the stars. Then looking to one side, thinking back to that day. And perhaps even seeing himself as a child for a moment, looking back at him in shock.

And then falling through nothing.

'The fall should have killed him,' I said. 'But it didn't. In the darkness, he'd got the angle wrong, so he didn't land on the train tracks. Someone saw him from the road, before he jumped, and had already phoned the police. They saved him. I suppose you can call it that. But he's been like this ever since.'

'I'm sorry, Will.'

Emma sounded helpless. She still didn't understand.

'I am too.'

Rob's more obvious physical injuries had healed, but he had never regained consciousness. He had remained in this state ever since, suspended somewhere between life and death. He wouldn't have wanted that. His suicide attempt had not been a cry for help; those had come before, and I, at least, had ignored the one made to me. But his parents were broken and they were rich. It was their decision to maintain his life support. In a different life, I might have had that argument with them – carefully, tactfully – but I'd given up that right a long time ago. They had lost their other child at a very early age and Rob was all they had, and I supposed that I understood their motivations well enough. In my own way, once upon a time, I had loved him too.

'Why did he do it?' Emma said.

'He didn't leave a note,' I said. 'He didn't need to. He'd been depressed for a few years. He lost his sister when we were just kids, and I think he always blamed himself for that – the fact that he hadn't been able to protect her. Which is stupid, I know, but like you said, people often feel guilty for things that aren't their fault. And Rob always felt things strongly. He cared very deeply.'

'You were kids. Surely that was a long time ago?'

There's no such thing as a long time ago, I thought. The very centre of the oldest tree is a long time ago, but it's still always there at the heart of it, shaping it.

'Then he lost someone else,' I said.

For a moment, I couldn't continue. It had been easy enough to tell Emma what Rob had done. What was harder to explain was why, and the guilt I felt. To reveal my connection to the case and how much it meant to me, knowing that it, along with my behaviour, would make it likely that I would be removed from the investigation. That both of us might be. And even worse, the simple fact that I hadn't confided in Emma from the beginning. *You don't have any friends*, she'd told me outside. I looked at her now, and I knew it wasn't true.

She deserves to know the truth.

I took a deep breath. And I told her a story about a girl named Anna.

Thirty-Three

It was dusk by the time Bunting finally arrived home.

The street was deserted, and his heart was pounding harder even than it had been in Moorton. While there had been reason to be nervous back there, it had not been borne out. As he drove through the warren of country lanes away from Frog Pond, taking bend after bend and crossing junctions, putting distance between himself and the scene, he'd been constantly astounded by how *easy* it all was. Maybe it wasn't easy at all. Perhaps some of Blythe's vanishing magic was somehow working on them both.

Regardless, there was a lot to be nervous about now.

He reversed carefully into his driveway, watching in the mirror as the red lights reflected on the metal garage door. He didn't want to get too close. It was an up and under, but he needed enough space to get into the boot if any of this was going to work. The car edged slowly backwards until it was completely hidden from view by the hedges to either side of the garden. The glow from the street light on the road disappeared, leaving the interior of the car in shadow. He pulled on the handbrake and then turned off the engine.

Silence.

For most of the journey, Blythe had been entirely quiet, only speaking when Bunting pulled into a service station. He had parked away from the other vehicles but as close to one of the bins as he could manage.

'Stay out of sight,' he'd told Blythe.

'What are you doing?'

Maintain frame. So Bunting hadn't replied. He'd just got out of the car, leaving the door open, and gone round to the other side at the back. When he opened the door, Blythe's backpack was there on the seat, but he could hardly see the man lying in the footwell at all. It was amazing how good he was at hiding and remaining unnoticed. But of course he'd had a great deal of practice at that over the years.

Bunting touched the backpack.

'What are you doing?' Blythe said, as though he could sense movements he couldn't see.

'Stay down. It's busy here. There are people nearby.'

A lie, but it was enough to keep Blythe from interfering with what he needed to do. The top of the backpack was open, and the inside was mostly empty now. Bunting had found the laptop and Wi-Fi device easily, and was relieved they were there. He'd placed them in the thick carrier bag he'd brought with him, put his own Wi-Fi device in there with them, then walked the short distance to the bin. Making sure nobody was watching, he'd pushed the bag inside. It was a risk, but he had little choice. His plan relied on the laptop not making its way into police hands, and especially not on to his own property. With its constantly changing parade of visitors, this place seemed as good as any. The people who emptied the bins probably went about their job like mindless zombies.

'What did you do?' Blythe had asked as they drove away.

'I needed to get rid of your laptop and Wi-Fi.' That was true, of course, but it needed to be furnished with a lie. 'The police know where you've been. There's a danger they could analyse transmissions from the area and trace the signal from them to those devices.'

Transparently bullshit, of course. But he had been hoping that Blythe didn't understand enough about surveillance technology to contradict him. Not that it made any difference at that point. It was done, and that was all that mattered.

Blythe hadn't spoken again.

Now, parked up in his driveway, it would have been easy for Bunting to imagine he was completely alone in the vehicle. There was no sound or movement from behind him at all. Except that he could *sense* Blythe lying there. The car was filled with the presence of him, and the skin on Bunting's back was squirming. His body was warning him that he was close to something incredibly dangerous. He felt like prey.

Which of course was exactly what he was.

'We're here,' he said.

Blythe didn't reply.

Bunting fought the urge to crane his neck and look over the seat to see if the man was still there. He tried to keep calm. As far as he had been able to tell, there hadn't been a weapon in the backpack, but he had no doubt that Blythe was armed in some way. He imagined a knife – a big-bladed hunting thing with a serrated edge – and tried to put the image out of his mind. He was taking a risk, but if everything went according to plan, the knife wouldn't matter. If anything, in fact, it would make things easier.

He got out of the car, closed the driver's door and waited.

There was a moment when nothing happened.

And then the shadows in the back of the car began rearranging themselves. Blythe threw the covers off and pulled himself up on to the seat. It was difficult to make him out in the gloom, but Bunting could tell the man was looking around, inspecting his surroundings, scoping out the terrain he'd found himself in. A natural predator – not about to make a move until he knew exactly what that move was going to be. He didn't appear remotely panicked or nervous. In contrast, Bunting was aware of the sweat slowly trickling down his own spine.

The seconds stretched out.

Finally the back door opened and Blythe stepped out of the car.

The two men stood looking at each other. As well as terrifying, Bunting found it *strange* being this close to Blythe. He had seen him before many times. Blythe had been a few years older than him at school, but he'd always recognised him when he'd seen him around Moorton. And of course, he'd followed him over the years – but always from a distance. He'd never been this close to him. Never stared into his face the way he was doing right now. The obvious power of him was a shock. With some men, it was only when you got close to them that the air between you began to shimmer and the animal part of you sensed how much physically stronger than you they were. He and Blythe were about the same height, but with his unkempt hair and black stubble and the thick barrel of his body, Blythe was an entirely different kind of animal.

And there was nothing in his eyes at all. Not hate, not anger, not even curiosity. He had already checked out what was around him and knew exactly what he was doing. There was no danger of being seen. Anything could happen right now.

Everything could.

Bunting glanced down. At least the man's hands were empty.

Blythe turned away, then wandered a little way down the drive towards the road.

'I thought I'd recognise you,' he said.

Bunting would have felt a small amount of pride at that – that he'd surreptitiously stalked this man, often literally, without being spotted – but the obvious lack of interest in Blythe's voice killed that. The hunter wasn't remotely bothered about having been hunted in turn, and the implication from that was clear: Bunting wasn't a threat to him. He had never been worth noticing.

'I was always careful.'

Blythe nodded, then turned around and wandered back, looking at the house.

'This is yours?'

'Yes.'

'You live alone?'

An apparently innocent question, but another chill ran up Bunting's spine. Blythe's right hand was in his coat pocket now, and Bunting realised that the wander down the drive had been positional. Blythe was now standing between him and the road: no escape there. And if he tried to run for the house, he'd never make it.

'Yes,' Bunting said quietly. 'It's just me.'

Blythe took another step towards him, eyes locked on him now.

'Well then. We should go inside.'

That's the last thing we should do, Bunting thought.

He was sure that the moment the pair of them stepped through his front door, he was a dead man. Blythe might not have been intelligent in the conventional sense, but he was cunning and he was astute. He would have guessed certain things about Bunting, and for the most part – sad to admit, but true – he would have been completely correct. If Bunting went missing for a few days, few people were going to come looking for him. And now that Blythe was away from Moorton, with access to a house and a car, there was no reason for him to keep Bunting alive at all.

So he needed an advantage. He needed to let Blythe know that he wasn't *quite* as in control of the situation as he might think.

'Not yet,' he said.

'We could be seen out here.'

'We won't. It's very private. It's the main reason I chose this house in the first place.'

'And because you wanted to be close to me.'

'I've been following your career for a long time,' Bunting said. 'You know that. And yes, I wanted to be close to you. But like I said, that's not the main reason.'

'Oh?'

'You need to look in the boot.' He nodded at the vehicle. 'Go on. It's open.'

Blythe glanced at the vehicle, then back at him.

'Why?'

'You'll see.'

With a huge effort of will, Bunting turned his back on Blythe and walked towards the front door of the house. Slowly, though. He didn't want to put himself out of range and force the man to attack him. Before he reached the step, he stopped and turned round. While he hadn't heard Blythe move, the man had somehow kept pace with him. Now he was level with the back of the car. The look on his face remained blank and empty.

'Don't you want to see?' Bunting said.

Blythe stared at him for a moment longer, obviously calculating the distance between them, and then made his decision and stepped between the car and the garage door. Once he had done so, it was as though Bunting didn't exist at all – although he had no doubt that, were he to attempt to run or try to get inside, Blythe would be on him immediately. He did neither, though. Instead, he watched Blythe open the boot of the car. The metal hinges creaked, breaking the intense silence. Bunting found himself holding his breath.

This is where it could all go wrong.

Blythe stared down into the boot for what felt like an age.

This is where it could all go so very wrong...

At last he looked up. His expression had changed slightly. It was no longer entirely blank. He was staring at Bunting as though re-evaluating him on some level, his opinion shifting, perhaps no longer seeing the *worm* he had been expecting. His eyes seemed to be shining in the dark, and Bunting knew that, if nothing else, he'd got the man's attention. He'd bought himself time to move them both to the next part of the story he was busy creating. Blythe gestured at the contents of the boot and sounded genuinely curious when he spoke next.

'What is *this*?' he said.

Part Four

Thirty-Four

The next morning, Emma and I drove to the department separately.

I had no idea what to expect, beyond the fact that we were in trouble. A call had come through on the radio just after we'd set off: Reeves wanted to see both of us in his office as soon as we arrived. Never good news at the best of times, this morning it felt like a death sentence.

I watched the back of Emma's car ahead of me and wondered what she was thinking. She had barely spoken to me last night on the drive back from seeing Rob, and she'd gone straight to bed after we'd got back to the house. This morning, she'd engaged in the bare minimum of communication. She was very clearly pissed off with me; I got that. She'd been annoyed with me in the past, though, and I'd never known her as closed off as this. The occasional red lights as she braked in the traffic seemed to be warding me off, keeping me back. The wedge between us now was painful. It felt like a loss.

Another loss: we were going to be taken off the investigation. Or I was, anyway.

I'd forced myself to watch the television coverage of my confrontation with Townsend. It wasn't an edifying spectacle. The cameras hadn't captured any of the dialogue, but even without sound it was obvious that I was being angry and accusatory, and that Townsend looked taken aback, even scared at one point. Without context or background, the images looked very bad indeed: a policeman apparently bullying the husband of one of the Red River Killer's victims. And perhaps that was what it had actually been. Because while I remained deeply suspicious of Townsend, it was still difficult to pin down the reasons why, never mind justify my behaviour. I'd lost it. That was what it came down to. I was too close to the case, I hadn't kept tight enough control of myself, and now I was going to pay the price for that.

Even worse, Emma was too.

I'm sorry, I thought.

We arrived at the department slightly early. Emma stalked off ahead of me, not looking back, locking her car with a beep aimed over her shoulder. She walked much more quickly than usual. I struggled with the balancing act of keeping up while maintaining the distance she obviously wanted between us.

'You got the message?' I said.

'Yes.'

We took the lift together in silence. Emma folded her arms and kept her gaze fixed firmly ahead. But before we'd reached the floor for Reeves's office, she reached out suddenly and hit a lower button. The lift came to a halt on the floor our office was on and the doors opened

'Come with me.'

She didn't wait for me to reply, so I followed her out of the lift and down the corridor until we reached our office. Emma put her bag and paperwork down on the desk and then, for what felt like the first time in hours, turned and actually *looked* at me.

I didn't say anything. She was evaluating me: searching my face, as though she might find something there that would explain everything and show her some way forward. I let her. After a moment, she sighed to herself and looked away.

'I'm sorry,' I said.

'Oh, I'm sure you are. But that doesn't really cut it, does it?'

'No. I know that. What are you going to do?'

'I genuinely have no idea.'

She had clear options, of course, and neither of us needed to say them out loud. By not mentioning my connection to the case, I'd potentially placed the whole thing in jeopardy. The evidence against Blythe could hardly be stronger, but a defence counsel would still try to find even the smallest gap in which to insert a lever. An officer with a personal investment in the investigation was a problem, especially given my subsequent behaviour. I had wanted to be in that room; it had felt like I needed to be. But it wasn't about me, and I should never have been there in the first place. I'd known that.

But Emma *hadn't* known, and if she wanted to, she could use my revelation last night to separate the two of us now. She had every reason to. What did she owe me, after all? For her own reasons, aspirational rather than personal, she'd wanted this case as badly as I had, and there was a good chance that if she painted me black, she could keep herself in the room. If that was what she was working herself up to doing, I certainly wasn't going to blame her.

'I really don't know,' she said again.

Then she reached down and picked something up from the desk. Townsend's book. She turned it over and stared at the photograph on the back.

'You're still suspicious of him, aren't you?'

'Yes.'

'But you're not even sure why.'

'The question he asked when he first came in. The stories. Him turning up in Moorton. And a feeling. Call it intuition, if you like.'

'I can call it bullshit if I like. Reeves certainly will.'

'Yes. But I still feel it.'

I had nothing better to offer than that, and I was well aware that it wasn't enough. Emma looked at me for another long moment. Then she nodded to herself, turned away and picked up her things.

'Right,' she said. 'Let's go and get this over with.'

*

Ferguson was already in with Reeves when we arrived. He was sitting slumped, with his arms folded and his blue shirt stretched tight across his back. He didn't bother turning around to acknowledge our presence. Reeves himself was sitting bolt upright on the other side of the desk, hands resting to either side of a pile of paperwork in the centre. He glanced from Emma to me.

I didn't think I'd ever seen him look calmer.

'Detective Beck. Detective *Turner*. Please have a seat.'

Emma took the middle one, next to Ferguson, leaving me on the end. That was fine. I'd resigned myself to that by now. In my own way, I was calm too – or rather, I'd pushed the tumult of emotions I was feeling as far down inside myself as I could manage. There was nothing I could do about it all right now. It was a tangle I'd have to attempt to undo at some point in the future, but for now, I just had to deal with this and take what was coming.

'Detective Turner,' Reeves said. His gaze was unwavering. 'You will have watched the news this morning, I assume?'

'Yes, sir.'

'How do you believe you came across?'

'Not well, sir.'

Ferguson snorted. I forced myself to keep my eyes on Reeves.

'Obviously,' I said, 'I don't have the benefit of DI Ferguson's extensive experience with media relations.'

It got a reaction, at least. Ferguson unfolded his arms and leaned forward to stare angrily at me.

'Who the hell do you think you are, Turner?'

'Have you found the fourteenth victim yet?' I said.

'Not yet, no.' He leaned back. 'We're still searching – doing our job. We've identified five sets of remains now. You'd know all this if you'd been paying attention to the case instead of assaulting relatives.'

'I didn't assault him.'

'Still,' Reeves interrupted, smiling politely and bringing the conversation back on point. 'You appreciate, at least, that it didn't go well?'

'Yes, sir. Not well at all.'

'I admire your ability to see your own flaws, Detective Turner, but it was considerably worse than that.'

'Yes, sir.'

'Can I ask what on earth was going through your head? What was it about Mr Townsend – the bereaved husband of one of the victims – that enraged you so?'

'I wasn't enraged, sir.'

'I'll be the judge of that. Explain, please.'

'I found Townsend's presence suspicious, sir. He drove right past the place where Blythe had been camping. I wanted to know what he was doing there.'

'It doesn't seem all that suspicious to me, Detective Turner. Blythe killed Townsend's wife, after all. It would seem natural to me that he'd want to be close to the case.'

'Yes, sir. But we'd just missed catching Blythe, probably by a minute or so at most, and I was frustrated with the efforts of the Moorton police. I think Blythe had help in escaping.'

Ferguson was shaking his head.

'More rubbish,' he said. 'The search is ongoing in Moorton. I talked to a DI Warren there earlier and they're confident Blythe is still in the area. There's no evidence he had help getting away and it doesn't make any sense. For what it's worth, Turner, he also said he thought you were weird.'

'I thought he was incompetent.'

Reeves tapped the desk gently with the knuckles of one hand.

'Back to Mr Townsend for the moment, I think.'

'To be honest, sir, I was suspicious of him before I saw him in Moorton yesterday.'

'Well, tell me everything.' He sounded almost kind.

I started with my first encounter with Townsend in the office downstairs, and the question he'd asked me about the bodies. I explained that he'd presented oddly, seeming too nervous, as though he knew more than he was letting on and was holding something back. *Just a feeling*, I said – and ignored Ferguson shaking his head again beside me. I told him about the strange, sadistic stories Townsend had written about Melanie West, his missing wife, the beginning of each one using the same words as the Red River letters. And then I finished by repeating myself.

'I can't say much more than that, sir. I've got a feeling there's something going on with Townsend. I don't know what.'

Reeves stared at me for a moment, not speaking.

'A *feeling*,' Ferguson said. 'You know, Turner, that's exactly your problem. This is why nobody likes you. It's all *feelings* with you. You walk around the whole time wrapped up in yourself, giving off this air that you care more than the rest of us do. And it's bullshit.'

I ignored him. I was still watching Reeves as he stared back at me. There wasn't anything else I could do now. He seemed to be evaluating me the same way Emma had downstairs. After a moment, he turned to her instead.

'Detective Beck,' he said. 'What do you make of your partner's behaviour?'

'I think he lost his head, sir. I don't think he'd deny that.'

'I wouldn't,' I said. 'And for the record, sir, this had nothing at all to do with Emma. Nothing about it is her—'

'At the same time, sir,' Emma inclined her head slightly, 'I want to point out that it was Will who tracked Blythe down in Moorton. We can all laugh at the idea of intuition, but if we hadn't followed Will's, then the Moorton police would still be looking in the wrong place. I followed it back there because I trust him.'

She was still facing forward, as though I didn't exist, but I felt a tingle in the air between us.

Oh Emma, I thought. *You don't have to do this. And for your own sake, you really shouldn't.*

'And what about Mr Townsend?' Reeves said.

'I don't know,' Emma said. 'I didn't see Townsend when he came to the department. But I do think the question he asked is strange, given what we've found – or what we haven't. I think the stories he's written are strange. And when I saw him in Moorton, I thought there was something off about his manner. But...'

There was a moment of silence in the office. I waited for her to finish that sentence. To tell Reeves about Anna and Rob, and that I was too invested in the case. That she hadn't known. That I was losing it and running with unsupportable hunches that were tripping us up, and that she was quite happy to cast me adrift if it meant she could remain part of the investigation.

'The truth is,' she said finally, 'I can't really explain about Townsend either. But I trust Will just the same. That's what it comes down to, sir. I have complete confidence in my partner.'

'Do you, DI Beck?'

'Yes, sir.'

Reeves stared at Emma, but she said nothing more. After what felt like a long time, he looked down at the paperwork on his desk, then leaned forward and looked up at me.

'Well then,' he said.

'Thank you,' I said, as Emma and I walked down the corridor. Ferguson had stayed behind with Reeves for the moment.

'Don't thank me,' she said.

'You didn't have to do that.'

'Yes, I know. Although for the avoidance of doubt, everything I said was actually true.'

'You could have told him about Anna. About Rob.'

'Well, so could *you*, Will.' She grimaced. 'Maybe you even *should* have. It doesn't have to all be up to me, does it?'

'No.'

'No. I'll tell you exactly what I'm going to do about the whole thing. Okay? About your friend in the hospital and all of that. I'm going to pretend I don't know a thing about any of it. If anybody asks, you never told me. Understand?'

'Yes,' I said. 'But for what it's worth, I'm sorry I didn't tell you at the beginning. I should have done.'

'No reason for you to tell me everything, is there?' She

shrugged. 'It's your life. Nothing to do with me. Absolutely none of my business.'

I didn't reply, even though we both knew she'd said it far too nonchalantly, and that she was hurt I hadn't confided in her sooner. It stung to hear her frame our relationship as apparently meaning so little.

'I'm sorry,' I said again.

'You should be.' She stopped suddenly and looked at me. 'And do you know what pisses me off the most, Will? It's actually not that you didn't tell me. It's *what* you told me. Because I always believed what Ferguson said just then back in the office. I always thought you *did* care a little bit more. And do you know what? That's one of the reasons I've stuck with you all these years. I suspected from the start that this case would get to you, but I thought it might be because of the *victims.*'

I looked back at her. Said nothing.

'But no.' She pulled a face. 'It was because of *you*, and what it all means to *you*. You and your friend. Well, I'm sorry, but your friend made the decision to do what he did, and so did you. In the meantime, we've got fourteen dead women who never had any choice at all, and this case is about *them*. It's not about your friend. And it's certainly not about you and your feelings. Fourteen dead women, Will. Think about that.'

She stared at me for a few seconds more, then shook her head and started walking again.

'So don't thank me, and don't say sorry to me,' she said. 'Just get your shit together.'

Thirty-Five

Although it was only mid-morning, it was obvious that the man who walked into my office had already been drinking. He wasn't reeling drunk, but there was something awkward and over-careful about his gait. As he approached the desk, I stood up ready to shake his hand, and could smell the whisky from metres away.

He was a big, barrel-chested guy, with long, unkempt black hair that had been swept back and appeared held in place mostly by grease. It was his face that really gave the drinking away. His cheeks looked swollen and damp, as though he kept his body so filled with poison that it was constantly leaking out of his pores.

'Detective Will Turner,' I said.

'Tom Clarke.'

Clarke's palm was as clammy as his face, and I had to resist the urge to wipe my hand on the side of my trousers after I'd shaken it. He stood there on the far side of my desk for a moment, clearly lost.

'Please.' I gestured. 'Have a seat.'

He did, albeit a little falteringly. I sat down opposite and was about to offer him a coffee when I realised he'd brought one in with him from the café across the street. His hand was shaking slightly as he put it down, and I suspected he'd doctored it before coming in here. Under the circumstances, I decided to turn a blind eye to that. Tom Clarke was – or had been – the husband of Ruby Clarke, the tenth known victim of John Blythe. Ruby had disappeared nearly five years ago. Unlike the relatives of earlier victims, Tom Clarke would have known almost immediately what had happened to her.

'I'm really very sorry we have to meet like this, Mr Clarke,' I said. 'I can hardly imagine what a difficult time this must be for you.'

Clarke nodded miserably.

'Have you found her?'

'I have to be very careful what I tell you,' I said. 'I want to be honest with you, and to keep you informed, and I can't stop you from talking to the press. But I'd prefer that you kept any details we discuss here between the two of us for the moment.'

'I'm not going to talk to the press.'

He looked up at me now, and seemed much fiercer than the cowed figure he'd presented when he'd first walked in. There was contempt at the very idea of speaking to the media. I could understand that. While I hadn't gone back and reviewed all the press coverage from the times of the abductions, I could imagine how it had been, for Clarke and all the others. While some outlets would have covered proceedings with tact, there would still have been numerous reporters trailing him, photographing him, harassing him for quotes and comments. It must have been intolerable.

'Thank you,' I said. 'I appreciate that.'

'Have you found her?'

'Yes.'

I'd had a chance to check the case file before he came to the office. We now knew the identities of five of the women found in the barrels in John Blythe's basement: Angela Walsh, Rebecca Brown, Emily Bailey, Anna Parker and Ruby Clarke. Ruby's remains had been identified overnight from distinguishing features listed in the file – in her case, an elaborate ankle tattoo.

Clarke was silent for a moment. It was difficult to read his expression. I wondered if he had even heard me. Perhaps he'd expected some kind of obfuscation on my part, and the speed of my answer had surprised him so much that he'd missed it.

'Yes,' I repeated. 'I'm very sorry.'

Clarke continued to stare back at me, then nodded to himself. He took a sip of the coffee and frowned. Reaching into his coat pocket, he brought out a hip flask.

'Do you mind?'

'No.'

'Thank you.'

He poured more whisky into the coffee, then screwed the cap back on the flask and put it away. He didn't touch the drink immediately. Instead, he put his big hands on the desk on either side of it and took a deep breath, gathering himself.

'Do you know,' he said, 'I've spent the last five years wondering how I'd react when I heard someone say that. I imagined all kinds of things. That I'd break down in tears. Or maybe there'd be some sense of relief. Because at least then we'd have a body to bury. At least then I'd know for sure that it wasn't all some kind of stupid mistake.'

'That's something,' I said. 'I know it's not enough.'

'But actually, the truth is I have no idea what I'm feeling. I don't know if it's anything different from how I felt before.' He shook his head. 'Are you sure it's her?'

'Yes. We're sure.'

'I knew deep down. Obviously.' Finally he picked up the coffee and took a sip. 'I saw the letter, way back, just after Ruby went missing. They showed it to me. Told me it was likely him, this man. And you know what the most terrible thing is? I wanted her to be dead then. At least, after a while. Because that was better than the alternative.'

I thought about Amanda Cassidy in the hospital, her partner waiting patiently by her side. She had been sexually assaulted, tortured, kept chained up for weeks, and had nearly died of dehydration. I understood what Clarke meant. Once you know that something horrible has happened to someone, and perhaps *is* happening to them, all you can really do is hope there's a limit to it. That there is an end.

'Did she suffer?' Clarke said.

His voice was so deliberately matter-of-fact that I knew how much the question mattered to him, even if it was something else he must have known the answer to deep down. Had Ruby Clarke suffered? Yes. Of course she had. But that wasn't a thing to hear or to say. In circumstances like these, we want to brush the truth away out of sight. To hear lies and to tell them. It's a kindness.

But I thought about what Emma had said earlier – that it wasn't about me – and I wondered if, by being kind to the living, we inevitably brushed the dead out of sight too. A woman had died horribly, and here I was, thinking of telling a man that it hadn't been as bad as it could have been. Ruby Clarke deserved better treatment than that, didn't she? It should be about her, not him.

In the end, those two conflicting instincts met halfway.

'We don't know,' I said.

He looked down at the desk again.

'What *can* you tell me? I want to know as much as I can.'

I told him what I could, even though most of it would already be familiar to him from the news reports. I told him about the bodies we'd discovered, and the efforts we were making to track down John Blythe, the man who had murdered his wife.

'We almost had him yesterday,' I said. 'In Moorton. You won't get this from the news, and it's not official, but we were close.'

'Do you think he's still in that area?'

'We don't know for sure. But I can promise you that we're doing everything in our power to locate him, and that we will find him soon. I'm certain of it. What you're seeing here today – we're a small cog in what's going on behind the scenes. There are several departments and a huge number of officers working on this. And he's just one man.'

'It's hard to think of him as that.'

'I know.' I hesitated. 'But it's true: that's all he is. Whatever he does, whatever he's called. He can't run forever and he can't hide forever. Sooner or later, we're going to get him. And ...'

But I trailed off as I noticed that Clarke was frowning again. He was distracted, staring at the desk. I followed his gaze and saw that it was Townsend's book that had caught his attention. Emma had left it on the desk, lying face down, so the back was visible, showing that large photograph of Townsend.

'What's that?' Clarke said slowly.

'It's nothing,' I said. 'My partner must have left it there.'

'May I ...?'

But Clarke was already reaching out, and I didn't reply. When he picked the book up, I expected him to turn it over and look at the title, maybe flick through the first few pages, but instead he just held it as it was, staring at the photograph on the back. When he looked up at me, the frown on his face had deepened.

'I know this man,' he said.

Thirty-Six

Townsend spent most of the morning in his front room with the curtains closed, watching the coverage of the hunt for Blythe on the television.

He'd winced last night when he first saw the footage of his confrontation with Turner – but at least the cameras hadn't captured their conversation, and in truth the coverage could have been much worse. Every time they replayed it, his heart still beat a little harder, but the media seemed much less interested than he'd feared they might be. He'd gone to sleep expecting it to be major news, but when he'd woken after a fitful night's sleep, it had already been relegated to supporting footage for 'police search potential suspects' cars in Moorton', and by mid-morning, it was being used as part of a collage of background colour while reporters talked about other things in voiceover. They were not interested in him.

Even so, he kept checking the curtains: opening them a little and peering down into the garden below. His flat was one quarter of a large Victorian house, and his front door was a long way from the street. Visitors had to walk all the way down a long concrete drive, through trees, and then down a set of old steps before they even reached his small garden. But of course, that hadn't stopped reporters when Melanie went missing. He still remembered how those knocks and phone calls had jabbed at him ten years ago, like an alarm clock jolting you when you're half asleep, and he couldn't help expecting it to happen again soon. His nerves were on edge.

He sat back down on the settee.

There was only one free seat, as the rest of it was piled high with old clothes, papers and books. He couldn't quite remember the last time he'd tidied or cleaned in here. After Melanie disappeared, he'd attempted to keep up some kind of pretence at normality, but over time that had faded away entirely. What was the point? The house had been gradually winnowed down to a utilitarian space: there was enough room for him to sit down in here; enough clear counter space in the kitchen to prepare a meal. The rest was dusty and messy. He put things down in random places and never picked them up again. It was a home where nothing had a home.

He shook his head.

The news wasn't helpful. Reading between the lines of the developments, the widespread belief appeared to be that Blythe had somehow evaded the police in Moorton, and the media focus was shifting slightly, moving into that period when they began to apportion blame. According to one reporter, 'questions are being asked' about why Blythe hadn't been apprehended yet, although it wasn't remotely clear who was asking them. Another had remarked upon 'a much heavier police presence today on the roads surrounding Moorton', with the insinuation that perhaps it had not been sufficient before. Which of course it hadn't. Before passing Frog Pond yesterday and encountering Turner, Townsend couldn't recall seeing a single police officer or vehicle on the roads at all.

The anger from that confrontation had passed now. In fact, it was hard to remember the emotion at all, apart from when he thought about Turner mentioning the stories – a ghost of the rage raised itself up then. But it was intangible and barely there. The man didn't understand what they meant, and Townsend could hardly blame him for that. He knew it must look like a strange and disturbing compulsion. The truth was that he'd been in tears every time he posted one of those stories online, but it was necessary. And if it hurt him to do it, and disgusted people to read them, wasn't that at least part of the point? He deserved every bit of that pain and revulsion. He was guilty of atrocities.

He wished that Turner hadn't mentioned the stories. Until that moment, he had been about to tell the man everything – to unload it all. Perhaps that would have been a mistake, but there was a sense that everything was coming to a head anyway. The end was approaching. As he'd walked around the house this morning, his legs had been weak and trembling, and for once he didn't think it was simply because of the weight that he'd felt bearing down on him for so long now. There was also the realisation that everything he'd done was going to be exposed. His crimes were about to be laid bare.

The all-too-familiar photograph of Blythe appeared on the television.

Where are you, you bastard? Townsend thought. *What are you doing right now?*

He walked down the hallway, through to his office. It was a small room and had been barely worthy of that title even before Melanie was abducted, never mind now. There was a glass computer table in one corner, the monitor humming softly away on the smeared surface. The black office chair pushed underneath it was speckled with mould. The smell of damp filled the air. It had spread in dots and flowery patterns over all four walls, and a portion of plaster below the window ledge had broken apart, its brown insides bulging out.

Let it, he thought. If the whole place was going to collapse, it might as well begin here. All three of his novels had been written in this room, and so it was only right that it was left alone now – that the place where it all began was allowed to succumb slowly to rot and decay, until it fell in altogether.

He walked over to the computer and nudged the mouse, and the monitor came to life. Given the damp in the room, it was a miracle the thing still worked at all; for a long time now, there had been condensation behind the glass in the top quarter of the screen. And the resolution was so low that it was hard to read any text on it. The words looked fuzzy. When you put your face too close to the screen, it seemed like the letters were fragmenting at the edges, coming apart and disintegrating.

He opened his email.

And there – finally – it was.

Townsend stared at the bold line at the top of the list for a long time, forcing himself to breathe steadily. He had been expecting this since first hearing the news, nearly three days ago now. Even so, the familiar random string of letters and numbers masquerading as an email address was almost too frightening to click on. Did he want to know?

No.

But he needed to, didn't he?

A file icon at the side of the message title indicated that the email had an attachment. He wouldn't look at that for the moment. The message itself would be enough to deal with for now. If he could be brave enough to open that and read it, then he could steel himself for the attachment later.

He clicked on the message and it opened in a new window.

DON'T BELIEVE EVERYTHING YOU READ.

He read the sentence again.

And then, not allowing himself to feel anything at all for the moment, he leaned forward and stared at the words, closer and closer, until the edges of the letters seemed to be flying apart like birds.

Thirty-Seven

'All right,' Emma said. 'I'll give you ten minutes. Tell me what you're thinking about Townsend.'

She spoke quietly, even though we were hunched on opposite sides of our desk in the corner of the investigation room, well out of earshot of the other officers. Ferguson was over on the other side. He kept glancing across at us – at me, really – with a look of contempt on his face. I wasn't going to give him the satisfaction of acknowledging him, and wasn't interested in what he thought about me right now. But even so, and even though Emma and I were still on the case, I was aware that we needed to tread carefully.

I'd already filled her in on what Tom Clarke had told me – that he'd encountered Townsend at a meeting for relatives of missing people, and that he'd had a conversation with the man that had unnerved him. Like me, Clarke had also intuited that there was something strange about Townsend.

'I don't understand what he's doing,' I said. 'Clarke lives miles away from here. So what on earth is Townsend doing turning up there?'

'Just passing through town?'

'Yeah, right. Out of all the support meetings in the world, he just happens to stop by one where another of Blythe's victims is attending. I'm not buying that. He targeted the place because Clarke was there.'

'Okay, perhaps so. But why?'

'I don't know. Not for support, though. And I bet you anything that he's been to see the others too – that he's been seeking out the other victims. But why? I can't figure that out.'

'No,' Emma said.

'It's strange, though, isn't it?'

She considered it. A part of her still wanted to disagree with me and downplay it, and if this had happened yesterday then she probably would have done. But this was one more detail – another connection; another coincidence – and it was one too many. I could tell that the image of Townsend searching out and haunting these groups was bothering her.

'Yes,' she said. 'All right, it *is* strange. But there might be a reasonable explanation for it. Maybe he just wanted to feel some sense of . . . I don't know. Kinship?'

'But never actually revealed who he was?' I shook my head. 'That doesn't make any sense to me. And another thing: what do we know about the Red River Killer? He liked taunting the survivors by sending those letters. And now we have Townsend seeking them out. Watching them. The whole thing makes me uneasy.'

'It's pretty thin.'

'It's cumulative,' I said. 'By itself, it's thin. But then there's the rest. *How* many *bodies have you found?* It gets stranger the more I think about it. He'd come in to see us because of his wife, hadn't he? Surely he'd only be concerned if we'd found *her*.'

'We've been over that.' She thought about it. 'Maybe the meetings he goes to are research of some kind. He used to be a writer, after all.'

'Still is. Don't think I've forgotten about those stories.'

'Oh, I'm well aware that you haven't.'

'But the point is,' I said, 'we're still one body down. And I'm more and more sure that Townsend was expecting that.'

I glanced over at Ferguson, who was deep in a fairly furious conversation with a couple of officers at his desk. His team had been stripping the interior of Blythe's house to its foundations, and they'd found nothing. The garden had been scanned: again, nothing. Which meant we had fourteen known victims of the Red River Killer, but only thirteen bodies, and no sign of the missing victim. Perhaps he'd disposed of her elsewhere, but the first victim, Rebecca Brown, was one of the bodies that had now been identified, and I didn't believe Blythe was the type to have altered his MO or made some kind of mistake during his spree.

Another explanation occurred to me now. And for a few seconds I stopped thinking altogether and let the repercussions of the idea run through my head.

'What if we over-counted?' I said quietly.

Emma frowned. 'Over-counted?'

'What if there are only thirteen bodies in Blythe's cellar because that's actually all the victims he killed? And the fourteenth was taken by someone else?'

It was Emma's turn to be silent for a moment.

'Fourteen letters, though,' she said.

'Yes. One for each of them. But didn't we say at the beginning that they seemed a little bit flowery for Blythe to have written?'

'*You* said that.'

'Well, we're a team. You can take credit for my successes as well as my failures. But look at it this way – what made the original teams finally believe the letters were written by the killer?'

Emma thought about it. I watched it dawn on her a second later.

'Shit,' she said. 'Melanie West's wedding ring.'

'Exactly. The letters were discounted at first. It was only when that one was sent that we began to take them seriously. There had been no evidence included before then.'

'But the style is the same. They were all written by the same person.'

'Yes,' I said. 'Just not by Blythe.'

'You think it's Townsend?'

I didn't answer. On one level, something about it made sense to me. It seemed at least to begin to pull the connections together: Townsend's nerves and guilt when I'd met him, as though some secret was weighing down on him; the stories he'd written, all beginning in the exact same way as the letters.

What if?

That's how writers often say they come up with their stories, isn't it? Asking a question and seeing where it leads them. I allowed myself to do that now. What if Jeremy Townsend had murdered his wife? That would explain why we were one victim short at Blythe's house. That was how he would have known we were missing a body, along with why he seemed nervous and guilty. And that was how he'd been able to include the wedding ring in the letter for Melanie. He'd written the others, too, planning all along to hide his wife's murder in the middle of an existing serial killer's spree.

But at the same time, something about the idea didn't fit. While it felt like I was circling the truth, there was still something I was missing. A problem with the whole theory. And after a moment, I realised what it was.

Emma was still waiting for an answer to her question.

You think it's Townsend?

'No,' I said. 'Because that's impossible.'

The first letter had been sent several years before Melanie West went missing. In itself, that wasn't an issue for me. People had planned murder on longer timescales than that, and they could often be a lot more cunning than you might expect them to be. Townsend – a talented writer, no less – could easily have been plotting things out that far ahead: writing the letters as the victims accrued; biding his time before including his wife among them. He was an intelligent man, and intelligent men are more than capable of that kind of long-term preparation.

The timescale wasn't the problem at all.

It was the foresight.

'Rebecca Brown was the first known victim,' I said. 'She

went missing in May 1999. But it's only with hindsight that we know she was taken by the Red River Killer. I can't remember for sure, but I imagine at the time it hardly even made the news. There was nothing to link it to any prior abductions. No evidence that it was the work of a serial killer – or a potential one, at least. Nothing to make it stand out.'

Emma could see where I was going.

'But the letter was sent anyway.'

'Exactly. The police received the first Red River letter long before Mary Fisher, the second victim, was abducted. I can buy the idea that Townsend decided on some long-term plan. I can't buy that he just happened to get that lucky. Whoever sent the first letter had to have known from the beginning that there was something unusual – something special – about Brown's disappearance.'

'But couldn't that be Townsend?' Emma said. 'We – you – think Blythe had help escaping from Moorton yesterday, and we know Townsend was there. Maybe he was involved with the whole thing from the start?'

I thought back to my impressions of Townsend upon meeting him that first time. Did he strike me as someone who might murder his wife? As much as you could tell: yes, of course he did; all sorts of people kill their partners, and many of them plan it out meticulously in advance. Townsend had been nervous, flustered. *Guilty.* So I could just about see him as an intellectual who had got out of his depth then realised his plan wasn't as foolproof as he might have thought. But could I see him aiding and abetting a multiple murderer over two decades?

'I don't think so,' I said. 'I don't think that's his story at all.'

'Interesting choice of words.'

'Is it?'

I was distracted, thinking all this through. None of it was clear right now, but I was convinced we were heading in the right direction. Blythe hadn't written those letters. And Townsend *was* involved somehow.

'Let's go back to the letter writer,' I said. 'Whoever it is, let's agree that they didn't just get lucky with Rebecca Brown. So they must have known what Blythe was doing. Either in on it too – a genuine accomplice – or just somebody who knew what he was capable of and had been keeping track of him. Either way...' I trailed off.

'Will?'

'Either way,' I said, 'that's a bond that must have developed a long time ago. We're looking for somebody from his past. Somebody from—'

'Moorton?'

'Yes. Somebody he grew up with.'

I turned my attention to the computer on my side of the desk. I loaded up the case file, then began to click through the reports we'd received until I found the ones I wanted.

Emma said, 'We don't know anything about his friends from back then. That information isn't going to be there.'

'I'm not looking for a friend.'

'Then...'

'Give me a second.'

On the screen, I had the list of earlier crimes that had been sent through from Moorton. A couple of days back, it hadn't been a priority, and I'd only scanned through them briefly, not particularly interested. I'd imagined that we would eventually find past murders that Blythe could be linked to – that he hadn't emerged fully formed – but at that point the focus had been on finding the man in the present. The rest could wait.

There were forty or fifty listings of unsolved offences, most of them burglaries or break-ins. None of those were likely to be our man, I thought. Blythe had always attacked his victims outdoors; he wasn't a home invader. Some vehicle thefts. Five rapes, over a period of several years. Two murders.

I clicked on the first.

As I scanned through the onscreen details, I felt a shiver run down my back.

'Jennifer Johnson,' I said. 'Found murdered on 21 August 1987. She was sixteen years old. Blythe would have been eighteen. The killer was never caught. Her body was found in an area north of the village, close to a spot known locally as Frog Pond.'

'Shit, Will.'

I looked up at Emma and gave her a sad smile.

'I don't remember clicking on this, but maybe I did. Maybe that's why the name Frog Pond stood out for me when I heard it from Carling. Jennifer Johnson must have been Blythe's first victim. That was why he returned to the scene. That was how whoever helped him knew where to pick him up.'

But how had *Townsend* known? I continued reading down the screen.

'She was pronounced dead at the scene,' I said. 'No sign of sexual violence. Found face down in the water with her throat cut.'

Emma was staring at her own screen now, reading the file for herself.

'The red river,' she said.

'Yes.'

And then I reached the next detail and stopped reading. The world receded around me. For a moment, there was just the words on the screen – the connection, blatant now, staring me in the face. All along I'd been focusing on the men. Blythe. Rob. Townsend. Me. I should have been thinking about the victims instead: the women who had suffered and died and who deserved to be kept at the heart of the investigation. The ones who should have been the focus of it all along.

I looked away from the screen, at the copy of Townsend's book on the desk.

'Shit,' Emma said, and I knew she had just reached the detail that had stopped me in my tracks. 'Shit, shit, shit.'

'Yes.'

I was still staring at Townsend's book. Thinking about the title. The subject matter. The dedication. *For Melanie, with all my love.*

'Johnson's body was found by her best friend, Melanie West.'

Thirty-Eight

With Blythe sleeping on the settee, and everything else in place, Bunting sat in the armchair and finally allowed himself to relax.

There was a lot left to do, of course, and any number of things that could still go wrong, but so far it had all worked out perfectly and his plot was unfolding exactly as he'd intended. In the beginning, the obstacles had seemed insurmountable, but they hadn't been. He'd overcome each of them in turn. That was the way it worked when you were clever. One task at a time and eventually it was all accomplished, just like writing a story was ultimately a simple matter of placing one word after another. *You should have had more faith in yourself*, he thought, and it felt good because it was true. He was smarter than all of them.

And as he often did in moments of calm, he thought about her.

Jennifer Johnson.

There was a time when he had been infatuated with her. For a start, there was that name – and it was always Jennifer, never Jenny. What appealed to him most about it was that it seemed to have come straight out of one of the comic books he used to lose himself in as a boy. There were exceptions, but so many of the characters in them had similarly alliterative names. Lois Lane and Lana Lang. Peter Parker. J. Jonah Jameson. Clark Kent – well, at least if you said it out loud. And so, Jennifer Johnson. It was a name that rolled off the tongue, with a small-town feel to it. If life really had been a comic book, she would surely have been an important character. Not the main one, obviously, as that part was reserved for him, but the superhero's partner in some unsuspecting way. An intrepid journalist, perhaps. A plucky lawyer.

In reality, she hadn't been beautiful. An artist drawing her would have had to slim down her body a little, sharpen slightly ordinary features and frame her hair differently. She wasn't the sort of girl who had boys chasing after her. But that was a positive thing, as Bunting had long ago recognised his own place in the pecking order. He was so far beneath it as to be practically invisible, and so Jennifer was attainable in a way that other girls clearly weren't. Or at least he could dream she was.

She had spoken to him once. In their early teens, she'd walked past him when he was sitting by himself on a bench in the street. *What are you reading?* she'd asked, and he'd shown her the cover of the comic he'd been engrossed in, his heart beating a little more quickly. *Nothing. Just this.* She'd stared at the comic blankly, and then nodded and said, *Okay, bye.* Not being rude, he decided at the time, just on her way somewhere.

He'd tried to speak to her again after that, but she'd cold-shouldered him each time. Not badly, though; not nastily. There were social pressures, he understood; she probably didn't want to be seen with someone like him, regardless of what she actually felt, but he was confident she'd change her mind eventually. After all, *she* wasn't that great either, was she? She wasn't so far above him. He began to resent her attitude. He took to following her sometimes, trying to work out whether he loved or hated her, but he was always careful, and she never knew, and nobody else did either.

Given what happened, he would realise later, that was incredibly fortunate. There could sometimes be advantages to being invisible.

One summer's day, he followed her to Frog Pond.

He didn't know that was where she was going at first. He

just spotted her wandering out of the village and decided he would go after her. It was a nice day, after all, and he had as much right to walk the country lanes outside the village as anybody. If he happened to bump into her... well, that was no crime, was it? So he followed her discreetly from a distance, a part of him hoping she might turn around and look over her shoulder – spot him a way back and maybe stop to say hello – but she never did. Perhaps if she had, everything would have turned out differently.

At one point, he rounded a bend in the lane and she had disappeared. It was only when he walked further that he spotted the trail and figured out where she must have gone. Frog Pond. He knew of the place, of course; all the local children did. He'd even been down there himself a few times, although always alone, never part of the congregations of kids that hung out there together, smoking and drinking and doing all the other things he imagined they did. That was clearly where Jennifer was heading that day. Maybe she was meeting someone. He'd looked around, but the lane was empty. No sign of anybody else.

Well – once again, he had a right to go there too, didn't he?

Even so, he'd waited a few minutes, so as not to look too suspicious, too obvious, when he arrived there after her. Then he'd set off, ambling slowly along the trail, taking his time, admiring the beautiful scenery and listening to the river as he drew closer. It really was a lovely day.

But when he reached Frog Pond, Jennifer wasn't there.

He'd looked around, curious as to where she might have gone. The trail continued on through the woodland for a while, but the terrain quickly became much more difficult, and there was nowhere worthwhile to head to in that direction. So where could she be? He'd walked back to the Pond and stood there quietly, breathing in the smell of that green water and trying to think.

And then he'd heard someone moving on the trail behind him.

Immediately he had known it wasn't her. It wasn't the sound itself so much as the feeling of fear at the back of his neck: the kind of primal, ticking sensation you'd feel if a dangerous wild animal was nearby. He had turned around slowly and seen nobody. Then, very quietly, he had stepped back out on to the trail and looked right and then left – and there, disappearing further into that hazardous woodland, he'd seen John Blythe.

The older boy never looked back. If he had, then once again things would have turned out very differently.

Instead, Bunting watched him moving away. He was more frightened now. There was nothing hurried about Blythe. He seemed completely casual and almost indifferent to his surroundings. But Bunting could sense that *something* was wrong, not with Blythe himself, but with the world around him. He could feel Jennifer's absence. She should have been here, but she wasn't. Blythe had been, and now he was gone. He could hear the noise of the river, but other than that, the woods were empty and silent.

He had walked tentatively back the way he'd come. Close by, he had found the break in the trees that led to the bank of the river itself, and stepped nervously through. He had seen Jennifer Johnson, lying at an awkward angle, with her head and shoulders in the water and blood streaming away in the river.

And then, as the wood seemed to come alive with horror all around him, he had run.

Bunting looked at Blythe now.

Sleeping – imagine that. After everything that had happened. Blythe was in a seated position, with his arms folded and his chin resting on the top of his chest, and he was breathing slowly and steadily. He seemed completely calm and relaxed. The man was truly an astonishing creature. If anything, Bunting was more in awe of him than ever.

Not that he blamed Blythe for being tired, of course. The last few days had presumably been wearing for him. Bunting himself was completely exhausted, but he wouldn't have dared risk going to sleep right now. The adrenalin wouldn't have allowed it anyway, but he didn't trust in his safety. That was ridiculous on one level, as Blythe could easily have killed him by now if he'd wanted to, but it made total sense deep down. Blythe wasn't the kind of man you let your guard down in front of. You might have the tamest lion in the world, but it was still an animal at heart, and it would respond accordingly to mistakes or displays of weakness.

Blythe had always been different; Bunting had recognised that long before he'd found Jennifer Johnson's body and come to understand exactly *how* different. He'd often see the older boy around, albeit only ever from a distance. Blythe had been solitary and friendless just like Bunting, but the similarities between them had ended there. Blythe had clearly never felt misunderstood the way Bunting did. He had neither wanted nor sought out friendship. Not only had he been at ease with his loneliness, he'd actually seemed *protective* of it. Watching him as a teenager, Bunting had at first felt a sense of kinship, but he'd known deep down that he was flattering himself. He'd wished he could be as self-reliant as John Blythe was. Wished that he too could somehow not want all those things he didn't have.

Or that he might simply be able to take them.

That was ultimately why he hadn't reported what he'd seen at Frog Pond that day. It was officially Jennifer's friend, Melanie West, who found the body, an hour or so later, by which point Bunting had been back in the village, sitting on his favourite bench and staring at a comic that he was only pretending to read while his mind ran over what had happened and what it meant. The fear that someone might have seen him there. The thrill he realised it gave him to have such knowledge. The possibilities it offered him.

The secret power.

The Monster.

In all the years since, aside from their email communication, Bunting had never spoken directly to John Blythe. Never had a conversation with him in the flesh. And so it was slightly bewildering to realise now that he'd spent most of the night doing precisely that. After Blythe had seen what was in the boot of the car, he'd looked at Bunting with curiosity at first, and then a kind of new-found respect – as much as a man like Blythe was capable of such a thing. Again Bunting was wary of flattering himself. He didn't think Blythe saw him as anything like an equal. But he was *interested*: intrigued enough to leave him alive for the moment – and even to follow his lead in some ways. Bunting had explained what needed to be done, and Blythe had taken direction from him, doing as he was told in order to accomplish the tasks ahead of them. Then he had listened carefully as the pair of them sat here in the front room and Bunting had shown and told him . . .

Well.

Not *everything*. Just the parts of the story he needed to know.

That story would be coming to an end soon. He was nearly there. *On the home run*, he thought. That was a good line, wasn't it? The last couple of days had taught him he was full of them.

With Blythe sleeping – for now – Bunting turned his attention to the laptop in front of him, and began to put the finishing touches to his life's work.

Thirty-Nine

It was early afternoon when Emma and I parked up outside Jeremy Townsend's house.

With our encounter yesterday making the news, I was nervous that we might be met by a phalanx of journalists clamouring for some sidebar story to accompany the main coverage on Blythe. But the street was empty. Perhaps there was too much other excitement right now to bother with something as inconsequential as a man whose life had been ruined by it.

Even so, the nerves remained. After the way I'd behaved, we were pushing our luck by coming here, and by mutual agreement we had decided not to mention this little excursion to Ferguson or Reeves. But as Emma pulled up by the kerb, any trouble I might get into with the department was of far less concern to me than getting to the heart of this and uncovering the truth. I could feel in my chest that we were close to doing so.

'Ready?' Emma said.

'Yes. Ready.'

'Not going to attack him again, are you?'

I glanced at her, then returned the small smile she was giving me.

'Not making any promises,' I said.

We got out of the car. The afternoon was warm, with just the slightest of breezes, and it suited the street: a leafy residential road in a suburb to the west of the centre, close to the canal that Melanie West had walked home along every day until her disappearance. Townsend's house was out of sight behind a high wall, with a concrete drive winding down. At the bottom, Emma and I were faced by an enormous old building, the huge bricks stained black. Stone steps led down beneath a couple of trees that seemed to be holding hands above. It was idyllic here. As quiet as the entire area was, Townsend's house felt like a pocket of even deeper calm.

Emma knocked on the door. I glanced at the floor above and saw a shadow appear behind one of the windows. The curtains moved slightly. He was home, at least. Whether he'd talk to us was another matter entirely. But after a moment, the shadow moved away from the window and I heard feet on the stairs, then finally Townsend opened the door.

In our previous encounters, I'd gathered a number of impressions of him. In the first: nervous, furtive, guilty. And then yesterday, he'd seemed panicked and scared, as though he'd been caught doing something he shouldn't – at least before the anger had surfaced anyway. All of it had made me deeply suspicious of him. But now that I thought I understood it all a little better, I could see the nerves and the guilt in a different light. Standing on his doorstep now, he seemed timid. He was almost shaking.

And I felt enormously sorry for him.

'Mr Townsend,' I said. 'First of all, I want to apologise for my behaviour yesterday.'

He looked down and shook his head. 'There's no need.'

'There's every need. It was wrong of me. I was overemotional and too deeply involved in the investigation. I can't imagine what it's been like for you.'

'No,' he said slowly. 'You really can't.'

'And in confidence, I have a connection with one of the other victims myself. It's no excuse, but it's there. We nearly caught Blythe yesterday, you see, and I was very upset that we didn't. I still am.'

'I understand.' He was still looking down. 'Is that the only reason you're here?'

It was obvious from his body language and tone of voice that he knew the answer to that question. He'd been expecting this – or something like it – for a long time. Now that it was happening, he seemed scared, but also strangely resigned. Perhaps, after all these years, it might even be a relief to explain it to someone.

'No,' I said. 'It's not. Can we come in, please?'

He still didn't look up, but after a moment he nodded.

As we followed him in, it reminded me a little of walking into Blythe's house. The inside of Blythe's property had seemed like a testament to his madness: the accoutrements of an ordinary life arranged in a chaotic fashion that only made sense to the occupant. The clutter in Townsend's house was far more prosaic, but still revealing in its own way. It was the home of a man who threw little away, and who no longer took the time to clean anything that wasn't necessary. Most of the settee was covered with clothes, leaving enough room for a single person to sit and watch television. Everything was dusty and old, and the air itched in my nostrils.

And so, while superficially different, the house represented Townsend just as well as Blythe's did. With his crumpled trousers, and the shirt with the old cardigan over it, he looked like a man from another era: one whose life had stopped at a particular moment and never carried on. His house seemed as much of a mausoleum as he did.

'Here,' he said. 'Let me clear a space.'

After a minute, he'd uncovered enough room on a second settee for Emma and me to sit down. He took a seat in what was clearly his usual place, then rubbed his face thoroughly. When he finally looked at us, I could see the blood spreading back across the pale skin. He seemed very old indeed.

'I know why you're here,' he said.

'Yes.' I glanced down at the book I was holding, the one he'd already seen in my hands, and then back up at him. 'Why don't you tell us what happened in your own words?'

He smiled at that. A horribly empty smile.

'My own words,' he said. 'Yes. That's exactly what happened.'

Forty

His own words.

In real life, a man named John Blythe murdered a young girl named Jennifer Johnson, and her body was discovered by her best friend, Melanie West.

It was an experience that haunted Melanie from that point on: a pivotal moment in her life. How could it not be? She was never able to leave it behind entirely.

I've never told anybody this, but I write poetry. Do you want to read some?

In an attempt to explore and make sense of what happened to her friend – and also to herself – Melanie began to write as a teenager. Poetry. Short prose pieces. Later, she would take up photography instead, always focusing on natural scenes. That was one of the reasons she loved the walk along the canal at the end of the day. There were similarities there to Frog Pond and to the river where the murder had happened. There was the smell of the water and the sight of that lush green undergrowth. When Townsend had visited Frog Pond, he had immediately thought of her photographs and realised how reminiscent they were. It was his wife's way of touching a traumatic experience from a safe distance.

And it had always been the same. Whatever the medium she employed, Melanie had spent her whole life exploring the moment when her best friend had died, and the place where it had happened. She had always been either pushing it away or approaching it from an oblique angle, confronting it and resolving the thoughts and emotions at a level she could be comfortable with. What had happened there absorbed her. Creatively, it defined her.

Like her friend Jennifer, Melanie had always loved reading, and that love eventually took her away from Moorton all the way to a university further south, where she studied English literature and found an entirely different kind of love. She found *him*. Townsend had been shy and socially awkward, but he was in love with writing and stories too, and was already something of a rising star in the department. There was an innocence to him that had attracted her. His life had never been touched by any real tragedy at that point – certainly not to the extent that hers had, though he didn't know that at the time, of course. It was a long time before she talked about Jennifer outside of her poetry. All he knew when they started seeing each other was that she admired his writing, and he hers, and that despite their differences there was a deep connection between them. He lived for that look in her eyes when she'd first read his story and told him she liked it. That moment when he had felt worthwhile.

In the years that followed, he finished his first two novels, and they were published, and both were dedicated to Melanie. In truth, he had nobody else to dedicate them to. Regardless, the sentiment was correct but incomplete. Not only had both been written *for* her; they had been written *because* of her. Before their relationship, his writing had indeed lacked focus. During it, he became inspired. The books wouldn't have existed without her, and it was entirely right that they be given to her.

But then he had begun to struggle.

Those books sold averagely well, and he found it harder and harder to come up with new ones. The problem, he realised, was that he had no *ideas*. There would be times when he'd sit and read Melanie's poetry and it would move him to tears. Despite her comparative lack of success, there was a depth to her work that he could never hope to equal. She was the better writer, if only because she had a well of experience inside her to draw from, when his own well had always been empty. With a new contract to negotiate, and with every day's writing failing him, he became increasingly desperate. While Melanie was a flow of poetry, he was two middling books about nothing, and that was surely all he ever would be. Without writing, what exactly did he have? How would she look at him? And yet the harder he tried to find a story within him, the clearer it became that there was nothing there to find.

And so, in the end, he had done something that would haunt him forever. He had made that first mistake of many. Like the ones that followed, it was a mistake he made for love, really – for that look in her eyes – but that fact made it no less forgivable.

He had taken a story that didn't belong to him and tried to make it his own.

'I didn't copy anything she'd written,' Townsend said quietly.

Except that was a flimsy excuse, and he knew it. Children felt the need to add footnotes to admissions of guilt; adults should not. If it was all going to come out finally, then he needed to be honest.

'I'd read all of it, though. And I *used* it. I used it to give me an insight into what had happened and how it felt. There's no way I could have written what I did without it. The murder and finding the body – it ran all the way through Melanie's work. You couldn't always see it directly, but it was the skeleton on which it was all built. So Melanie's work became the skeleton for my own novel. Her story, but told in my words. Except that really it was *still* all her. You don't have to copy a work directly to steal it. I stole something incredibly important from her that I had no right to take.'

Not plagiarism of words, he thought. Plagiarism of a soul.

The two police officers had been sitting listening quietly while he'd explained what had happened. They remained silent for a moment now. Turner was staring down at the book he was holding. Emma Beck was looking across the room at him.

'Did Melanie know?' she asked.

'Not at first, no. She knew I was working on something, but by then she'd stopped looking at my writing until it was finished. Sometimes not until the final copies arrived. She was a writer too, after all. She knew that things change. You edit stuff to get it right.'

He wanted to laugh at that. It was an easy observation, but it was true: if only it was that simple to edit your own real-life stories, rather than just living them once and being stuck with the consequences forever. There was so much he would have changed. And of course, writing that book had only been his first betrayal. He watched now as Turner held it in his hands, looking at the back cover: the photograph of the man Townsend had once been. Finally the detective looked up.

'How did she react?'

Townsend closed his eyes.

'She never said anything.' Was that the hardest part of it all? It might have been, if nothing else had happened afterwards. 'She liked the book. She said it was good. But I never knew what she really thought, even though it must have been obvious to her what I'd done. Sometimes I tell myself that she didn't mind. She was a writer too, after all, and there's that saying – that a writer has to have a sliver of ice in their heart. Whatever happens to them or to people they know, it's fair game to be used. Melanie would have understood that. Maybe she even thought that having her in my life meant the story was partly mine too.'

He opened his eyes.

'But other times I remember how it seemed the light in her eyes had gone out when she looked at me. Maybe that's just hindsight, though. Because of what happened.'

That was the most important thing. He would never know for sure what Melanie thought of his book, so he was free to imagine anything. He could picture the best and allow the guilt to lift from him a little. But she did go missing and he was responsible for that, and that knowledge always brought the guilt back to him again. Because there was no escaping the consequences for her of what he'd done.

Turner was looking at him with something close to pity now.

'You think your wife was taken because you wrote about what happened?'

'Yes.' Townsend nodded. 'I *know* she was. I changed a lot of the details. I made the dead character a boy, a man. But somehow... he knew. The man who did that all those years ago. He must have known Melanie's name from the reports at the time. Perhaps he kept track of her all these years. And what I did made him angry.'

Turner was silent for a moment. Then he placed the book down to one side of him, leaned forward and stared at the floor.

'You know,' he said, 'a few days ago, I'd have said that was a ridiculous idea. Because there's never been any evidence that the Red River Killer *ever* targeted his victims for a specific reason. There are no obvious connections between the women he abducted. And believe me, we've looked. There's never been any indication that it's *personal* for him, at least in that sense. I don't think it's a crazy idea now, though, but I do think you're wrong. There's still no evidence.'

'It's not a coincidence.'

'No,' Turner agreed. 'It's not. I think *Blythe's* victims were chosen at random, but I don't think your wife was taken by him at all. I think we're looking for somebody else. Someone who knew what Blythe did at Frog Pond all those years ago, and who's followed him since. I think this other man is the one who wrote the letters that were sent to us, and that he's the one who abducted your wife. And I think you know more about him than you're telling us.'

Turner looked up.

'Don't you?' he said.

His expression was less hostile than yesterday; today it was tinged with sadness. It was more weary. But despite the lack of anger there, it was similarly intense, and Townsend knew there would be no escaping from it. He was going to have to tell them. Even though he had known that deep down from the moment they'd arrived, the idea still seemed impossible, and for a moment the words wouldn't come. He could feel himself trembling.

'Tell me about the stories, Jeremy,' Turner said.

'The stories?'

'Those horrible stories about Melanie and what she was going through. Why did you do that to yourself? Was it out of guilt?'

Townsend shivered, unable to look away from Turner's gaze. He thought about it. The stories. The pain. The guilt. All of it together threatened to overwhelm him. And it was only going to get worse from here, once they knew. But there was no choice now. He couldn't trust himself to talk sensibly or carefully, so he just spoke without thinking.

'Guilt,' he said quietly. 'Yes, exactly that. The stories are part of my punishment for everything.'

'Whatever you did, Jeremy,' Turner said, 'stealing Melanie's story, if that's how you think of it, you don't need to punish yourself as much as that. And I think even you know that.'

Townsend looked down at his hands and willed them to stop shaking. After a second, miraculously, they fell still. *You don't need to punish yourself as much as that.* Turner had no idea. No idea about what he'd done. No idea about all the people who had suffered because of him.

He looked back up again and forced himself to speak.

'No,' he said. 'The stories are a punishment from *him*.'

Forty-One

As Townsend led us along the corridor, I was still trying to make sense of what he'd told us.

On one level, it appeared simple. He'd written a book based on Melanie's experience as a teenager of finding her friend's body. He – and more importantly, *she* – had been punished for that. I could understand the guilt he felt: that he had taken a story belonging to someone else and terrible things had happened as a consequence.

What I couldn't understand was why he hadn't told us before.

However guilty he felt about this apparent betrayal of his wife, what he'd done was no crime. And if he'd approached the police and revealed what he knew, it would have opened up an important new line of enquiry. We'd have connected the Red River Killer to Moorton and Jennifer Johnson, reopened that old investigation and possibly even identified Blythe as a suspect. Townsend might have saved lives. The only thing keeping a lid on the anger I felt was that he clearly *knew* all that. It was part of the explanation for the guilt that was so obviously weighing him down.

So why hadn't he come forward?

He pushed open a door ahead of us. We followed him into a small room, an office of sorts. If anything, it was even more untidy than the rest of the house. Piles of cardboard boxes filled most of it, their sides damp and creased. The air in here stank of mould. Looking around, the walls were dappled with it.

'What's going on, Jeremy?' Emma said.

Townsend didn't answer. In the only clear space in the room, an old computer was humming on a dirty glass desk. The monitor above it was on standby. Townsend reached out to move the mouse by the side of the keyboard, but then hesitated and stared into the black display for a few seconds.

'The horror of not knowing,' he said quietly. 'I used to go to meetings for missing people – meetings where the relatives of the other victims went. I wanted to see and hear them. Their faces. The way they spoke. I needed to find out if they knew more than they were letting on – if they were just pretending, the way I was. But they never were. I'm sure of that. All along, it was only ever me that knew for certain.'

Finally he nudged the mouse and the monitor came to life.

An image of a woman filled the screen. It was a head-and-shoulders shot. She was lying with her head turned to one side, a blindfold around her eyes. Beneath her, a spread newspaper covered whatever she was resting on.

My skin began to crawl. However reluctantly, I'd seen popular movies with similar images in them, and as shocking as they could sometimes be, there was always something far more horribly jolting at the sight of the real thing. It didn't matter how well made a film was, or how convincing the actors and special effects were, you could always tell the difference when you saw real people and real suffering. It hit you on a deeper level. And from that sensation alone, I knew immediately that this image was real.

Townsend touched the screen gently, as though he wanted to reach into the photograph and smooth the woman's loose strands of hair. And just as I knew the picture was genuine, I also understood who I was looking at.

'It came this morning.' He pointed at the date on the newspaper in the corner of the image. 'You can see it was taken yesterday. He used her camera – the one she had with her when she went missing. That's why the resolution isn't so good.'

'*Yesterday?*'

'Yes.' Townsend nodded, his hand falling to his side. 'She's alive. She's been alive this whole time.'

The three of us stood in silence for a few moments. I was trying to take the information in, and Townsend – presumably – was thinking back over the last decade of his life. Melanie West was alive. It was impossible for me to accept. She was alive, and Townsend had known all this time...

I looked at the photograph again. The question came urgently. 'Where is she, Jeremy?'

'I don't know.'

My heart was pounding. I wanted to grab him, shake him, but forced myself not to. Wherever Melanie was, she was clearly in danger. I had to keep calm. We had to find her.

I took out my phone.

'You need to tell us, Jeremy. *Right now*. Everything.'

'Yes,' he said. 'I know.'

As we waited for other officers to arrive, Townsend talked.

The first email had arrived a few months after Melanie went missing. By that time, the Red River letter had been delivered, along with his wife's wedding ring, and a connection with earlier abductions had been established. He had known what had happened. Or at least he'd thought he did. His wife had been abducted and murdered and was gone from his life, and he was alone.

It was difficult for him to remember quite how black those weeks had been. When he tried thinking about it, all he could really dredge up was the crawling horror of it all. Things had been awful and devastating, or else they had been surreal, and either way there was nothing worth remembering there. It had been a period in which Melanie was missing, and then she was dead, and if he hadn't even begun to come to terms with that then at least the world had stopped swaying quite so violently and he had been able to stand. Then the first email had appeared, taking his legs away again.

He opened it for us now, and then stood back so we could read it.

Mr Townsend
By now you will have received my letter and my GIFT to you of the ring that your wife will no longer be requiring. You will know the truth about what happened, but I am here now to tell you that truth is a LIE and just a TALE that I told for the benefit of OTHERS. I would apologise, but the reality is that it is YOU who owes ME an apology, as you will soon understand.
I want to tell you another story about a girl named Melanie. She saw something she shouldn't have done, and told something she shouldn't, and she became briefly FAMOUS as a result of taking what was MINE, what belonged to ME, and pretending it was HERS. And even worse, her inadequate husband then took what was MINE and tried to make it HIS. For that, you will SUFFER, I promise you. You will SUFFER for the rest of your life, because if YOU DON'T then SHE WILL.
 I enclose a photograph as evidence of these words. You will NOT go to the police. I will be watching to make sure you don't. You will NOT trace this email or this photo, as I know more about technology than you and I have been very clever. If you want her to live then you WILL WAIT for further instructions. If you do not, then she will go into the RED RIVER cursing your name.

Townsend stood quietly as Emma and I read. There was an attachment. I clicked on it; the image that appeared was all but identical to the one Townsend had received this morning.
'They're all like that,' he said.
More than ten years, I was thinking. *More than ten years.* She'd been alive the whole time. I couldn't comprehend it.
'How many have there been?'
'Fourteen more, after the first. One for each of the stories he sent me. And then the new message today. Click back to the folder. They're all there, along with the attachments.'

I did so, opening each message in turn and reading what was there, then viewing the attachments. The photographs blurred into one after a while. All that really changed was the date in the corner of the newspaper the man used as backdrop. Proof – as he had promised – that Melanie would remain alive so long as Townsend did exactly what he was told.

According to the second email, that had involved publishing the short stories that were sent to him.

'They had to be under my own name,' Townsend said. 'I couldn't bring myself to do that. Not exactly. But the slight change seemed good enough for him, and I was never going to publish under my own name again anyway; that was part of the deal. And it's not like it mattered. People did find them. *You* found them. He wanted to destroy my reputation and hurt me, and he did both. Every single one of them tore me apart inside to put online. But I did it anyway.'

Townsend was staring past us at the computer screen.

'And you decided not to report this?' I said.

His gaze still fixed on the screen, he shook his head slowly.

'I tried to track the emails. I even paid for an expert to help – although I scrubbed the content of the message first. She told me that whoever had sent it was using some kind of anonymous server and that it was impossible to trace. She said even the police wouldn't be able to. I couldn't send the photographs to her, but I did my best with them myself. The data had all been filtered off. There was nothing.'

I was almost shaking trying to take all this in. He had published the book based on Melanie's experience, and she had been abducted because of it. For over ten years, he had dealt not only with the secret guilt from that, but also the guilt and pain of this private correspondence from the man who had done these things, and who had forced him to publish those hateful stories to punish him. Bearing it alone the whole time.

At that point, I really was about to grab him: clutch fistfuls of his cardigan and demand more, even if he had nothing more to tell. Because whatever he'd been through, as unimaginable as it was, people had died while he remained silent – *Anna* had died – and Melanie was still out there somewhere. She had been out there for over ten years, suffering God only knew what, and we needed to find her.

I took a step towards him.

'Why? Why did you go along with it?'

'Because I'd betrayed her once already, and I couldn't do it again.' Townsend was still staring at the screen, oblivious to my anger. 'I had to sacrifice everything for her. I had to keep her safe.'

Finally he looked at me.

'I did it out of love,' he said simply.

I don't know what I would have done then, but behind me, I heard the computer beep once. And when I turned round, I saw that a new email had arrived.

Forty-Two

Blythe was standing by the cellar door, the knife in his hand.

'I want to go down now.'

He was looking at the old padlock that held the door shut, the key for which was in Bunting's pocket. Blythe had been amenable enough up until now, and had accepted Bunting's appeals to wait, but it was clear from his body language that time was up. The man was utterly still, staring at the lock that was keeping him from the woman below as though it was the only thing in the world.

Bunting was sitting on the settee, still working on the laptop.

'Wait a little longer,' he said.

'No.' Blythe sounded blank. 'Now.'

Bunting glanced over again. This time, he noticed the way Blythe's jaw was clenched. He was turning the knife around in his hand as though he might attack the door with it at any second. Not just the door, of course. Blythe's interest had worn out, and his patience along with it. If Bunting didn't open the door right now, he could tell the Red River Killer was going to turn on him.

'All right.' He took the key out of his pocket. 'Here.'

He threw it through the doorway. Blythe caught it and immediately undid the lock.

'Just don't start without me,' Bunting called. 'I want to see this.'

But Blythe was already heading down. *Shit*. Bunting turned

his attention back to the laptop – back to the story – and wondered if it was ready. It needed to be; it was going to be the last.

I want to tell you a story about a girl named Melanie...

In each of the other stories, he'd explored a huge variety of possible scenarios following Melanie West's abduction, all of which he had known Townsend would find torturous and painful to read and then be forced to publish. And yet none of those scenarios had been remotely accurate. Whereas this – finally – was as close to the truth as he could allow himself. In many ways, it was the most horrific one of all. It was the tale of a special victim, taken for a specific reason, who had been kept alive for years in order to torment the man who had stolen something that didn't belong to him and tried to make it his own. It was a story of prolonged hope that ended, finally, with that woman's vicious murder.

After all these years, it was Bunting's final revenge on Jeremy Townsend for taking what had always belonged rightly to *him*. It would have to be good enough.

He found a random line in the first paragraph of the story and typed quickly. *SIMON BUNTING 23 CROSS STREET HE'S HERE HELP ME.* Then he pressed send.

Immediately he felt the message flying free, and was aware of the sudden inevitability of it all now. There was no going back. There hadn't been from the beginning, he supposed, but everything would accelerate from here. He had very little time left.

He shut down the secure browser and took one last look around the living room.

He was ready.

Time to go down to the cellar.

He had always written stories.

When he was a teenager, his parents had thought it was a childish pursuit and had never supported him. He could remember his father reading one in disgust – but then he'd always disgusted his father, hadn't he? And then there had been all the rejections over the years for the stories he'd submitted. Throughout it all, he had never given up hope and had continued to have faith in his own talent and ability. In the end, he realised now, he had done something considerably better and more remarkable than any of the authors of the books that lined his shelves.

Most books and stories were safe, discrete things. They existed solely in words on the paper glued between the covers of a book or across a handful of pages in a magazine. There was a beginning, a middle and an end, all read in order, and once the story was finished it was contained and could be placed to one side. Over the years, Bunting had begun to understand that his personal genius lay in a different direction.

He had begun his project tentatively. There had never been a Red River Killer. There had been Blythe and the things he did, but it was Simon Bunting who had created the character, building him up piecemeal from the clay provided to him, fashioning him through the letters he sent. Bunting had built a story using real people. And rather than it being trapped between the covers of a book, it was spread through thousands of newspaper articles and online comment threads, and alive in the minds and fears of people everywhere. It was a story composed from countless fragments, its chapters not laid out in order but interwoven throughout the psyche of a whole country.

He had transformed an ordinary killer into a *story*.

Now it was time to give that story the ending it deserved.

When he arrived down in the cellar, his heart was beating hard. Blythe was leaning over Melanie West, the knife in his hand. Melanie remained blindfolded, with her hands and feet bound together, but she was awake now. Bunting could hear her talking.

'What's going on?' she said. 'What's *happening*?'

God – he was actually going to miss her. It surprised him how calm she sounded. But then he'd always treated her well, hadn't he? They'd always got on together. And although the last couple of days had seen a substantial variation in their routine, she had no reason to suspect she was in any immediate danger. She didn't realise that Blythe was poised above her, a knife in his hand, his arm tensed, his gaze searching out the first place to stab her with it.

Goodbye, Melanie, Bunting thought.

The End.

He brought the wrench down on Blythe's head with as much force as he could manage.

Part Five

Forty-Three

Statement by Simon Bunting
Date: Thursday 30 June 2016

I grew up in Moorton, but have no memory of ever
meeting John Blythe during my time there. To
my knowledge, I have never encountered him in
this city either. Equally, I have only ever been
peripherally aware of the Red River murders,
as I find media coverage of such horrific crimes
prurient, distasteful and upsetting. I actively
avoid such reports. I had not read or watched the
news recently, and had no idea of the developments
in that particular case.

On 29 June, I was off sick from work with a
headache. This morning, I was better, but phoned
in sick again anyway. I decided to use the time
to visit my parents' graves in Marwood Cemetery
in Moorton, as I often do. I therefore became
aware of the police presence in Moorton itself,
and was stopped at a checkpoint by an officer who
can corroborate this account. However, I had no
idea of the reason behind it, and, frankly, little
interest. After visiting my parents' graves, and
because the weather was reasonable that day, I
decided to avoid the congestion in the village

and instead drive home along back roads. I
estimate this will have been late morning or early
afternoon, but can't be sure of the time.

A short distance north, I saw a man with a
backpack standing by the side of the road, waving
his arms at me for help. He was dressed like a
hiker or a camper, and looked as though he had
been living rough. I did not recognise him at the
time, but now understand this man to have been
John Edward Blythe. A woman was lying motionless
in the road at his feet. As I approached in my
car, the man stepped further out, to the extent
that I might have struck him if I continued. There
was little time to think, and anyway, my instinct
was to stop. The first impression I had of the
scene was that the woman had been hurt, perhaps
having been hit by another vehicle, and that the
man was trying to flag down assistance. I would
always want to help in such circumstances, and so
I stopped the car.

I had not connected the situation with the
police activity in the village, and at that point
sensed no threat, so stepped out of my vehicle to
see what had happened. The man grabbed me almost
immediately and held a knife to my throat. He
was very strong, and the level of violence was
so shocking that it actually took a moment for
the fear to set in. I can't remember the man's
exact words, but it was obvious he was threatening
me, and when I recognised that he had a knife, I
became convinced I was going to die. I tried to
keep calm, and told him to take the car but please
not hurt me. He ordered me to help him get the
woman into my vehicle.

As I approached her, I realised her hands were
bound and she was blindfolded. At that point, I

could not tell whether she was alive or dead. I
had no choice but to do as he asked, and while I
deliberately took my time in the hope that another
car would arrive at the scene, the road remained
empty the whole time. The man opened my boot and
made me place the woman inside. He took my car
keys and told me to get in the driver's seat,
which I did. He then sat behind me, returning the
keys to me and telling me to drive.

He gave me directions throughout the entire
journey. He still had the knife, and he told me
that if we were stopped by police, he had nothing
to lose and would kill me and then himself. I
was torn between hoping for assistance and fear
of encountering some kind of blockade. As it
happened, by following his directions, we didn't
see a single police officer or vehicle. Given the
heavy presence in the village itself, this seemed
surprising to me, although the man seemed to know
the area very well.

I do not remember where we drove, partly because
I was very afraid, and partly because the man was
directing me down seemingly random roads, some
major, some minor. He seemed intent on losing us,
although his motivations were not clear, as for
the most part he was rambling and incoherent. I
could not make sense of much of what he said, and
it felt like he was talking to himself rather than
me. We did not stop at any point, and the journey
went on for a long time. Eventually he asked me
where I lived, and when I told him, he laughed. I
did not understand this at the time, but now that
I am aware we live in the same city, I realise he
must have seen it as a happy coincidence. He told
me we would go there, and continued to give me
precise directions.

I do not know exactly what time we reached my house, but it was early evening and already growing dark. He told me to reverse into the driveway. I was panicking, but he told me that he would not kill me if I did what he said. I did not believe him, but thought that inside the house I might at least be able to find a weapon or escape from him somehow. He took my keys and made me carry the unconscious woman inside, and then down into the cellar. He placed a newspaper under her head and made me take a photograph of her. He then ordered me back upstairs into the front room, where I was told to sit on a chair and not move.

The man locked all the doors and disconnected the phone line. Throughout the night, he kept listening at the cellar door, and checking the curtains in the front room. I was allowed to use the toilet, but was escorted. The man continued talking to himself a great deal, but it was impossible to follow his train of thought, as little he said made sense, and again, I was too frightened to pay close attention. The conversation was a jumble and a blur. He had a laptop, which he set up on the coffee table and he spent a good portion of the night typing. He seemed sometimes pleased with what he was doing and sometimes disappointed, although to begin with I had no idea why.

In the morning, he passed me the laptop and asked me to read what he had written. It appeared to be a horrible short story of some kind. He had written about a woman being held captive for years, and then brought to a house and murdered. It was clear it related to the current situation. So as not to anger the man, I said I thought it was good. He explained that he had abducted the

woman in the cellar many years ago, and that
he had sent stories to her husband in order to
punish him for some perceived slight that I did
not understand. He told me this would be the final
story, and that this one would be true and so it
needed to be perfect. He continued to work on the
story for some time afterwards.

I had no way of telling the time, but I believe
it was early to mid afternoon when it happened.
The man had been growing increasingly agitated
and distracted, and his attention was focused
more and more on the cellar door. He seemed to
have forgotten about me altogether by this point,
and instead appeared to be coming to some kind
of decision in his head. After a time, without
saying a word, he picked up the knife and moved
over to the cellar door, which he opened before
disappearing downstairs.

Alone for the first time in nearly twenty-four
hours, I was too shocked to know what to do. The
front and back doors were locked and the man
still had my keys. Similarly, he had disabled my
telephone. I sat there for a moment, too afraid to
move. Then I moved over to his laptop, where I saw
that the story he had written had been pasted into
the body of an email message but not sent. Without
any real clue what I was doing, I typed in my name
and address and a plea for help, connected to my
home wireless, and then sent the email.

At that point, I considered escaping. It would
perhaps have been possible to force open one of
the downstairs windows, climb out and seek help.
But from the content of the story I had read, I
knew that the man was intending to murder the
woman in the cellar, and I could not allow that
to happen without at least attempting to save

her. I was very scared, but I went through to the kitchen. A few days previously, the tap in the kitchen had broken, and I'd used a wrench to fix it, which remained on the window ledge. I tried to be as quiet as possible, but I was physically shaking as I made my way downstairs.

When I entered the cellar, the man was standing over the woman with his back to me, and seemed unaware of my presence. He was staring down at her, turning the knife around in his hand, and it was clear he was about to hurt her. She was awake now, but still blindfolded, and was asking what was happening, but the man was ignoring her and breathing heavily. This went on for a few seconds, perhaps even longer. Then he suddenly crouched and moved the knife towards her. At that moment, I swung the wrench down as hard as I could and struck him on the back of the head.

He immediately fell to one side, and one of his legs began shaking violently. I was not sure if I had killed him, but it was clear that I had incapacitated him. I considered striking him again, but the knife had fallen from his hand and he was seriously injured, and the violence had horrified and sickened me. I crouched down by the woman myself and tried to reassure her. After a minute, the man's leg stopped kicking and I believed that he was dead. I continued to tell the woman that everything was going to be okay. The police arrived several minutes later.

I have not been informed of the woman's condition. I wish to note that I would like to know she is all right.

Forty-Four

'So let's get this straight,' Emma said. 'Blythe talked all night, but Bunting can't remember any of it. It's all a blur. Because he was so *scared*.'

'Natural enough for him to be frightened,' Ferguson said.

'Except that, conveniently, he *can* remember certain bits. The necessary parts. Give me strength.'

She shook her head. The three of us were sitting in DCI Reeves's office, talking over the first interview with Simon Bunting and his subsequent statement. Or rather, *they* were talking. I was leaning forward in my chair, staring down at my hands, which I was rubbing together slowly. While I was paying attention to what they were saying, I was also lost in thought, turning Bunting's account of events around in my head.

I didn't like it. I didn't like *him* either, come to think of it, and the two facts were certainly connected. Simon Bunting was average height, slightly overweight, plain looks: the kind of man you passed on the street all the time, with nothing to make him stand out. But there was also a fussiness and an arrogance to him – a sense of self-importance. From the way he'd looked at us in the interview, it was clear to me that he thought he was far more intelligent than we were, even if he was trying his best to hide it. I didn't like the combination of those two things: the superiority he so obviously felt in contrast to how apparently average and undistinguished he was in every conceivable way.

In my experience, that was a mixture with a tendency to curdle in people.

And Emma was right about how convenient Bunting's story was. He could tell us *just enough*, but at key moments when we'd have liked more information – the details of the drive; exactly what Blythe had said – his memory became curiously patchy. Ferguson had a point that a normal person might be too preoccupied to pay close attention to everything, but I could tell that even he was only playing devil's advocate. Bunting's statement stank, and we all knew it.

Reeves took a deep breath.

'You think he's lying, DI Beck?'

'Oh yes,' Emma said.

'DI Ferguson?'

Ferguson shrugged. 'Yes. Of course I think he's lying.'

'DI Turner?'

'I think he's lying too.' I didn't look up for the moment. 'But the truth is, it doesn't matter what we think, does it? It matters what we can prove.'

Because that was the problem we were faced with. Bunting's story was unlikely and none of us bought it for a second, but could we actually *prove* he was making it up? At first glance, the details he had given us so far seemed to match the facts on the ground, and the gaps in his story might turn out to be difficult to fill. For one thing, Blythe was dead and therefore not in much of a position to contradict any of it. Melanie West might be able to, but she was currently in hospital and her immediate condition was unclear. There were traces of drugs in her system and she appeared to have been sedated for much of the last couple of days. It remained to be seen what her account of events would turn out to be.

'Yes.' Reeves nodded. 'Exactly so. What matters is what we can prove. Where are we at with that? DI Ferguson?'

'We're nowhere yet,' Ferguson said. 'We've recovered what Bunting claims is Blythe's laptop and camera from the scene. The camera appears to be the one that was reported missing along with Melanie West. We've already traced the laptop: bought second-hand in town years ago. Too long ago for CCTV. Prints are ongoing.'

'Make them go faster.'

'They'll match Bunting's story,' I said.

'How do you know that?' Ferguson said.

'Because if they didn't, he'd have told us a different story.'

'Well, we'll see. As for the contents of the laptop, the Red River letters and the short stories allegedly sent to Townsend are all on it. The timestamps look about right. Otherwise, it's clean. There's a web browser, but it looks like whoever owned it took serious security measures there, as we're not getting anything from it.'

'What else?' Reeves said.

'The whole property is obviously being processed as a crime scene. Car, house, everything. We've recovered Bunting's own laptop and mobile phone, but haven't found anything incriminating on either of them. Bunting wasn't half as careful, privacy-wise, and he's been completely cooperative. Nothing dodgy. He didn't even look at porn, the sexless little freak.'

'CCTV?'

'Also ongoing, sir. But there's a lot of cameras to check between here and Moorton, especially as Bunting claims he can't even remember what route they took.'

'Yes,' Emma said. 'And Blythe was directing him the whole time. How convenient.'

'Everything will match,' I said. 'Everything we can investigate. Everything we can test. It will all fit.'

There was a moment of silence.

'I see,' Reeves said finally. 'So. Let me summarise the situation. We're all sure the man is lying, but for the moment there's absolutely no evidence to back that up.'

'Turner's right, sir.' Ferguson shrugged. 'His story fits the facts. Whether that will continue to be the case is another matter. But right now, that's where we're at.'

Reeves leaned forward slowly. 'I'll tell you where we are

right now, DI Ferguson. *Right now*, I have what appears to be half the world's media camped out in front of the department, waiting for me to make a statement. The other half is either at the hospital or outside Simon Bunting's house. He's already been informally identified in the press. Did you know that? They're calling him a hero.'

'The man who caught the Red River Killer,' I said.

'You'd be terrible at writing headlines, Turner.' I still hadn't looked up, but I could tell that had earned me a sharp look. 'I'm sure that will be the general content, though. He'll be stealing your thunder on that one, won't he?'

I didn't reply.

The man who caught the Red River Killer.

Because that was precisely the ending Bunting wanted, wasn't it? I thought I could piece together what had happened, even if I couldn't prove it. For the letter-writer, I'd realised earlier that we were looking for someone who had grown up in Moorton, and I was sure that was Simon Bunting. He was a few years younger than Blythe and denied knowing him, but still. It was him.

Somehow Bunting had known that Blythe had killed Jennifer Johnson all those years ago, and he had followed his career of murder afterwards – a parasite on a much darker host. He knew what Blythe was doing. He had written the letters to entwine himself in the case from a safe distance and enjoy his own small moments in the limelight. To feel part of it. He must have followed Melanie West too, because of her involvement in that initial case, and then become angry when he realised her husband had stolen his pet killer's crime and written about it. Whereupon he'd taken his revenge by abducting Melanie and tormenting Townsend for years afterwards.

All of which meant that the laptop had to be Bunting's, not Blythe's. He had another one, of course – an innocent one – and like Ferguson had said, I'd no doubt that it had never been used for anything incriminating. But I was also sure there had been extensive communication between the two men over the years, presumably initiated by Bunting, who had wanted to share in the details of the murders. Involving himself even further. All of which had culminated in a demand from Blythe for help after he'd gone on the run, and Bunting creating this story to get himself out of his predicament. To provide the conclusion he desired.

The man who caught the Red River Killer.

'Bunting wrote the Red River letters,' I said. 'He abducted Melanie West. He wrote the short stories. He's been in contact with Blythe all this time. He's been ... living on the *outskirts* of the murders since day one. Do you know what that means?'

'Illuminate us,' Reeves said.

'It means that there never *was* a Red River Killer. Not really. What we had all along was John Blythe, a sick and dangerous man just going quietly about his business. And then we had Simon Bunting, a man greedy for attention, influence and power. He sent all those letters and turned a man into a myth. A monster. A *name.*'

There was silence in the room for a moment.

Then Reeves sighed.

'You're nominal lead on the case, DI Ferguson,' he said. 'What's your opinion? Are we going to release Bunting to the hero's welcome he'll receive outside, or are we going to arrest him?'

Ferguson folded his arms and was silent for a moment, mulling it over. Considering it. Finally, he spoke.

'Turner,' he said. 'What do you think we should do?'

When I looked up at him, I realised that he wasn't joking. He was staring at me. Everybody in the room was. I made an effort to sit up straight and bring myself fully into the conversation.

'Arrest him,' I said. 'On suspicion of the abduction and false imprisonment of Melanie West. And the murder of John Blythe.'

'Even though we can't prove it?' Ferguson said.

'We will, though.'

'You're confident of that?'

'Yes.'

There was another moment of silence.

'Yes,' Emma agreed.

'All right.' Ferguson took a deep breath, then looked at Reeves. 'I'm in agreement, sir. We arrest him.'

I waited – we all did – while Reeves looked at the three of us in turn, quietly considering. We all knew it was a serious decision. As he had said, the media machine was already churning into gear, creating its own narrative from the fragments of events it could glean. To arrest Bunting right now was to thrust a crowbar into the cogs of that machine and bring a temporary halt to it. If we made the wrong call, there was going to be a hell of a scream when we pulled the crowbar out and set it all moving again.

'All right,' Reeves said finally. He checked his watch. 'Twenty-four hours. Half past eleven tomorrow night, we formally charge Simon Bunting or else he walks. We need to connect him to Jennifer Johnson. Prove that he's been holding Melanie West all this time. Show that he's lying about what happened with Blythe today.'

'Yes, sir.'

Reeves looked at me.

'Go on then, DI Turner,' he said. 'Go and take his story and tear it to pieces.'

Forty-Five

Extracts from interviews with Simon Bunting
Present: DI William Turner; DI Emma Beck
Thursday 30 June 2016–Friday 1 July 2016.

Question: Mr Bunting, you understand why we're
here? You have been arrested on suspicion of the
abduction on 30 August 2005 and subsequent false
imprisonment of Melanie West, and on suspicion of
the murder of John Edward Blythe on 30 June of
this year. This has been explained to you by the duty
officer?
Answer: Yes.
Q: And you have made the decision to waive the right to
legal counsel for the moment. Is that correct?
A: Yes. I don't need a lawyer. This whole thing is
ridiculous. I've already told you exactly what happened,
and you should be thanking me for doing what I did.
I could have just run away, and she'd have been dead
now, wouldn't she? I saved her life.
Q: I understand you're upset, Mr Bunting. I would ask
you to calm down, so that we can proceed.
A: I am calm. Let's just get this over with.
Q: You were born in Moorton on 14 May 1971 and you
grew up there. In your previous interview, you said that

you had never heard of John Edward Blythe before recent events. Is that correct?

A: Yes.

Q: But Moorton is a small community, Mr Bunting, and Blythe was only two years older than you. I find it hard to imagine that your paths never crossed as children or teenagers.

A: If they did, I don't remember. I wasn't a very sociable child. I'm quite a solitary man now. I've always been happiest on my own. I kept to myself as a teenager and didn't have many friends. But that was fine. I could have done if I wanted – I was popular enough. But I preferred to be on my own. People tend to bore me, I suppose. I used to read a lot. Walk a lot.

Q: And where did you walk a lot?

A: Just around Moorton. The countryside there is beautiful. I've always liked nature. You can lose yourself a bit. Daydream and think.

Q: Have you ever walked along the canal in the city here?

A: Probably, but not for a long time. From what I remember, it never felt particularly safe there. It's quite isolated, and it seemed to be the kind of place where you'd get groups of kids hanging around. Drug types too. Not that I'm particularly scared of people like that, but it's best to avoid conflict if you can, and there are nicer places to go.

Q: Do you recall your whereabouts on 30 August 2005?

A: Of course not. How could I possibly remember that?

Q: One reason might be that something specific happened on that day. Something memorable. Were you at the canal on that date?

A: No, I was not.

Q: But you just said you couldn't recall your whereabouts, so how can you be sure?

A: What I meant before is that it's such a long time ago. But actually, I can't have been at the canal that day. Because you're right. Something memorable did happen that day. It was the day that Melanie West went missing, wasn't it? If I had been walking there that day, I would remember. I would have come forward to eliminate myself from enquiries at the time. And so I'm quite sure that I can't have been.

Q: When you spent time walking in the countryside as a teenager, did you ever visit a place known locally as Frog Pond? It's close to where you picked up John Blythe the day before yesterday.

A: I didn't 'pick him up'. But yes, I know where you mean. It's about a mile or so down a footpath? I went there every now and then. Lots of the other kids went. They'd drink and stuff. Sometimes I'd go, but I was never really into that kind of thing, and like I said, I was pretty solitary as a teenager. So I wouldn't have had much reason to go there. I tended to avoid places like that. I preferred being on my own.

Q: And why were you there the day before yesterday?

A: I wasn't *there* as such. I already told you. I'd driven through the village and seen how busy everything was. After I'd been to the cemetery, I decided to avoid that and go for a drive. I was taking a longer route home and just happened to be in the wrong place at the wrong time.

Q: So you weren't there specifically to pick up John Edward Blythe?

A: Absolutely not. That's ridiculous.

Q: So it's not true that you have been in contact with John Edward Blythe for many years, and that you were concerned that if he was apprehended, that communication might come to light?

A: That's not true at all.

Q: Or that you realised you needed to dispose of the evidence and get rid of him?

A: No, that's complete rubbish.

Q: Why do you have a lock on your cellar door?

A: Sorry?

Q: You have a padlock on your cellar door, even though there's nothing of value and no external entrance to the property down there. Why?

A: I don't know. I can't even remember. I imagine it must have been there when I moved in however long ago. It's not something I ever think about. The key's on my key ring. That's it.

Q: When did you last clean your cellar?

A: I'm not sure. A couple of weeks ago, perhaps.

Q: It still smells of disinfectant, as though it was more recent than that.

A: Maybe it was. It's not the kind of thing I mark in my diary, to be honest. There's often a funny smell down there. Like... well, like old meat. I'm not sure where it comes from, but I do my best to keep on top of these things. I like my house to be clean and tidy. Don't you?

Q: Are you aware that your cellar has exactly the same layout as John Blythe's?

A: Does it?

Q: Yes. One larger room and a smaller secondary room.

A: I wasn't aware of that. But as far as I know, all the houses in that area have the same layout, don't they? So I'm not particularly surprised.

Q: Does the name Jennifer Johnson mean anything to you?

A: Yes, of course it does. She was in the same year as me at school. Actually, we were quite close. I remember what happened to her. It was terribly upsetting.

Q: You were friends with her?

A: Yes. We spoke when we saw each other. She liked comics too. She liked reading. She was one of the nicer people I remember. Girls at that age can be...

Q: Mean?

A: Not mean. Stand-offish, maybe. It's all about social status at that age, isn't it? Most people, they care a lot about a pecking order. And obviously I was never really interested in any of that. I was outside it all because I was happy enough by myself. I think Jennifer respected me for that. She thought I was a bit different. A bit more interesting than the other boys.

Q: Did you want her to be your girlfriend?

A: No, not all. She was a nice girl, but without being rude, she was quite plain. That sounds horrible, I know, but it's true. If anything, I'd say it was the other way around. Like I said, I think she was a bit intrigued by me. But I wasn't remotely interested in her on that level.

Q: And you found what happened to her upsetting?

A: Yes, of course. It would have been horrible even if I *hadn't* known her. We were all really shocked and frightened by the whole thing. It was very sad. I remember there was a memorial service for her one assembly. People told stories about her life and loads of people were crying. And it was – well, it was just really sad. I remember crying myself, which really isn't like me. Horrible.

Q: Her body was found at Frog Pond. Were you there on the day she was killed?

A: No. Of course not.

Q: Did you see John Edward Blythe kill her?

A: No.

Q: When you picked Blythe up yesterday, who got in the car first, and who had the keys?

A: Oh God, I've already told you this.

Q: Tell us again.

Q: Does the name Melanie West mean anything to you?

A: Yes. You know that. She was the woman I saved from John Blythe in my cellar. She was one of his victims. He said she was special to him in some way.

Q: Did you know her before then?

A: No, not really. Obviously, I can make the connection now.

I do vaguely remember her from school, although I don't think I ever spoke to her. She was Jennifer's friend back then, I think. If I heard the news when she went missing, then I can't have recognised the name. We were never close.

Q: Does the name Jeremy Townsend mean anything to you?

A: Not that I'm aware of.

Q: He's Melanie's husband. He's an author. You've never read a book called *What Happened in the Woods*?

A: Again, not that I'm aware of. I have a lot of books – I read a lot – but that's not a title that stands out for me. What's it about?

Q: It's loosely based on what happened to Jennifer.

A: Is it? That seems a little distasteful to me. I suppose I would remember it if I had read it, so I can't have.

Q: You never wrote to Jeremy Townsend?

A: Absolutely not. How could I have done? Like I just said, I've never even heard of him.

Q: Well, let's go back to Melanie for a moment. It's your contention that, while camping in the wilds over the past few days, John Blythe had Melanie West with him the whole time. And that despite having to move quickly on occasion, he somehow managed to take her along with him. How is that possible?

A: I don't know. It's not *my* contention, though. I'm just telling you what happened to me.

Q: If Melanie was abducted by Blythe, and kept imprisoned all this time, why haven't we found her DNA or fingerprints in his cellar?

A: I have no idea. Why are you asking me?

Q: Where did Blythe get the newspaper from?

A: How would I know *any of this*? I literally have no idea what Blythe did before he attacked me, whether Melanie was with him at that point, or where he got the newspaper from. I can't help you with any of that. Why don't you ask her?

Q: We'll ask her, don't worry.

A: It doesn't make any sense. If what you're implying is true, then why would I have sent that email asking for help? Why wouldn't I just have killed Blythe and... carried on doing whatever horrible thing you think it is I've done?

Q: That's a good question. Why don't you tell us?

A: I can't. Because none of it's true. [Long pause.] You haven't even told me how she's doing. Do you realise that? I think that's the least I deserve. I'd like to know that she's okay after everything I did to help her.

Q: Were you bullied as a teenager?

A: No. Obviously not. Why?

Q: Most kids are at some point, aren't they? And with all respect, you say 'obviously', but it sounds like you were the kind of kid who might have been. No friends. Keeping to yourself.

A: No. Like I said, it was more by choice than anything else. The other kids left me alone. I think maybe they respected me more than anything else – the way I didn't seem to rely on anybody. It's always been that way.

Q: Put it like that and you sound a lot like Blythe. Maybe you *were* bullied and you looked up to him a bit because you wished you were more like him. Is that why you helped him?

A: No.

Q: Why *did* you help him then? Was it because you knew all along what he'd done, and were worried it would all come out when the police caught him?

A: No. As I've told you a hundred times now, I didn't help him. I've never communicated with him. I'd never made the connection with Melanie West. I'd never heard of her husband or his book. You can print everything, check everywhere, do whatever tests you want; you won't find anything to contradict what I'm saying. Because everything I've told you is the truth.

Q: We'll do all of those things, don't worry.
A: Anyway – the police didn't catch him, did they?
Q: What do you mean?
[Pause. Note that the interviewee seems pleased.]
A: *I* did.

Forty-Six

Go and take his story and tear it to pieces.

Early afternoon on the day after arresting Simon Bunting for the abduction of Melanie West, Emma and I parked up outside the hospital. We had about ten hours left. It wasn't going to be enough.

A part of me really had thought he'd fall apart under more detailed questioning, but I'd underestimated him. Aside from a few hesitations and flashes of anger, he'd managed to keep calm and stick to his story – and of course, that was all he needed to do. It was a wild story, but it fitted the facts, and so far – despite the department throwing everything we had at the case – we hadn't found a single thing to contradict it.

While we'd been interviewing him, other officers had talked to his neighbours and work colleagues. It had given us nothing. The neighbours said he was quiet but not unfriendly, and they hadn't seen anything suspicious on the evening he'd arrived home with John Blythe. His boss confirmed that Bunting had called in sick to work on the two days he claimed to have done. One of the police manning the checkpoints in Moorton recognised him from a photograph, and confirmed that Bunting had indeed told him he was on his way to visit his parents' grave at the cemetery.

A large amount of CCTV footage had been pored over, but there were as yet no sightings of his vehicle in any of it. The search amounted to hundreds of cameras and even more hours of film, and even if we did manage to catch his car somewhere, the footage would likely be from a distance and probably useless for establishing the veracity of his story.

The laptops had still given us nothing. Bunting's own machine could be traced to him, but the saved files and browsing history were all entirely innocuous. The one he alleged to be Blythe's was second-hand, and could theoretically have been purchased by either of them. While the letters and stories were on it, the browsing history remained impenetrable. Bunting's prints had been found on the machine, but that fitted with what he'd told us – that Blythe had shown him the final Melanie story, and that Bunting had amended it and sent the email asking for help. Blythe's prints had also been found on Bunting's keys and in various places throughout the house and the cellar, and just as I'd expected, all of them matched Bunting's account.

There *were* discrepancies, of course. It seemed unbelievable that Blythe could have dragged Melanie around the countryside with him when he went on the run. Where had he got the newspaper? And there was absolutely no physical evidence that she had ever been in his cellar. But Bunting had remained calm under fire. He didn't know any of that; it wasn't his problem; he was just giving an account of what had happened to him.

Even though we were all sure he was lying, we still couldn't prove it. And time was not on our side.

As Emma and I walked towards the hospital, the media gathered by the entrance seemed to come to life. Cameras appeared, turning in our direction, and reporters moved to meet us. In the small but intense throng, I recognised one of them as the man who'd annoyed me outside Blythe's house. That was less than a week ago, but it felt like years had passed since.

'Can you give us a word on her condition, Detectives?'

'Not yet, Joe.' Emma was as frustrated as I was, but she managed to sound as cheerful as ever. 'We've only just arrived, haven't we? We've talked about that keen journalistic eye of yours before, I think.'

We passed through the crowd to the front door, and I tried not to wince at the cameras flashing around me.

'How badly hurt is she?' Joe called from behind.

I kept my head down and ignored him.

We were met outside Melanie West's room by Dr Cleaves, the same man we'd spoken to days earlier about Amanda Cassidy. Word on Amanda's condition was cautiously positive: she remained in a serious condition, but was stable and responding well to treatment. It appeared that she was, finally, coming out of the woods.

Melanie West was another matter entirely.

How badly hurt is she?

'With one notable exception,' Cleaves told us, 'she doesn't appear to have been hurt at all. Physically, I mean. Obviously, what has been done to her is its own form of violence, but her health is good. She hasn't been directly harmed in any way.'

'What's the exception?' Emma said.

'Her eyesight. We're in relatively uncharted territory here. My understanding is that she's been kept in an extremely dark environment, and generally blindfolded, for over a decade. As you can imagine, there isn't a large body of medical literature dealing with such a situation.'

I glanced at the closed door. At this point, we were relying on Melanie being able to tell us something that could help prove she had been held by Simon Bunting and not John Blythe. But she had been blindfolded. An extremely dark environment. There was also the fact that Bunting's house was structurally identical to Blythe's.

Just how careful had Bunting been?

'Can she see?' Emma said.

'She can. But living in those conditions for a prolonged period of time weakens the eye muscles. The pupils are no longer used to dilating and contracting. Light – even weak light – can be exceedingly damaging. So we're keeping her surroundings very dim for the moment, and she's wearing dark glasses.'

'Is it permanent?'

'Probably not. It might take some time, though. Interestingly, she isn't displaying any of the other signs you might find in somebody deprived of light for such a long time. She has been looked after – if you can call it that. She's been well fed. She's been given vitamins.'

'You make her sound like a plant,' Emma said.

Cleaves looked awkward at that, but she was right. Assuming it had all happened the way I thought, that was exactly how Bunting had treated Melanie. I didn't think he'd been interested in her at all, except as a way to torture Townsend. A plant, dutifully kept and watered. That was what he had reduced her to, and he had done it well.

'She's mentally quite sharp,' Cleaves said, 'but there is something else. She suffers from hallucinations.'

'Hallucinations?' Emma said.

'This is actually a well-documented phenomenon; you see it in test subjects after only a few days. When the brain is deprived of sights, it creates them. It usually starts relatively small – flashing lights and so on – but over time it develops into elaborate visions. She's not insane; she knows they're not real. But they seem as real to her as the world we're seeing around us now. According to her, they're already beginning to fade, but over the years they've been vivid and intense.'

Neither Emma nor I spoke for a moment. I continued to stare at the closed door, feeling any hope I had beginning to ebb away inside me. Melanie had been kept blindfolded in the dark. She suffered from hallucinations. If we were relying on her account to nail Bunting, then we might be relying on testimony that any half-decent defence team would tear to shreds in minutes.

Might be, I thought.

Give her a chance.

'What has she been hallucinating?' Emma said.

294

Still staring at the door, I nodded to myself, already knowing what the answer was going to be.

'Water and woodland for the most part,' Cleaves said. 'Bright green woodland.'

'The doctor told us you've been seeing things.'

Melanie West nodded. She was sitting up in bed, with the sheets around her waist, wearing a white hospital gown and sunglasses. Her brown hair was tied back in a ponytail. Although it was difficult to see clearly in the gloom, she seemed – as Cleaves had said – healthy and physically unharmed. On the outside, at least.

'Yes,' she said. 'For a long time now. I've always known they're not real, but... well. Actually. Are they or aren't they? When that's all there is to see, what difference is there? I know my mind's making it up, but at the same time, they seem real.'

'Are you seeing those things right now?'

'I was earlier, but not right now. Everything's just dark at the moment. Well – not *that* dark, really. Hang on.'

She reached up to take the sunglasses off.

'Melanie...'

'It's fine. I can see you both.' She smiled. 'Assuming you're really there, of course.'

'We really are. All right.' I took out the photographs I'd brought with us and held one up for her. 'Can you see this?'

She peered at the image of John Blythe.

'I can, yes. Is this the man from the house?'

'I was just wondering if you recognised him.'

She shook her head. 'No. I don't.'

'What about this man?'

I swapped the photograph of Blythe for one of Simon Bunting. She stared at this one a little longer, her gaze intent, and I allowed myself to feel hope. All it would take was for him to have made one mistake. One slip.

But after a moment, she shook her head again.

'No.'

'Okay.'

'The thing is, I never saw his face.' She sounded apologetic. 'It was always very dark, and I was blindfolded most of the time. I hardly ever saw him, and when I did, he was always wearing a mask. A balaclava. And I was glad. I didn't want to see him. It made me less afraid.'

'Why?'

'Because if he didn't want me to see him, that meant he might eventually let me go.'

I was silent at that. After a moment, Melanie smiled sadly and closed her eyes. Then she put the sunglasses back on.

'What kind of build did he have?' I said.

'He was quite stocky, but not tall. At least I don't think so. He always seemed much bigger, but I think that was my imagination as much as anything. I don't think he was huge.'

'All right.' I put both photographs away. That didn't help us either. Bunting and Blythe were roughly the same height, and while Bunting was in considerably worse physical shape, he could easily have looked broader and stronger in the right clothes. 'Let's start at the beginning then, as much as we can.'

We did. And very quickly, the frustration set in.

Perhaps it wasn't surprising that after such a long time, Melanie could remember little about her actual abduction. She knew it had taken place at the canal, near a bridge, and that she had stopped to photograph something when it happened. But the exact details were lost to her now. Similarly, the intervening years had blurred together into one long monotonous period. There had – of course – been panic and fear at first, and then anger and boredom, but ultimately her existence had settled down, and she had become accustomed to her new life. It seemed impossible to comprehend. But then, what choice did she have? People survive. That's what they do. And throughout it all, there had always been the hope that at some point, one day in the future, he might let her go.

'I tried to talk to him,' she said. 'I remember pleading at first. *Please let me go*. And then just trying to understand. *Why me?*

He would speak to me occasionally, but I could tell he was changing his voice – obscuring it somehow. That was reassuring too. And the strange thing is, even from the beginning, I never had the impression he *wanted* to hurt me. Only that he would if he had to.'

'What did you talk about?'

'I can't remember a lot of it. Sometimes he let me have a radio of some kind. I could listen to music or the news, and we spoke about that. What was going on in the world. Things like that. And he played me books.'

'Audiobooks?'

'Yes. One of them was my husband's. The book Jeremy wrote about what happened to Jennifer.' Melanie paused. 'It was only one of many, but I realised it couldn't be a coincidence, especially because he sat and listened to that one with me. It was like he wanted to see how I reacted. That was when I made the connection: that it was something to do with me back then. With *Jennifer*, I mean. And so I tried not to react at all. It was one of the only times after the first few weeks when I didn't feel safe. It felt like he hated me right then.'

'Okay.'

'That's one of the reasons I never mentioned the visions to him either. The woods. The water. I didn't want him to know about any of that. I didn't want to talk about it. And also... well. They were *mine*. He couldn't see them. They belonged to me.'

I didn't say anything for a moment.

'Can I show you some more photographs?'

'Yes.'

Melanie took her sunglasses off again, and looked carefully at each of the images I showed her. We had taken numerous photos in both Blythe and Bunting's houses. Almost all of them seemed familiar, she said, but she couldn't be certain. When she'd been allowed upstairs to use the bathroom and shower, she'd always been blindfolded. And the photographs of the first room in the cellars were all but identical. The only difference between the two was that Bunting's was empty, whereas Blythe's had a mattress in it.

'Oh yes,' she said. 'That's my bed.'

'Did your room have a particular smell?'

She wrinkled her nose.

'Yes. There was another room that was part of the cellar, and that always stank. An awful smell. Sometimes he'd go in there and do things, but the rest of the time it was locked. He told me there was something bad in there. I didn't want to know what. It smelled like death. But after a while, I didn't really notice the smell. It just became normal.'

I leaned back in my seat, feeling hopeless now. I remembered what Bunting had told me. *There's often been a funny smell down there. Like old meat.* Had he recreated Blythe's crime scene that meticulously? First choosing a house with the same exact layout, then studying photographs that Blythe might have sent him to the point that he could even source the same mattress? And then tidying everything away when Blythe went on the run. In a tip somewhere there'd be a mattress just like that, I realised. And from his arrogance, I imagined *old meat* was precisely what he'd used.

All gone now.

I like my house to be clean and tidy.

But I had to keep trying.

'Do you remember seeing this woman?'

I showed her a photograph of Amanda Cassidy.

'No. He was the only person I ever saw. As much as I ever saw him.'

Which again proved nothing. Amanda had been found restrained in Blythe's garage. There was no evidence he'd ever taken her down to the cellar.

'What can you remember about the last few days?'

'Not much.' Melanie put the glasses back on and frowned. 'I was asleep more than usual. I think he might have put something in my food. I remember that he seemed excited, nervous. That was before we left. I don't know how long ago that was.

Then I was in an enclosed space for a while. A vehicle, I think. I could feel it moving around me. And I was excited, because maybe he was going to let me go. And then scared, because what if he wasn't?'

'Do you recall anything else?'

'We camped for a while. I'm not sure how long, but there was a tent. I heard water at one point. It's all a blur. Fresh air, though!' She smiled. 'It was unbelievable. I couldn't see anything, but I could tell we were outside. I was seeing the woodland as a hallucination, but for once it felt like it matched the world around me. We were in undergrowth. There were trees – I could smell them. It was early morning, I think, and we were moving fast. He was telling me we had to move quickly. He gave me something to drink, and I was asleep again, and then I don't remember anything else. Not until... the end.'

The end.

I looked at her. It was difficult to know what she must be thinking and feeling. Yes, she was free now. And yes, this man had imprisoned her – but he had also cared for her and been her only companion for a decade. Her life had been twisted off course, causing huge emotional pain, but then it had settled into something new: a different kind of existence, one she had become acclimatised to over time. Now that too had been wrenched away from her, and everything was different once again.

Or perhaps not. I wasn't sure whether she could see us through the dark glasses, or whether it was simply a matter of reading the silence and unspoken implications in the room, but a moment later, she smiled again. And this time, it wasn't sad. It was the smile of somebody who had held tightly to hope for a very long time, never allowing herself to be swept away by the surrounding storm, and had that hope land finally on a shore.

'I'm so happy,' she said.

Jeremy Townsend was waiting outside when we left.

He was holding a coffee, and looked smarter than the last time I'd seen him. His clothes were still archaic, as though from a different age, but he seemed cleaner, and the outfit somehow better put together. His hair was neater, and he'd trimmed his beard. There was a stronger aura to him now. His experience had of course been entirely different from that of his wife, but in his own way I supposed he'd also been trapped in the darkness all this time, enduring his own punishment.

Of course, other people might have been saved if he'd acted, and we still weren't sure exactly what was going to happen to him: whether it was in the public interest to prosecute him for what he'd done and what he hadn't. Looking at him right now, though, I didn't think he would care what we did. He'd acted out of guilt and love and hope, and everything he'd done, however misguided, he'd done as an act of atonement in order to keep Melanie alive.

'Mr Townsend.' *Keep calm.* 'I'm glad your wife seems okay.'

'You've finished speaking to her?'

'Yes. For now.'

'And?'

I hesitated. Even if I *could* have talked about the investigation, there was nothing to tell him. The truth was that Melanie's answers hadn't brought us any closer to charging Bunting, and right then, I couldn't think what might. So I opted for the most honest answer I could give.

'And I'm glad she's as well as she is. Truly.'

'She's always been strong.'

'Yes. She must be.'

'I saw that you've arrested Simon Bunting.'

There was no point in denying that.

'Yes, we have.'

'You think he's the one who abducted Melanie and sent those stories to me?'

'I can't talk about that right now. He hasn't been charged yet.'

'No. I understand that.' Townsend frowned, looked down at his coffee. 'But I've been thinking about that. About *him.*'

'I'm sure you have.'

'And the thing that keeps coming back to me is that this man is a storyteller. Because if he really did this, then he's made up a lot over the years, hasn't he? And if he's denying it, then he's still making things up now.'

I nodded slowly. He was right, of course. Bunting had woven a story not from words or pictures, but from reality itself. He'd created a narrative that had played out over the years, and which was now moving towards what seemed its inevitable conclusion. Very shortly, he would become known as the man who stopped the Red River Killer. He would be the hero the media wanted him to be. And it was possible that that would be how history remembered him. He had plotted the whole thing out carefully enough that I wasn't sure we could stop that right now.

Townsend was still looking down. Still thinking.

'You know what?' he said. 'I can tell you something about storytelling. He thinks he's good, this man. But from the ones he sent me, he's not nearly as good as he thinks he is. I had to correct them. Just little bits, here and there. I don't know why I bothered, but I did. He always hit the main beats, but the stories didn't hold together when you looked at them closely. There were always details that didn't add up, at least before I edited them.'

They're not very good, are they? I remembered reading that comment on the forum I'd found, and agreeing with it when I sampled the stories themselves.

'What are you suggesting?' I said.

'That he'll have made a mistake *somewhere*. That his story *will* have a hole.'

Townsend looked up at me.

'It's just a matter of finding it.'

Forty-Seven

'So.' Ferguson stood with his hands on his hips, glancing around the front room. 'What are we looking for exactly?'

He, Emma and I were downstairs in Simon Bunting's house. It was early evening now, and growing dark outside. Most of the reporters that had been gathered in the street had gone home for the night. We'd been met at the cordon by a solitary pair, who hadn't badgered us for a quote or even bothered taking our photographs. The house around us now was still and silent.

But it did have a story to tell. I was sure of it.

'I don't know exactly,' I said. 'A hole.'

Ferguson looked at the floor.

'Not a literal one,' I said. 'A hole in Bunting's story. I think that what Townsend told me at the hospital was right. There will be one somewhere.'

Ferguson grunted. Despite the tentative degree of co-operation between us now, it was clear he hadn't entirely shaken off the animosity he felt for me, and also that he considered our visit to the house right now something of a fool's errand. Looking around the room, it was easy to imagine he was right. Almost every visible surface, from the walls to the chairs to the coffee table in the centre, bore the pale grey swirls of printing dust. The whole house had received similar treatment, from the attic high above to the cellar below our feet, and the test results had been rushed through. Bunting's account of what had happened here stood up forensically as well as verbally.

I wandered over to the flat-screen television, which was angled on a stand in the corner. A home wireless device behind it was glowing with soft blue light. There was a sheen of dust on top of the screen. Nothing useful there. I turned around and surveyed the room. Ferguson still had his hands on his hips and was shaking his head. I ignored him, concentrating instead on the scene. It was easy enough to picture Bunting and Blythe sitting in here, exactly as Bunting had described.

'I think it went down in here more or less as he told us,' I said. 'There will have been differences, of course. I don't think he was a prisoner, for one. And I think it was his laptop all along, and that he was the one working on it, writing the story. But he'll have shown it to Blythe – or shown him something. The camera, too. He needed to get Blythe's prints on all the right things to make the story work.'

'Which doesn't help us,' Ferguson said.

'It doesn't.' Emma sighed. 'It means that any hole we're looking for will be somewhere *outside* the details in his story. He'll have told us things that fit the facts. So we're not going to disprove it by attacking those things. There's nothing here, Will.'

'Maybe not.'

But I was distracted. My mind was drifting, and the silence in the house was hypnotic. I turned around and looked at the television again. Something about it was bothering me, but I couldn't work out what. Bunting really didn't catch any of the news about Blythe while he was off work? I didn't buy that. But again, there was no way to prove he was lying about it, and therefore no point on dwelling on it.

I walked past Emma and Ferguson, through to the kitchen. They followed behind, but I was barely aware of their presence.

'The lock on the cellar door still doesn't sit right with me,' I said. 'Okay, it's old enough that it *could* have been there when he moved in. But it's weird, isn't it? No need for it in terms of security.'

'Traced the previous owners,' Ferguson said. 'They're elderly. They can't remember whether it was there or not when they lived here.'

I looked at him, surprised.

'You did that already?'

'Yeah. While you were getting nowhere in the interviews, I did something useful.'

'Right.' I looked back at the lock. 'Not that useful, unfortunately.'

'I also checked a few of the local shops, to see if we can find where he bought the newspaper. No joy there, either. It's not like we can check the CCTV everywhere that sells newspapers between here and Moorton, and he knows it. He's smart, Turner. That's assuming it really is all him. I'm almost beginning to doubt it myself.'

'No,' I said. 'You were right the first time. He's just smart.'

That was certainly what he wanted us to think, anyway. But maybe he wasn't quite as clever as he thought. In my encounters with him, I'd caught sight of the shy, bullied boy beneath the superior demeanour, the hubris. I could easily imagine the attraction he'd felt as a child to an older boy like John Blythe: similarly ostracised and hateful, but much larger and stronger, much more comfortable in his own odd skin. Bunting was a smart man, and I had no doubt that he'd thought things through very carefully. He would have taken pride in it: enjoyed it, even. But the fact remained that, underneath it all, there was still an angry little boy doing at least some of the driving.

'Why didn't he kill her?' Ferguson said. 'That's what I don't understand.'

'You make it sound like you would have done,' Emma said.

'No witnesses. Would have made it even harder to contradict his story, wouldn't it?'

'He'd have run the risk of messing up the scene in the cellar,'

I said. 'Her blood could have ended up on Blythe where he was lying. Anything might have happened. That's far too unpredictable for a man like Bunting.'

'All right. But like he said in the interview, why send the email asking for help? He could have brained Blythe and killed Melanie West, or just carried on as before, and we'd never have been any wiser. We'd never have found him or known about any of it.'

The police didn't catch him, did they?

I *did*.

'Because that's not the way he wanted this thing to end,' I said. 'He had to save her.'

Bunting had spent years manufacturing the story of a serial killer and becoming part of it. I doubted this was the ending he'd planned all along, but events had dropped it into his lap, and I was certain it was the ending he wanted now. Killing his own creation; saving Melanie West; becoming the hero. However convenient it would have been to kill Melanie too, or stay in hiding, it wouldn't have been as satisfying a resolution for him.

Ferguson started to say something – another objection, I assumed – so I ignored him and walked back to the front room, frowning at the television as I passed it, and then through to the spare downstairs room. In Blythe's house, it had been full of apparently random debris. Bunting's was effectively a library. Just like in the house I shared with Emma, the walls were lined with shelves, and those shelves were filled with books.

I scanned them, searching the spines for Jeremy Townsend's name.

'It's not here,' I said. '*What Happened in the Woods.*'

'No,' Emma said behind me.

'But he *must* have had it at some point.'

'He had a couple of days to prepare this place, Will. To get everything to match his story. He was hardly going to leave that book lying around, was he?'

'No.'

She was right, but I'd still been hoping. Just one hole in Simon Bunting's story. That was all we needed. Something small that he'd overlooked, either because he couldn't think of everything, or because of a blind spot of some kind.

Hubris. Pride.

'We're running out of time this round,' Ferguson said. 'Let him walk. What does it matter? We can come back to him.'

'That's not good enough.'

I shook my head, still scanning the shelves. Bunting would emerge to a hero's welcome, and the press would run with that narrative. After everything he'd done, I wasn't going to let him have the ending he wanted, not even for a minute. There had to be something. It would be something between the details, or behind them...

Behind them.

I turned around slowly. Through the doorway, I could see all the way back into the front room, to the television in the corner. With the home wireless device glowing softly behind it. *That* was what was bothering me, I realised. What was alleged to be Blythe's laptop had always used an anonymous portable device to connect to the internet, until the final email Bunting sent for help. And Bunting's own laptop – his innocent one – had been entirely clean of incriminating material.

But.

I stared at the blue light for a moment longer, putting things together in my head. Remembering something again now.

Words coming back to me.

'Will?' Emma said.

'Just a minute.'

I tried to suppress the thrill I felt in my chest, because at that moment I couldn't be sure. It could still be nothing. But as I turned back to the bookshelves, the feeling became stronger. *Hubris*, I thought, looking over the shelves again. Searching for something.

And there, right at the bottom, I found it.

I crouched down and slid it off the shelf. I opened it very carefully indeed and looked inside.

'Will?' Emma said. 'What is it?'

'Good news and bad news,' I said.

'Bad first,' Ferguson said.

'We're going to be very busy.'

I looked back down at what I'd found, thinking about the huge amount we needed to accomplish in the next couple of hours. It seemed insurmountable, but we could do it. One thing after another: that was what it came down to. We *would* do it.

I stood back up.

'And we need to call DI Warren in Moorton.'

Forty-Eight

Just over an hour to go.

That was by his estimation, anyway. In truth, Bunting was so exhausted by now that it was difficult to keep track of the time and the numbers. But as he sat down in the familiar interview room, he was also feeling a sense of exhilaration: he was going to beat them. They'd thought they could break him, but he'd stuck to the meticulous narrative he'd constructed, and he was confident he hadn't made a single mistake. If he had, they'd have found it by now.

The pair of them – Turner and Beck – looked suitably solemn as they entered the interview room and took their seats across from him. That alone told him they had nothing. It was easier to see in the woman; she'd never given anything away before. The man, Turner, that just seemed to be his manner. Always dejected, that one. Well, he had good reason to be tonight, didn't he?

Whereas Bunting himself felt elated at the sight of them. In an hour, he'd be out of here. Too tired to give any statements to the press right now, but willing to talk about the whole ordeal in the morning. *All* of it, too. Not just his terrifying experience at the hands of the monster John Blythe, but his decidedly shoddy treatment by the police afterwards. He would be understanding, of course, but only up to a point. The media had already been starting to question the police investigation, and he was sure they'd draw convenient conclusions about what was happening here to the man who'd stopped John Blythe and saved Melanie West. It would feel good to give that knife an extra little twist.

Turner did the formalities – starting the recorder and stating the names of those present and the time of the interview. Bunting sipped from a cup of water throughout. He was so close now that it was hard to suppress the smile, but it was important to stay in control. There was a camera in the upper corner of the room, also recording the interview, and it wouldn't do to leave footage that presented him in a bad light. He'd seen that used against people in the past, and he wasn't about to make an amateurish mistake at the last minute.

'Mr Bunting.' As usual, Turner just stared down at the notes in front of him, slightly pathetically, as though he found it hard to meet people's eyes. 'Earlier on today, we spoke to Melanie West.'

Despite himself, Bunting's heart beat a little harder at that. He forced himself to calm down. Of course they would have done, but he'd been very careful. He doubted she'd been able to tell them anything that would contradict his version of events.

Maintain frame.

'How is she?' he said. 'Because once again, nobody's told me, and after everything that's happened – everything I did – I think I have a right to know. Is she okay?'

Turner nodded slowly, still looking down. Beside him, Beck bit her bottom lip and folded her arms.

'She is going to be okay,' Turner said. 'Did you know she suffers from hallucinations?'

'How would I know that?'

That was his go-to answer for those sort of questions. They'd tried to trip him up a few times in that way, with questions that assumed he knew more than his story allowed, but he hadn't fallen for it once. And any details outside his story that didn't make sense, that was their problem to solve, not his. He was just telling them what had happened to him.

Even so . . . it bothered him slightly, and he suppressed the slight irritation he felt. Hallucinations? He hadn't known that. It felt like he should have done.

'Melanie sees the woods where it happened,' Turner said. 'Frog Pond. The river. The trees. I admit that when I first heard that, it seemed very horrible to me. Because everything started in those woods. Melanie spent years trying to come to terms with what happened, dealing with the trauma of it through her poetry and photography. And then, all because of you, she spent years in a pitch-black cell with that whole landscape literally coming out of the walls in front of her.'

'Not because of me,' Bunting said.

'Because of you, she was imprisoned in her own past.'

Turner looked up now, staring right at him.

'That may even be the worst part of what you did to her.'

'I didn't do anything to her.'

But as Turner continued to stare at him, Bunting felt something begin to unravel inside him. When the pair of them had come in, he'd thought they looked so serious and defeated because they had nothing on him. Now he wondered if the reverse was actually true, and it was the enormity of what he'd done that was weighing them down. Turner looked quietly judgemental, as though Bunting was a child who had let him down. Now that it had come to it, he didn't seem to have any problem meeting Bunting's eye at all.

'I didn't do *anything*,' Bunting repeated.

After another moment, Turner looked down at his notes again.

'Mr Bunting,' he said, 'according to the account you have already given us, on Wednesday 29 June, shortly before encountering John Blythe and Melanie West at the roadside, you went to Marwood Cemetery to visit your parents' grave.'

'That's right.'

'Can you tell me where in the cemetery your parents are buried?'

Bunting stopped thinking for a moment.

The silence in the interview room began to swell, until it

was ringing in his ears. Turner didn't look up at him; the man didn't seem to be moving at all. He was just waiting patiently for Bunting's answer, as though he already knew exactly what it would be.

Bunting took a sip of water.

'It's hard to describe,' he said.

'Is it? That's strange, because I got DI Warren, from the Moorton police department, to visit the site in person. He gave me a decent enough description.'

'I don't really think about it.'

'You said you went there often.'

'It must be an autopilot thing.' Bunting shook his head. *Jesus Christ!* His parents had undermined him all his life. It wasn't right that even in death they should be his undoing. It wasn't *fair*. 'It's quite emotional for me. I just... I go in. Walk around for a bit. I don't always take a direct route. My head just kind of takes me there.'

Turner remained silent, still waiting. Bunting glanced at Beck instead; she had her arms folded but was looking directly at him. He glanced away quickly, then reached out and took another sip of water, trying to keep his hand steady for the camera. Not long to go now. This didn't matter at all. This was nothing.

'What does it matter anyway?' he said.

'If we took you to Marwood Cemetery, do you think you could take us to your parents' graves?'

'Yes, probably.' There wouldn't be time for that tonight, of course, and he was sure there would be ways around it in future. 'If you don't mind wandering around, like I said.'

'Oh, I don't mind wandering around,' Turner said. 'But perhaps we can talk about that another time. Let's move on. In an earlier interview, you told us that you had never heard of Melanie West's husband, Jeremy Townsend, and were not familiar with the book he'd written, titled *What Happened in the Woods*.'

'That's correct.'

Bunting was on safer ground here. There was no way to disprove that, was there? He'd owned a copy, of course, but that had been removed from his house two days ago, along with the rest of the incriminating material. The audio cassettes he'd played to Melanie West, similarly, were long gone. Both had been bought for cash years earlier. How could you prove someone had read a book when they said they hadn't?

'Allow me to read something to you.'

Turner picked up one of the sheets in front of him.

'*Anyone remember* What Happened in the Woods *by Jeremy Townsend? This just came back to me. I remember reading this book a few years ago, but then there's been nothing since? No new releases available on pre-order or anything. The guy's got no website either. Anybody know What Happened to Him?*'

At first Bunting didn't recognise any of what Turner was saying, but as the man went on, he remembered. While he'd allowed Jeremy Townsend to get away with the slightly amended name attached to the short stories, he'd become frustrated at the lack of interest they were attracting and so he'd logged on to that stupid fucking website and started that thread, attempting to draw some attention to them. Except it hadn't really worked. From what he could recall, only one other person had responded.

But that was *years* back now. On a laptop that was long gone. And he'd been careful, only ever using his portable Wi-Fi. There was no way Turner could prove that was him.

'And?'

'Did you write those words? Along with the other entries under the username *writer_at_heart*?'

'No.'

'It's true that we can't find any reference to that site on your personal laptop, or indeed on the laptop you allege belonged to John Blythe. The posts are from too long ago. So we contacted the administrator responsible for the forum and had him look up the details of the individual making those posts.'

Keep calm.

'Oh yes?'

'The majority were made from an IP address we can't trace: a mobile Wi-Fi device, presumably, with a throwaway SIM card. But one post wasn't. *Hmmm. I don't know about that. They're certainly different, though!*'

Turner looked up at him.

'That one – and that one alone – came from the IP address that's registered to your home wireless network.'

Bunting closed his eyes.

Yes. He remembered that now.

It was all because that other user had said the stories, *his* stories, were terrible. Badly written. They weren't, of course; he knew that deep down. But the insult had stung regardless. He should have left it, but he'd been at home and drinking that night, and he'd stared at that comment – that insult – and been unable to let it go. He'd *needed* to reply. It had been impossible to leave it there without defending his work, however obliquely.

He opened his eyes again and saw that Turner was looking at him. The expression of disdain on his face now was infuriating. As though Bunting was nothing to him.

'Hubris, Simon,' Turner said. 'Do you know what that word means?'

I hate you, Bunting thought.

'It's pride, basically. Misplaced pride. It's what happens when you think you're better than you are.'

I hate you.

Turner reached down and picked a box file off the floor.

I hate you, I hate you, I hate—

'And we're only just getting started,' Turner said.

Forty-Nine

After so many hours of composure, it was a pleasure to see Simon Bunting's mask beginning to slip.

When we'd first entered the room, it had been obvious how much smarter than us he thought he was, and that he was expecting us to have found nothing. Over the last few minutes, I'd watched his smug expression fade as the reality of the situation dawned on him. My impression of him had been correct. He was fine when he believed he was in control, but the scared little boy inside was rising to the surface now. His face was pale, but the skin on his neck started to redden as I put the box file on the desk between us. He recognised it.

But his reaction provided mixed feelings. As we'd worked through the evidence during the last couple of hours, it had become clear exactly what Bunting had done, and why, and there was no real pleasure to be taken in any of it. Even though we'd suspected it all along, finding the proof hadn't brought the surge of adrenalin it normally might. We were going to get him for what he'd done, yes, but that wouldn't change the fact that he had done it. It couldn't give Melanie West the last decade of her life back.

And all for...

So little, really.

Bunting was staring at me as I opened the box file, his eyes locked on me. The anger he was feeling was obvious; his hands were actually trembling. I didn't think I'd ever seen that level of tension in a man before – such rage, but with the desire to act on it constrained by a complete inability to do so.

I smiled at him.

'There was dust on top of this when I found it,' I said. 'It was obvious that it had been there for a long time. I'm guessing you believed it deserved to have its place amongst all those other *inferior* books, but then forgot you'd put it there.'

Bunting just kept staring at me.

'Or was it more hubris?' I frowned. 'You were so careful with most of your story. I imagine you must have had some kind of list to make sense of it all. To get your house *just so*. So maybe you didn't forget about this, and it was just arrogance – you thought either we wouldn't find it, or we wouldn't make the connection if we did. And your ego just couldn't bear to get rid of it.'

I didn't expect an answer. Once again, I didn't get one.

'Anyway,' I said. 'Here's your masterpiece.'

I took out the manuscript that Bunting had kept in the box file and placed it on the table. It was a thick bundle of paper, the pages loose and misaligned, held roughly together by an old rubber band. Many of the sheets were weathered, but a few at the top, separated by a second rubber band, were far more dog-eared and stained, the paper curling up at the corners. The first page was blank except for two lines of text in the centre:

The Day in the Woods
Simon Bunting

'I'm guessing this top section is the three chapters you kept submitting to agents.' I gestured at the pile of paper. 'I'd read parts of it, so it wasn't difficult to convey the contempt I felt. 'With an emphasis on the *kept* submitting. The rest of it is in slightly better shape, isn't it? Because none of the agents ever wanted to see the whole book, did they? Assuming we can even call this piece of rubbish a book.'

The crimson was rising into Bunting's face now. He was still looking at me; he hadn't so much as glanced at the manuscript on the table between us. I wondered if he might even lose control completely and attack me. I hoped so.

'I admit I haven't read it all. I tried a bit and what I saw was very bad. Although to be honest, I've never been much of a fan of this kind of thing. DI Beck read much more of it than I did.'

'It's terrible,' Emma said. 'Just awful.'

Bunting glanced at her, then back to me. Just with his eyes. His head didn't move at all.

'DI Beck is a big reader,' I said. 'But to be scrupulously fair, neither of us are literary critics. So perhaps our assessment is wrong. Fortunately there are more expert opinions available, which we were very grateful to see you'd kept for our amusement.'

I reached into the box file and took out the pile of loose papers that remained inside. They had been stored below the manuscript itself. Each of them had a different letterhead at the top, but although the design varied, the content was generally the same. Rejection letters from numerous literary agents.

'I'm actually interested in why you didn't throw these away,' I said. 'Keeping the book... I suppose I can understand that. It's worthless dross, but I'm sure you worked incredibly hard on it. These rejection letters, though? I'd have thought they'd have been an affront to you. Maybe you thought that one day you'd prove them all wrong.'

I laughed at the idea.

'Anyway. Let's read a few of them, shall we?'

'No.'

Bunting's voice was small and tight, and although the rest of his face had reddened, his lips looked pale.

'Yes,' I said. 'I think so.'

'They're private.'

'Not any more. And they're very funny. Let's start with this one. *Regardless of the dubious merits of your story, your command of English is not strong enough to compel me to read further*. That's not very encouraging, is it?'

'Stop it.'

'Then we have a few that are just form rejection letters. *Thank you for submitting your work. We regret to inform you . . .* blah blah.' I put each letter to the side as I worked through the collection. 'I like this one, though. *I'm afraid the characters are flat and I found the writing utterly underwhelming.* I bet that stung.'

'I said stop it.'

'You're not in charge here, Simon. Here's my second favourite. *Many rejected submissions show promise, but I believe in being honest, and I see absolutely nothing of value here. This work is badly written and—*'

'STOP IT!'

The explosion finally came: Bunting screamed the words at me, pushing forward in his chair, gripping the edge of the table. His face was puce now. I just stared back at him, and that was as far as it went: he held himself in that position for a few seconds, the interview room silent, and then leaned slowly back again. He rested his elbows on the table and steepled his fingers around his forehead as he stared down. His shoulders were trembling.

'One more, I think,' I said quietly. 'My favourite.'

'Just stop.'

'No. I'm going to read this one out in full.'

I looked down at the sheet in front of me.

Dear Mr Bunting

I would normally say thank you for a submission, whatever my personal reaction to it, but in this case I will refrain from doing so. It is not simply a matter of the writing being inept, although it is. Your characters are confusing; your spelling and grammar is appalling; and your general flair for language is laughably non-existent. However, this is also a matter of professional ethics.

A modicum of research would have revealed to you that I currently represent the writer Jeremy Townsend, who earlier this year published the novel *What Happened in the Woods*. Your story appears to all intents and purposes to be identical. Mr Townsend is a superb writer, and it would be ludicrous to suggest you had plagiarised your execrable prose from his work, but the similarities in the stories are simply too great to allow for coincidence.

You state in your covering letter that you have spent years writing this story. From the quality of the writing, I cannot believe that. Rather, I believe it to be an attempt to distract from your whole-cloth theft of another writer's work. If you intend to persist in this foolhardy endeavour then I suggest you choose who you submit to far more carefully in the future.

I put the page down slowly on top of the others, and looked across the desk at Bunting. He had sunk further forward while I was reading. His fingers were now stretched through his hair, and his face was close to the table itself. But he was no longer shaking.

'I did work on it for years,' he said softly. 'He stole it. It was *my* story. *Mine*.'

For a moment, I said nothing. I was thinking about Anna. From the beginning, I'd imagined that being involved in ending the Red River spree would bring me some sense of closure – some relief from the guilt I felt – but it wasn't the case. I just felt immensely sad about all of it. But then it wasn't about me, was it? It was about all those dead women. And so as I looked at Simon Bunting, sitting defeated in front of me, I thought about them instead. And about Melanie West, the girl who had found the body of her best friend and been haunted by the discovery, and who over time had attempted to make sense of that horror through her words, her poetry, her photography. A woman who now would still be able to see those woods vividly every time she closed her eyes – a moment from the past overlaid on the present – and whose tale had been told by far too many others.

It was my *story.*
Mine.
'No,' I told Bunting. 'It wasn't.'

Fifty

It wasn't my story either.

As Emma had told me angrily after we'd nearly been taken off the investigation, it wasn't about me. But there was something I still needed to do, though I also realised that it had to be done *before*. It couldn't be the ending itself. And so the day before the funeral, I drove fifty miles out of the city, along quiet country lanes, arriving just after midday in the small village where I'd grown up.

The geography of it was immediately familiar, although much had changed. Driving down the main street, I recognised the architecture of the buildings themselves, but none of the businesses that now occupied them. Nevertheless, the village still corresponded to the map I'd kept folded up in my head all these years, and emotions flared as I passed certain places. It was subconscious; I often wasn't sure why. But I knew each flash was a rope I could pull on if I wanted, bringing some buried memory back up to the surface. *That happened there, didn't it? I remember now.* The day was sunny and warm, so I drove with the window down and my elbow resting on the sill, and even the sounds and smells of the place brought my childhood back to me.

I passed through the centre and then took a turning away from the shops, towards the residential part of the village, where the houses rubbed up against the edge of the countryside. The street curled around, and I parked up on a quiet corner and turned off the engine. The houses to my right were expensive and detached. To the left, there was a stretch of neatly tended grass, and then an old stone wall that separated the street from the steep, tangled embankment beyond. A short distance ahead, there was a break in both the grass and the wall, where a path led to the bridge over the railway.

I got out of the car.

The Bridge hadn't changed at all. I walked slowly along it, looking at the vaguely cobbled ground beneath my feet. The nubs in the black stone on the tops of the walls to either side looked as though a thousand children's thumbs had been pressed into the stone as it formed. As a grown man, I'd expected it all to seem smaller, but it didn't. When I stopped in the centre, the wall still came up to my chest, just as it had all those years ago. How was that possible? The place felt like a tree that had grown thicker with time: expanding with long, steady breaths, and somehow keeping pace with the size of it in my memories.

I stood for a minute, staring over the top of the wall at the tracks disappearing into the distance, then hoisted myself up slightly and leaned over. It still seemed a long way down. I hadn't been back since Rob had tried to kill himself, and it was easy to imagine him here now. Sitting on the wall, looking around and remembering what he'd seen as a child – the man with long hair and a sad face. Perhaps thinking of the email he'd sent to his once best friend that had never been answered. And then eventually leaning forward and tumbling through space for a second or two before his body hit the hard stretch of pebbles so far below.

Do you think the fall would kill you?

Yes, I thought now. Yes, it would.

I didn't know exactly what I'd expected to feel here. There are people who think you can tell when something terrible has happened in a place, and it's true that I did sense a trace of sadness in the air, but I'm sure that was only because I'd brought it with me. A part of me wondered what would happen if I waited long enough. Would the day darken? Would anything appear to me? I could see it all so clearly anyway: separate instants superimposed over each other and gathering emphasis, the way a faint pencil line grows stronger the more you go over it. A different kind of pareidolia. Seeing not a face formed from the environment around us, but patterns discerned from events over time, only making sense in hindsight.

I didn't wait. Instead, I placed the flowers I'd brought with me at the base of the wall, said a quiet final goodbye to my friend, and made my way back to the car. Even so, I was almost surprised not to see a pair of bicycles, one more expensive than the other, leaning against the wall at the end.

The next morning, Emma and I arrived at Mill Hill crematorium.

The grounds around the building were beautiful. The crematorium was on the outskirts of the city, with the driveway winding almost leisurely through quiet green woodland, and the parking areas lined with carefully tended banks of flowers. From the outside, the building itself resembled a cabin in the middle of nowhere. We walked into a long room where everything seemed to be made of polished wood, and where every sound, even the gentlest of footfalls, echoed respectfully.

Emma and I took a seat at the back of the room. Ferguson was already here, I noticed – sitting with Reeves on the other side of the aisle.

A number of police who had been involved with the investigation were also attending; I recognised a few faces from the operations room. Other officers were stationed at the two entrances to the grounds and outside the crematorium building itself. For obvious reasons, there was enormous press interest in today's events, but everybody involved was determined that the funeral of John Blythe would be a private affair.

I looked down the aisle at the coffin. It was plain and brown, and of course, there were no flowers on it. There was nothing at all for the moment, although Blythe's body would not be going behind the waiting curtains to the furnace unadorned.

I glanced around. Blythe had no known surviving family, and none of his friends, neighbours or work colleagues had wished to appear today. But the room was still full.

The officiant stood patiently at the front. He was old, with curly grey hair and round glasses, and I sensed an air of kindness about him even from the back of the room. He seemed like a man who would be good at saying the right things – guiding you through the prayers and hymns and eulogies with care. After a time, he nodded towards someone standing at the back of the room. I heard a gentle click behind me as the door was closed, and then the murmur of conversation faded away.

The officiant approached the lectern.

'Ladies and gentlemen,' he said. 'We are gathered here today in terrible circumstances and for horrible reasons. On a different occasion, I would begin by speaking at some length about the deceased – stories about their life and achievements. But we will not be talking about the deceased today. Instead, may I please ask Elizabeth Brown to join me at the front of the room?'

A woman in her early seventies wearing a black dress moved slowly to the front of the room, and the officiant stepped back to allow her space. She put on a pair of reading glasses, then placed a piece of paper on the lectern.

'I want to tell you a story about a woman named Rebecca,' she said. 'Rebecca was my daughter, and I loved her very much. Many people did. One of my strongest memories is of when she was six, and obsessed with becoming a doctor. My husband and I bought her a toy medical set for her birthday, and I remember she wore the stethoscope for days on end, and insisted on subjecting her poor little sister to endless unwanted interventions.'

She looked into the audience and smiled. Following her gaze, I saw a woman, perhaps in her forties now, smile back at the memory.

'Rebecca always cared for other people,' Elizabeth went on. 'I thought she might end up as a nurse or a doctor when she grew up, but she took a different direction in the end, and I was equally proud. She loved children very much, and she was working as a primary school teacher at the time she was taken from us. I know some of her former colleagues are here with us today.'

She placed one hand on her heart.

'Thank you all so much. I still have each and every one of the messages you sent me about her, and I treasure them all. I'm sorry that Rebecca never had a chance to become a mother herself. She would have been as amazing at that as she was as a daughter. There is nothing else to regret about her life, though – just the manner in which it was so abruptly and cruelly ended. I miss her very much, and I think about her every day. Goodbye, Becky.'

She closed her eyes for a moment, gathering herself. Then she picked up the sheet of paper, folded it, and placed it carefully on top of the coffin.

The relatives all took their turn to speak. Mothers and fathers, husbands and boyfriends, grown children. They all approached the lectern to tell something of the truth that lay behind the bare list of victims.

I want to tell you a story about a woman named Mary.

I want to tell you a story about a woman named Kimberly.

I want to tell you a story about a woman named Grace.

Mary Fisher had always loved language as a child. She spoke French and Italian fluently, and had just started her own small translation company when she went missing. Kimberly Hart's twin children remembered their mother's calming presence and the way she read them bedtime stories using different voices for all the characters. Grace Holmes had been born prematurely and spent several difficult weeks in hospital before finally being allowed home. That was why they had chosen her first name: Grace.

I want to tell you a story about a woman named Sophie.

I want to tell you a story about a woman named Chloe.

Both Sophie King and Chloe Smith had been teenagers when they were killed by Blythe. Sophie had already been an accomplished artist and had plans to study to be an architect. Chloe had gone off the rails for a time, her brother said, but she was bringing her life back around. He'd argued with her so much over the years. He was sure he'd still be arguing with her now if she was around, and he wished that she was.

I want to tell you a story about a woman named Anna.

And there were Anna's parents. I recognised them, of course, and even though they seemed so old now, it was easy to see the people they had once been. Her father spoke about how they'd had two little boys before her, and how he'd been thrilled to have a daughter finally, just so he could encourage her to climb trees, ride bikes and do everything her brothers did. And she had. Her husband, he told us, had taken his own life after her disappearance.

I watched as he placed the folded piece of paper on the coffin, glad that in its own small way, Rob's story was part of this too.

I want to tell you a story about a woman named Amy.

I want to tell you a story about a woman named Ruby.

I want to tell you a story about a woman named Olivia.

Amy Marsh had been a scientist. She was a single mother who'd worked hard for her PhD, and a keen runner. Her daughter remembered how she had been training for her second marathon when she disappeared.

Tom Clarke, dressed in a suit, his long hair neatly combed, explained how Ruby Clarke had saved him. He'd never been able to believe that someone so caring, so gentle, could be interested in a man like him. He'd lost track of things since she went missing, but he was going to try to do better.

Olivia Richardson, her mother said, had always been so *bloody obstinate*. They hadn't got along at all. It was only in hindsight that she realised that that was because they were so very similar, and she wished she'd had a chance to tell her that and say sorry.

The coffin gathered its pages, its tales. If you watched

carefully, it was possible to see some of them unfolding a little, like flowers, after they were left.

I want to tell you a story about a woman named Carly.

I want to tell you a story about a woman named Emily.

I want to tell you a story about a woman named Angela.

Carly Jones had worked as a session musician. Her father had tried to steer her towards the violin – his own personal love – but she'd gravitated to the guitar. She'd practised for hours on end as a teenager, hunched over the instrument, and she had such long hair that when you walked into her room, it was like Cousin Itt from the Addams Family was sitting cross-legged on the bed.

It had taken Emily Bailey five attempts to pass her driving test, but she had never wavered in her determination. She was always such a *serious* child, her brother said. When she started something, she never gave up. She loved films and had her own amateur review blog, which had been attracting increasing traffic, and which he continued to update as best he could, even though he found it difficult.

'We tried so hard to have children,' Angela Walsh's mother said. 'Eventually we adopted Angela. Her birth name was Davina, which I think is simply beautiful. I wonder what would have happened if we hadn't changed it – if things would have been different. It would still have been her, of course, but maybe there's another story there. I think about that a lot.'

Amanda Cassidy remained in hospital, but her husband Peter was present, and he spoke in her place. As he walked to the lectern, I recognised him from his vigil at the hospital. He seemed lighter now.

'Amanda is recovering slowly,' he said. 'She's better every day, and my daughter Charlotte and I are so grateful to have her back. When Amanda was a little girl, her mother, Carol, would fold sheets of paper in half and get her to write stories in them. Carol kept them all and I have one with me here. So I'm not going to read a story *about* Amanda today, but one *by* her. She was ten years old when she wrote this, by the way, so I can only apologise in advance.'

There was a little laughter at that, but it disappeared as he started to read: a story about a girl who wandered into a terrifying forest and was pursued by a monster that cast an enormous shadow over her. The little girl ran and ran, until at the end she finally turned around and saw that the creature pursuing her was a small, snivelling thing that fled when it saw her looking.

'*So however scary monsters are, and whatever awful things they do, that's all they ever really are,*' he finished. '*The End.*'

He placed the book on the coffin – a handful of old pink sheets, folded over and sewn at the crease with green and white string – and returned to his seat.

And then it was Melanie West's turn to speak.

She had been sitting at the end of a row, next to Jeremy Townsend. Now, she stood and made her way to the lectern. With the exception of Amanda Cassidy's childhood book, the other papers people had brought were new – freshly written or printed – but Melanie's pages were old and worn. They had been with her for a long time. She took off the dark glasses she was wearing and looked around, and for a moment it wasn't clear whether she was seeing us or something else entirely.

'I want to tell you a story,' she began, 'about a girl named Jennifer.'